By CINDY SUTHERLAND

NOVELS
Wrapped Up in Chains

NOVELLAS
All the Things I Didn't See
Cowboy Way
Hunt and Pray
Luck of the Irish

Published by DREAMSPINNER PRESS
http://www.dreamspinnerpress.com

WRAPPED UP
IN
Chains

CINDY SUTHERLAND

Dreamspinner Press

Published by
Dreamspinner Press
5032 Capital Circle SW
Suite 2, PMB# 279
Tallahassee, FL 32305-7886
USA
http://www.dreamspinnerpress.com/

ISBN: 978-1-62798-568-0
Digital ISBN: 978-1-62798-569-7

Printed in the United States of America
First Edition
March 2014

For Ryan and Dani, who were with me every step of the way and never let me quit, even when I was sure I should.

Acknowledgments

When I started out to write this, I never set out to write the perfect BDSM story. This is a story about healing from something horrible and finding love along the way. I did as much research as I could, but I know that what I don't know or understand about that world would fill volumes of books. I have nothing but respect for those who are involved in the lifestyle and hope that shows here.

One

DEVON WALKED into Mystique looking every inch the Master of the world. The truth wasn't too far off. Inside his club there were many who called themselves Master, but here in this place, they all answered to him.

Tonight he wore black jeans and a dark red silk shirt, unbuttoned at the neck. His black jacket and boots completed the look. Devon didn't favor the leather and chains look so many in his community seemed to be stuck on unless he was in a scene.

He radiated power as he walked down the hall and into the main room of the club. He was used to most eyes turning his way as he entered the room. The fact that they didn't tonight was Devon's first indication that something was wrong. When he looked to see what had captured people's attention, his green eyes flashed with anger.

There was a crowd of people gathered around the raised stage in the middle of the club, watching one of the young men who worked there as a Dom beat a young man who was tied to the St. Andrew's cross that sat on the platform.

Most of the people watching looked horrified but made no move to stop the torture.

The unfortunate sub had been beaten so badly that his back was bleeding in half a dozen places, and it was obvious this was some kind of punishment instead of a scene. He was limp in his bindings, and the pain in his shoulders must have been excruciating as the muscles were stretched to the limit when his legs failed to support him.

Devon spotted his manager standing uncertainly to the side. This was the man who should have been putting a stop to the chaos in front of him, but Devon could see that he was intimidated and trying to decide whether or not to stop it. He took the choice out of the manager's hands.

Striding quickly to the stage, he caught the eye of the DJ as he went, and the music died. All eyes were finally on Devon as he shouted.

"*Stop!*"

The Dom had just pulled his arm back to administer another blow and was startled when Devon yanked the flogger out of his hand.

The man spun to confront whoever had dared to interfere and visibly paled when he saw it was his boss. Devon smiled coldly at the man.

"Matt, I'd like you to explain to me what this poor sub has done to merit being beaten half to death." He moved around so he could see the bleeding man's face. Devon's fury grew. The man wasn't much more than a boy.

"He struck a Dom, sir." Matt's voice shook.

Devon gently pushed the hair back off the young man's face and was gratified when he opened his eyes. However, the pure terror in the hazel depths made Devon even more furious. He ran his fingers through the man's hair, trying to calm him down a little.

"Why? He obviously didn't hit him for no reason."

Matt just shrugged. "I don't know. I didn't see what happened. One minute the Dom was talking to him, the next he was flat on the floor with a broken nose. Don't worry, sir, Jason took him to the hospital." He made it sound like Devon should be proud of him for taking care of the Dom.

"And you didn't ask why the kid hit him? Did it occur to you that he might have had a reason?"

Matt scowled. "Subs don't hit Doms, sir. It's the rule."

Devon pulled himself to his full height. "In case you've forgotten, Matt, I make the fucking rules here! And rule number one is consent from all parties for everything! Are you telling me this man consented to this?"

Matt flinched even though Devon hadn't raised his voice. When Devon lifted the flogger to look at it, his anger almost overwhelmed him.

The whip was actually a cat-o'-nine-tails that was about two-and-a-half-feet long. It was one of the nastier versions Devon had seen, with knots tied at intervals along the tails and the ends cut at an angle, all designed to cause the maximum amount of pain and damage.

"You used this weapon of torture on someone in my club? Are you out of your fucking mind?" Devon's voice was starting to get louder, and as it did he could feel the sub shake harder. He knew he had to calm down and get the injured man taken care of.

Taking a deep breath, he threw the flogger across the stage to land at the feet of his manager. "You are *not* a Dom. You're just a fucking bully. Now get the hell out of my club. You're done here."

Matt opened his mouth to speak but stopped when two of the bouncers who had been with the club since it began stepped forward at a gesture from Devon. With a giant man on either side of him, Matt had no option but to move in the direction they wanted him to go. He went quietly.

Devon turned back to the sub. He'd started moaning in pain, although Devon could see that the man was trying hard to be quiet.

"If the rest of you wouldn't mind, could you please step back and give us some room to work?" He looked over his shoulder and saw Andy and Joe walking toward the stage. They must have just arrived or this wouldn't have been happening.

"Could you two give me a hand here?"

"What in the hell's going on, Dev?" Andy's eyes widened when he saw the sub's back. "Who did that? I'll fucking kill 'em!"

"Someone who is no longer employed here. We'll talk about it later." Dev leaned in to talk quietly in the sub's ear.

"What's your name, sweetheart?" He couldn't resist tucking a lock of hair behind the other man's ear. His face was so innocent he couldn't imagine him lashing out at anyone in anger.

"Chase, Sir." His voice was wrecked, hoarse and raw from screaming.

"Chase, we're going to get you down from here and figure out what's going on, okay?"

Chase nodded. "I'm sorry, Sir."

Devon rubbed the back of his knuckles gently over Chase's cheek. "Shhh, just be quiet for now, sweetheart. We're gonna take care of you."

Looking back at Andy, he motioned for him to start untying Chase while Joe ran off to grab the gurney they kept to help move patrons who were sometimes overwhelmed in intense scenes.

Devon stood beside Chase, moving in front of him and holding his weight when Andy finally got both the limbs on one side untied.

Chase was trying hard to hold himself up, but Devon knew he was seconds away from collapsing. "It's okay, Chase. You can lean on me. I won't let you fall."

Chase put his forehead on Devon's shoulder, both arms hanging down by his sides, apparently too weak and in too much pain to grab on to anything.

"Who's your Master, Chase?"

Chase trembled at the question, and for a moment, Devon didn't think he was going to answer.

"James, Sir, James Kingston."

Devon sighed. "Why am I not surprised?"

Joe came with the gurney then, and they managed to manhandle Chase onto it, laying him carefully on his front. Once he was settled, Devon looked at the crowd.

"Did any of you see what happened?" He needed to get to the bottom of this. If Chase was seriously hurt, this little shit show could cause him real problems.

Everyone shook their heads, but Devon knew some were lying. He watched as a pretty little dark-haired sub he recognized leaned in to whisper in her Dom's ear. Her Dom looked at her in surprise before nodding at her.

She walked up and stood in front of the stage, head bowed and hands clasped in front of her until he spoke.

"Yes, Katie?"

"Pardon me, Sir, but I saw Chase's Dom walk him in and sit him at the bar. He whispered in his ear and then walked to the booth in the corner, leaving Chase alone." The poor girl was shaking, but she bravely kept talking.

"The Dom and his friends watched as people came up to Chase and talked to him. Chase always said no to offers of company, and they walked away. But then one of the men from his Dom's table came up and wouldn't leave him alone. I don't think Chase knew the man was with his Master, Sir. He couldn't see the booth from the bar."

Devon was pretty sure he knew what had happened next, but he nodded for her to continue. She was nervous, and he was happy when her Dom came up behind her and wrapped his arm around her waist, offering her comfort.

"The man pulled Chase off his stool and tried to push him to his knees, and that's when Chase hit him." She looked up at Devon, begging him to understand. "Sir, I don't think Chase meant to hit him, he just... panicked. He's shy, and his Master doesn't take him out much. Please don't be too angry at Chase, Master Devon."

Devon walked to the front of the stage and crouched down to smile at her. "I'm not mad at Chase, Katie. He's not the one in the wrong here. Thank you for telling me. Do you know where his Dom went?"

She shook her head. "No, Sir. When everyone started freaking out, he just left as fast as he could, leaving Chase behind." The look on her face told Devon exactly what she thought of the cowardly asshole who'd abandoned his sub.

Devon leaned in and kissed her on the forehead and nodded gratefully at her Dom. They were a couple who came in often, and Devon knew they were a devoted pair.

"Don't worry, Katie, we're going to take care of Chase, I promise."

She smiled at him, tears causing her eyes to shine a little brighter. She turned in her Dom's arms, and he held her and soothed her as they walked away.

Devon looked over to where Andy and Joe were trying to tend to Chase's injuries. He stood and walked off the stage to join them.

"Does he need to go to the hospital?"

Andy shrugged. "I don't know. He won't let us get close enough to look and keeps insisting he isn't going to see any doctors." Dev could see the frustration on his friend's face.

Dev crouched down so he could look Chase in the eyes and started stroking Chase's dark, sweaty hair. "Hey, sweetheart, what's going on?"

"Master said no one touches what's his and no doctors. They ask too many questions."

Devon continued petting him, running his fingers down the back of Chase's neck to try and ease the tension there. "I'm touching you."

"You're the Master here. This is your place. It makes it okay, I think." His voice was so quiet it was hard to hear, and Dev could tell he was struggling to make sense of things.

Dev smiled encouragingly at him. He knew he had to help Chase feel comfortable so that he'd let them help him. "Let's get you to my office and get you checked over. If I decide you need to go to the hospital, you're going, no arguments, all right?"

Chase nodded, and Devon stood up. He could see the other man making an aborted move toward Devon's hand, and his heart twisted in sympathy. Chase was terrified and had apparently attached himself to Devon without his Dom to turn to. He laid his hand over Chase's, smiling when the injured man turned his hand palm up and curled his fingers around Dev's almost painfully.

Devon looked toward the crowd. "Please feel free to continue to enjoy yourselves, but keep this in mind. I won't tolerate this kind of brutality in my place. Remember, these amazing people put themselves in your care, and it's your duty as their Doms to make sure they're safe while they're with you. Don't abuse the gift they've given you if you want to keep it."

The last was said as a warning, and the Doms in the room knew James Kingston was going to be sorry for ever trying this kind of brutal game in Devon's world.

Two

ANDY AND Joe pushed the gurney through the crowd with Dev walking at its side. He kept his hand on Chase's, knowing he needed the comfort only a Master could offer. It should have been his Master, but Devon would have to do.

When they finally made it to the office, they closed the door, and he crouched down beside the gurney again.

Dev reached up, stroking Chase's hair as he spoke calmly. "Chase, I'm going to check you over now. I'm sorry if it hurts, but I need to see if there are any serious injuries, okay?"

Chase nodded, and Dev was touched by the fact that the other man was willing to trust him after everything he'd been through. He smiled at Chase, smoothing a comforting hand down his arm before standing and looking down at his back.

He inspected the torn and bleeding skin in front of him, wincing at the bruises already forming. He made Chase move his arms, testing to make sure there were no strained or pulled muscles. The cuts were his biggest concern. He turned to Joe.

"I think I saw Lisa Jones out there. Would you please go and see if she's available to look at Chase's back?" Joe nodded and headed out the door.

Crouching down, Devon spoke to Chase again. "A friend of mine is going to come and take a look at your back. She's a doctor, a plastic surgeon, actually, and I want to make sure those cuts on your back are going to heal cleanly, without any infection and hopefully without too many scars."

"Is she gonna give me trouble? I was bad, Sir. Master said no doctors. I don't want to be bad again." It was bothering Devon that Chase seemed so lost in his own mind he couldn't find his way out of it

Devon ran his hand over his face, trying to calm down. He was going to strangle Kingston when he finally got his hands on him. "Chase, no one's mad at you. Your Master left you alone, with no protection...." He looked again and realized that Chase didn't even have a collar on. "He didn't even give you your collar...."

Chase sobbed quietly. "Master said I didn't deserve a collar." The poor man was shivering, his grief and fear overwhelming him. "He said I was a worthless sub and the worthless subs didn't get collars."

Devon looked up at Andy, who was frowning grimly, and they exchanged a look that promised punishment for the missing Dom.

He looked back down at Chase. "Chase, I want you to listen to me. You're not worthless, your Master is."

Chase started to shake his head, but Devon curved his palm around the other man's cheek and held him still. "No one has the right to treat anyone this way, sweetheart. I guarantee no one will treat you like this again."

Chase looked at him, and Devon could see that he wanted to believe him but was scared to. He was stopped from saying more by the arrival of Joe and a woman with long dark hair and kind eyes.

Devon stood up and held out his arms to receive the hug she offered before turning back to Chase. "Lisa, this is Chase."

Lisa knelt down beside the gurney so the other man could see her face. "Hello, Chase. Is it okay if I look at your back?"

Chase looked up at Devon, who smiled at him encouragingly. He took a deep breath and nodded. Lisa smiled and patted his cheek before standing up.

Like Devon she was gentle and thorough, trying as much as possible to not cause Chase any more pain.

"What do you think, Lisa, does he need to go to the hospital?" Devon's hand was back on Chase's head, petting him soothingly.

She looked up at him, and he could see the rage in her eyes. "No, I don't think it's really necessary. They should all heal fine. I don't think any of them need stitches, but a couple need some butterfly bandages to keep them closed for a few days." She took a deep breath, obviously considering her next words.

"The damage wouldn't have been so bad if he wasn't twenty pounds underweight. I'm concerned that Chase might not be getting enough to eat." She crouched beside the younger man again.

"How old are you, sweetheart?"

He flinched at the sound of her voice but answered her quietly. "Twenty-three, Ma'am."

Devon was shocked. He wouldn't have guessed that Chase was any older than eighteen or nineteen. "Chase, do you live with your Master all the time?"

Chase nodded. "Yes, Sir. I've been with my Master since I was sixteen." A look of shame and grief came over his beautiful face.

"Sixteen?" Devon was floored. At sixteen no one is capable of making the decision to be a full-time sub. He opened his mouth to speak again but was cut off by Lisa.

"Dev, let's get him fixed up, and then you can talk to him some more, okay? I'm thinking he's probably scared enough and in a lot of pain. Let's deal with that first."

Devon nodded at her and motioned for Andy to bring over the medical kit they kept in the club. Lisa slid on some gloves and got to work, cleaning the blood and sweat from Chase's back and putting on antibiotic cream. She bandaged the worst of the cuts and gave Chase two of the heavy-duty pain relievers that were kept in the box after asking if he had any allergies.

The whole time she worked, Devon sat beside Chase in a chair that Joe had brought over, holding his hand and whispering to help calm him.

When she was finished, she told Chase to take it easy for a couple of days and to not get his bandages wet. He could shower the next night, but for now he'd have to make do with a sponge bath. He nodded sleepily.

"Thank you, mistress." He was so polite, his manners so ingrained, and Devon could see that it tugged at her heart. She leaned over, kissed his cheek, and turned to leave. She looked at Devon, and he stood, whispering to Chase before following her to the door.

"What are you going to do, Devon? He shouldn't be alone right now. I'm not sure how long he's been living as a sub 24/7 but I think it's been a while. Maybe even years."

"I'm going to take care of him here for a couple of days, at least until he can travel, and then we'll take it from there." He looked over his shoulder to where Andy and Joe were standing guard over Chase. He knew they felt the way he did.

"And I'm going to find Kingston and have a chat with him." Devon scrubbed his hands over his face in frustration. "How in the fuck did this happen in my club? Why didn't anyone stop it?"

"I don't know, Devon. I got here just as you did, and Andy and Joe were right behind me. My guess is that the others were either in agreement with punishment or scared or unsure about interfering." She sighed. "What about Matt?"

Devon sneered. "He's gone and never coming back, if he knows what's good for him. I should've followed my instincts about him instead of listening to Jack."

Jack was the manager who'd been reluctant to interfere in the beating.

"You should get rid of that idiot and put Andy and Joe in charge, Devon." She looked at the two men fondly. "I know they're your friends and you're worried about taking advantage of that, but they wouldn't let you down. And I think they'd enjoy it."

Devon smiled at her. "You're one hell of a smart lady, you know that?"

Lisa smiled back at him. "Of course I am!"

He kissed her cheek and opened the door so she could leave. "Thanks, Lisa."

She winked at him. "Anytime, sugar." She closed the door softly behind her as she left.

Devon turned and walked back to Chase, who was sound asleep on the gurney. The younger man looked so innocent in sleep, and something warm seemed to unfurl in Devon's chest as he looked at him.

"Where do you want him, sweets?" Devon grimaced at the hated nickname but didn't call Andy on it.

"Let's take him to the recovery room behind my office. We don't ever use it, and it has an attached bathroom."

Andy nodded, and he and Joe moved quickly as Devon gathered his laptop and a few other items he needed from his office, including the pain pills, and followed them down the hall.

Joe looked up as he entered the room. "You want us to put him on the bed?" Chase was tall, but Lisa was right, he was entirely too skinny for his frame. Moving him wouldn't take much.

"Yeah, just a second, though." He dumped his things on the dresser by the door before making his way to the gurney. He leaned over Chase and spoke quietly in his ear.

"Chase, I need to move you to the bed, okay?" Chase moaned softly as he tried to wake up. "Shhh, it's okay, baby. I just didn't want to scare you."

Chase nodded without ever opening his eyes, and the three men moved him quickly and efficiently, jostling him as little as possible. Andy had pulled the blanket back on the bed, and they settled him against the sheets on his stomach.

Joe carefully lifted Chase's hips up, and Devon undid the sleeping man's pants and they slid them off. None of them were surprised that there was nothing under the jeans.

Devon was sickened by the crisscrossing pattern of fine scars that covered the younger man's ass and upper thighs. It looked like tonight wasn't the first time he'd been tortured.

"Fuck, Devon. This kind of scarring takes years! You can see how some are older than others and how they overlap." Andy's voice was tight with anger.

"Who in their right fucking mind does this to someone?" Devon was choking on his fury. "Kingston puts us all in a bad light with this kind of behavior. We're under enough scrutiny as it is without him acting like a wild animal."

Taking a deep breath, Devon tried to get control of his emotions. There was nothing he could do about Kingston right now. Taking care of Chase had to be his priority.

"I need to talk to you two. Dr. Jones seems to think that you guys might not be averse to a change of employment."

Andy and Joe looked at each other and grinned.

"I guess she's right." Dev smiled at his two oldest friends. "I'd like you to send him to me. I'm going to inform Jack that his services are no longer required. His severance will include a $5000 check and a promise that I won't have him blackballed at every club in town if he leaves quietly. After I deal with him, I'm going to count on you guys to make sure he goes quickly and with as little fuss as possible."

They nodded at him and headed for the door. Devon called them back for a second. "I'm going to be staying here with Chase for a couple of days. You're in charge. Any questions, come and ask me. You're on the payroll as of tonight, got it?"

Joe came over and hugged him. "We got it, Dev, don't worry. You just take care of the poor boy."

Dev hugged him tightly for a minute and then pushed him toward the door. "Go on and make yourselves useful instead of just drinking all my tequila. And for fuck's sake, schedule a meeting for all staff. We need to make sure this never happens again."

Andy nodded before giving him the finger, and they all chuckled. When they'd gone, Devon walked over and sat on the edge of the bed to look at Chase.

How had this beautiful young man ended up in the clutches of the worst example of a Dom the city had to offer? Dev had heard the rumors about a sub being kept under lock and key at the Kingston mansion, but he hadn't ever believed they were true.

He was going to get to the bottom of this and do his best to help Chase. This kind of thing was like a personal affront to him and the lifestyle he led. The public already had so many wrong impressions about the BDSM community, and something like this getting out could hurt a lot of people.

A few minutes later, a knock on the door announced Jack's arrival. Once he'd quietly dealt with his former manager out in the hall, Devon sat on the bed, being careful not to disturb Chase. He sat back against the headboard and closed his eyes. He listened to the quiet breathing of the man on the bed beside him and wondered about the best way to help him. Chase was due some looking after, as far as Devon could tell, and he was going to make sure he got it.

Three

HE MUST have fallen asleep, sitting there on the bed with Chase, and Devon wasn't sure what woke him up. He blinked and looked around, eyes instantly finding the other man in the dim light of the room.

Chase was lying on the edge of the bed, trying to curl up as small as possible. It was an impossible task for someone so tall and in so much pain. He was whimpering as he moved slowly, obviously trying to put some room between him and Devon.

Devon slid farther down the bed, being careful to not get any closer to the terrified man, and lay on his side on the pillow so he could be eye to eye with him. He put one hand on the mattress between them, palm up, and spoke softly.

"Chase, it's okay. You're safe here, and I need you to stop moving before you fall off the bed. If you do, it's going to hurt a lot."

He wasn't all that certain Chase was completely awake. His eyes were glassy, and Devon was willing to bet the pain meds were messing with his mind.

"Chase, do you remember me? I'm Devon, the Master here."

Devon wasn't sure about bringing up the Master part, but he suspected it would at least make it through the drug-induced fog in Chase's brain.

After a moment Chase nodded, his head barely moving. "Sorry, Sir." It wasn't much more than a whispered breath.

"What are you sorry for, Chase?"

"I'm being a baby. You don't need to stay here. You have more important things to do." Chase spoke quietly and was shivering again, but Devon didn't know if it was cold or fear causing it.

"Right now you're the most important thing I have to take care of. I'm so sorry, Chase. This shouldn't have happened to you, not in my place."

Chase's eyes widened. "It's not your fault, Master. I was bad, and I hit that man. I had to be punished." He was still whispering, and Devon suspected he couldn't talk any louder right now.

He watched as one of Chase's hands crept closer to his on the bed. The younger man was so desperate for contact it hurt Dev's heart to watch.

"Chase, defending yourself from someone is not being bad. That man had no right to try and force you to do anything. He wasn't your Dom or your boyfriend, and you didn't have to do anything that you didn't want to."

The younger man looked so perplexed it made Devon smile. Chase ducked his head, not meeting Dev's gaze. The older man sighed. It was going to take a lot longer than a couple of hours to work through Chase's issues. He was going to have to be patient. He was hoping to talk and get some answers, but he knew Chase needed more rest. He slid his hand under Chase's and let himself relax.

"Do you need more pain meds, sweetheart?" He could see Chase wince with every move he made.

"Yes, please… and could I have some water as well?"

Devon pulled his hand back and started to sit up. "I'll be right back, okay?" Chase nodded, and Dev got off the bed.

He grabbed a bottle of water out of the minifridge along the wall and after a moment grabbed a straw too. The pain meds were on the dresser, so he collected those as well and headed back to Chase. He could feel those hazel eyes watching him, and he made sure to keep his movements as nonthreatening as possible.

He sat carefully on the edge of the bed and put the water on the nightstand. He opened the pills, handed a couple to the younger man, and then took the water bottle and opened it. He put the straw in so Chase could drink it without sitting up.

"I'm going to hold this for you, all right? It'll be cold if you drop it on yourself, and I don't want you to be any more uncomfortable."

Chase just nodded, and the confusion coloring his face would have been adorable if it hadn't made Devon so damn sad. It was obvious this man hadn't been shown one moment of true kindness in a long time, and he didn't know yet how to help him believe he was safe here.

"Chase, do you mind if I ask you a couple of questions?" He knew the young man would answer them if ordered, but he was reluctant to do that.

"No, Sir, I don't mind." That soft voice was going to be the death of Devon, he was sure of it.

"How did you end up with Kingston? Sixteen's very young to be involved in this kind of relationship."

He didn't think Chase's eyes could get any sadder until they did. "I ran away from home when I realized I was gay. My family… I didn't think they'd understand. Our church isn't very tolerant, and I didn't want to embarrass them."

His shaggy head lay on the pillow, and his eyes filled with tears. "I was lost in the city, trying to find work, when Master found me and took me in. He was kind at first, and he contacted my family. They didn't want me back. They told him I was too much trouble and he could keep me… so he did."

Devon highly doubted that Kingston had contacted anyone about Chase. It was just one more way he'd taken advantage of the other man's innocence and trust. It was one more thing Devon would be looking into.

He lay down again, not wanting Chase to feel like he was being towered over. He put his hand between them again, palm up, and relaxed as much as he could. "Can you tell me what happened then?"

Chase's hand crept out from under his chest and toward Devon. Their fingertips barely touched at first, but soon Chase's palm was over his, his fingers curled around the delicate bones of Devon's wrist.

"He said I could stay with him, but if he was going to look after me, I had to do things for him to pay him back. I had to be a good boy and do as he said, and he would give me food and clothes and somewhere to stay."

Devon rubbed his thumb gently over Chase's palm, being careful to keep his grip loose. Chase's tears were falling freely now, but Devon didn't think the other man was even aware of them.

"I tried really hard Sir, but I'm stupid and not nearly good enough. I kept making mistakes, and he would have to punish me. He said he didn't want to, that it was my fault, and that I was hurting him by not being good."

The younger man was starting to be overcome by his emotions, and Devon knew he needed to get him calmed down.

"Chase, sweetheart, I need you to listen to me, okay?" There was no indication that Devon's voice was penetrating the grief the other man was lost in, so he closed his fingers around Chase's, holding them gently and pulling a little to get his attention.

It worked, and Chase took a shuddering breath as he tried to calm down. Devon relaxed his grip immediately but didn't pull away.

"You were a child, Chase, and Kingston took advantage of that. He shouldn't have expected you to be in any kind of relationship with him. It wasn't your fault, anything he did, and he's never going to get the chance to do it to you again."

He could see Chase wasn't really understanding what he was saying, and he suspected the drugs were kicking in. "I want to wipe off your face. Is that okay?"

Chase nodded, and the wonder in his eyes at the request for permission made Dev smile as he pulled his hand free and reached behind him for the baby wipes he knew were in the drawer of the nightstand.

He opened the container and pulled one free before gently wiping the tears and sweat from Chase's face. When he was finished, he tossed the wipe in the garbage beside the bed and put the rest away. Chase's hand was searching blindly for his again, so he slid his under it.

"Do you need anything else, baby?" he whispered, not wanting to wake him if he was already sleeping.

"No thank you, Sir, I'm fine." Dev could barely hear him, and at that moment Chase's overly lean frame shuddered.

"You cold?" It was comfortably warm in the room, but Chase was naked and probably suffering from shock.

"A little, Sir."

Devon slipped his hand free and reached down to pull the soft blanket up over Chase to his shoulders. He smiled as the man sighed and relaxed a little more. He reached out and once again tucked a stray lock of hair behind Chase's ear and was glad when he didn't flinch.

"Thank you, Sir."

Devon chuckled a little as he watched those hooded eyes slide shut.

"My name is Devon, Chase."

The younger man breathed out the name as he drifted back to sleep.

It was easy to see what had attracted Kingston to Chase. His features were exotic and beautiful. The almond-shaped eyes and golden skin were enticing. Even too skinny and bruised and battered, his body was gorgeous.

Devon sighed, his frustration almost overwhelming him. This was someone who should have been protected and cared for, not beaten and treated like trash. He couldn't understand Doms like Kingston. They never seemed to comprehend the gift they'd been given and always felt like they needed to take something more.

Devon had been in this scene for a long time, but he'd never forgotten the feeling he'd had the first time someone had knelt for him. The rush of power had been heady and almost addicting, but the protectiveness that had followed on its heels had surprised him.

He'd been nineteen years old, and the Dom that had been teaching him had tried to tell him about it, but the man knew it was something you had to figure out for yourself. Dev was a natural Dom, having the innate ability of knowing how far he could push someone without going too far. He knew how to break someone down and then build them back up again, and he took his duties very seriously.

To men and women like Kingston, it was a game. A very dangerous game that had broken more than one person beyond repair, and Devon was desperately hoping Chase wasn't one of them. There was something about the man that pulled at Devon's heart and made him want to take Chase into his arms and protect him forever. Chase was innocent in almost every sense, and Devon knew it was something to be cherished, not abused.

He ran his fingers through the soft dark-brown strands of hair that lay on the pillow. Falling for Chase would be so easy. Having someone so perfect to be his was a temptation that would be hard to resist, but Devon knew he needed to.

Chase needed freedom and time to make his own choices. If he wanted to run away and never have anything to do with this lifestyle ever again, Devon would certainly understand. Life had been horrible to Chase so far, and if he could find some peace somewhere, he deserved it.

Devon continued petting Chase's head. His first order of business was going to be getting Chase well. He was going to contact his family and see if they really didn't want him back, and he was going to make sure that Kingston paid for what he'd done, to Chase and to any others he'd been abusing. The bastard wasn't the only one with connections in this city, and Dev was going to take advantage of every single one.

It was a promise he made to himself and to Chase. Kingston was done.

Four

CHASE WOKE to the unaccustomed feeling of a soft bed under him and a warm body at his side. Actually, that warm body was almost under him as well. He could hear the steady beat of a strong heart under his ear as he realized that his head was actually pillowed on someone's chest.

No, not just someone, the Master.... Devon, he'd said. He wondered how much trouble he was going to be in. It would almost be worth it. It had been a long time since he'd been allowed the comfort of waking up with someone holding him.

He felt one of the man's hands on the back of his neck, not holding, just gently brushing through the baby-fine hair there, and the other was on his arm, stroking softly. The Master's chin rested on Chase's head, and although he realized he was almost desperate to use the bathroom, he was reluctant to move. He was sure that once he did, the spell would be broken, and Chase would have to go back to the misery that was his life.

Soon, though, he was so uncomfortable that he started to squirm, and that made all the aches and pains from the beating flare up again. He didn't know he was whimpering until the Master spoke.

"What's the matter, Chase? Is the pain getting too bad?" The man's voice was soft and caring, and it made Chase so nervous.

"I'm sorry, Sir. I just have to go to the bathroom. I didn't mean to disturb you." Chase's throat hurt when he spoke, and his voice was cracking.

He started pulling slowly back, trying to get himself up, but a gentle hand on his arm stopped him. "Just a second, sweetheart. Let me get up, and then I'll help you up."

Chase nodded and waited as the Master slid carefully out from under him and rolled off the bed. Chase didn't think he'd ever seen anyone so beautiful in his life. The man was almost as tall as Chase, with spiky dark-blond hair.

He was wearing nothing but a pair of dark-green pajama pants that sat low on his hips, and his chest and abs looked like they could have been sculpted out of marble. His lips looked soft and seemed to have no problem curving into an encouraging smile as he came around to help Chase off the bed.

But it was his eyes that held Chase's attention. When he looked into those jade-green eyes, they radiated power. Power that was tempered with kindness and compassion, and Chase knew this Master would have subs begging to do his bidding just to have him pleased with them…. But only subs that were worthy of him would get the chance.

Chase sighed sadly. He wasn't a worthy sub, and he knew he'd never have a Master like this one.

Still, it felt so good when Devon slid his arm under Chase's chest and helped him up off the bed. As he got his shaking legs under him, he tried really hard to be quiet and not whine, but a few pained sounds slipped out before he could stop them. Master Kingston hated it when Chase was whiny.

Then a hand was back in his hair, petting it softly. "It's okay, Chase, I know it's gotta be hurting you so bad right now." Devon was standing in front of him, and Chase whimpered a little noise of protest when that comforting hand left his head. He watched the other man pick up a cozy looking robe, and then he slipped it on Chase, first on one arm and then the other and then tied it carefully in the front.

Chase hadn't even really noticed he was naked. He wasn't allowed to wear a lot of clothing at home, and those things he did wear were picked by his Master for the way they looked, not how comfortable they were.

Devon smiled at him, and Chase tried to return it, but he was having a hard time dealing with the kindness being shown him. He kept waiting for the smiles to turn to sneers and the caresses to turn to blows. It had been one of his Master's favorite games, to pretend to be kind for a little while and then to be twice as brutal afterward.

Devon just picked up Chase's arms and put them on his shoulders. "I don't want to put my arm around your waist because I don't want to hurt you, so just hang on to my shoulders, and we'll go as slow as you need, okay?"

Chase could only nod and try and swallow past the painful lump in his throat. He thought he might just curl up and die if he had to go back to Kingston Manor after this.

He walked forward slowly, concentrating on putting one foot in front of the other and trying to keep his legs from buckling under him from the pain and fatigue. He could hear the other man speaking to him quietly, and even though the words weren't making sense to Chase in the state he was in, the tone was comforting and helped to make him feel less afraid.

They finally made it to the bathroom, and Devon helped Chase get situated at the toilet before stepping out the door to give him some privacy. He'd left the door open, though, and for that Chase was grateful. He was scared if he tried to move on his own he'd fall, and he knew that would be more pain than he could handle.

When he was finished, he flushed the toilet, and it signaled Devon to come back in and help him to the sink. He washed his hands and then looked up when the other man spoke.

"Chase, there's a spare toothbrush here if you want it, but I'm afraid you won't be able to shower or bathe until later. Dr. Jones wanted to make sure you don't get any infection." Chase was getting more confused all the time. The other man seemed so sincere in his care of Chase.

"I understand, Sir. Thank you."

He saw the other man frown for a moment before he reached up and stroked Chase's cheek. "Chase, do you remember what my name is?"

Chase nodded, unconsciously leaning into the touch. "Your name's Devon, Sir."

"That's right, sweetheart, and if you don't mind, I'd like you to call me that. Is that all right with you?"

"I'll try and remember that, Sir... I mean Devon." He hung his head. This was all getting so complicated.

A gentle hand curled around his jaw and directed his head back up. "I want you to do whatever you need to do to be comfortable, Chase. I won't be mad no matter what you do, okay?"

Chase nodded, desperately trying to blink back tears. He couldn't seem to get any kind of control on his emotions.

The Master... Devon... took one look at the tears that were finally starting to spill over and moved in closer to Chase. Those kind hands once again put Chase's hands on his shoulders and put his own on Chase's hips, pulling him close.

He took the invitation and let himself lean on the other man. He was shaking so badly, and he wasn't even sure what was worse, the pain or the confusion. He laid his head on Devon's shoulder and let the tears fall.

"Shhh. It's okay, sweetheart. I know you're scared, but I promise you, Chase, you're safe here." Devon's mouth was right by Chase's ear, his voice low and comforting. "I know you don't believe me yet, but you never have to go back to Kingston unless you truly want to. And I don't want you to worry about what you'll do if you don't go back. I'll help you figure it out."

"Why?" Chase was terrified at having asked, but he just didn't understand. He was worthless, and he knew it. No one wanted him... not his family... not his Master. Why was this man being so kind to him?

"Because you've been taken advantage of and betrayed through no fault of your own, and it makes me feel a little guilty. I'd heard that Kingston was keeping someone at his house, but I chose to believe that he wouldn't be so stupid, and I was obviously wrong."

Devon thumbed away the tears on Chase's cheeks. "And because you were a boy who was taken and hurt by the worst possible example my community has to offer, and if you'll let me, I'd like to try and make it up to you a little."

Chase couldn't help turning his face into Devon's neck and taking in the scent of him. He smelled so good, not bitter and harsh like his old Master always did.

"You're not worthless, Chase, you're really not, and I'm going to prove it to you."

Chase nuzzled Devon's skin, fingers tightening in a bruising hold, scared to believe what he was being told and scared to let go in case he lost his only chance.

"Come on, baby. Let's get you back to bed before you fall over on me. Even underweight, you're still a big boy."

Chase nodded and let himself be led back to the bedroom. When they were standing beside the bed, Devon reached for the belt of the robe and then stopped.

"Do you want this on or off?"

Chase thought about it. Being naked didn't bother him much, and the robe was kind of itchy against his sore back. "Off, please."

Devon smiled at him like he was proud of him for making a decision, and it made Chase's stomach twist in a good way.

He watched as Devon untied the belt and then let him slip the robe off of his shoulders. He stood, looking at Devon from under his lashes as the older man put the robe on a chair and smoothed the sheets before encouraging Chase to get back into the bed.

Once he was settled, Devon checked the wounds on his back, making sure that none had been reopened, and then he pulled the cool sheets back over Chase and knelt beside him.

"I'm just going to go and check on things quickly and grab some food from the kitchen." Devon tucked a strand of hair behind Chase's ear, and it made the younger man smile a little. It seemed to be an obsession of Devon's.

"Is there anything you'd like in particular? Anything you hate?"

Chase started to shake his head and then stopped. He looked at Devon, working up the courage to speak. He wanted to make Devon happy again. "I don't like shrimp... or spinach." His voice was shaking with fear, but Devon just smiled at him.

"Got it, no shrimp-and-spinach omelets for you. What about chicken vegetable soup and maybe a grilled cheese?"

"I'm not really hungry, Sir." Chase winced at the use of the word, but Devon just ran his fingers through Chase's hair as he spoke to him.

"I know, but I'd like you to eat something before you take any more meds. The painkillers can be hard on your stomach if it's empty, and I really don't want you throwing up. Will you try a little for me? Please?"

Chase's eyes widened at that word. Masters never asked; they just told. That's all he knew. "Yeah, I'll try."

Devon rubbed the back of his knuckles over Chase's cheek and then stood up. "Okay. I won't be long. Do you want me to get someone to come and stay with you while I'm gone?"

Chase shook his head quickly. The thought of being this vulnerable with anyone else right now terrified him. He only trusted Devon, and he wasn't entirely sure about that yet. "I'll be fine."

"Yes, you will." Chase knew he was talking about more than just having to wait here alone for him. "I'll lock the door when I leave, and no one else will be able to get in. You rest while you can, and I'll help you eat when I get back."

He watched as Devon reached for a hoodie that was on the dresser and slipped it on. He slid his feet into sneakers that had been sitting by the door before opening it and leaving Chase alone with his thoughts.

He lay there, contemplating the turn his life had taken. For almost seven years he'd lived at the mercy of the man who'd taken him in. At first he'd thought it was okay. Master James had taught him about sex with a man, something that Chase's sheltered life hadn't prepared him for. For Chase the pleasure had always been tempered with pain, and lately, the pain was all there'd been.

Now he was starting to realize that maybe it didn't have to be that way. He'd always thought that was the way his life had to be, like it was a punishment from God for being attracted to other men. When the Master had looked at him, it was almost like he'd hated Chase as much as he'd wanted him, and he'd always been convinced it was his own fault. That having to take care of Chase had made the Master resentful, and that's why he'd taken his anger out on him.

But Devon was taking care of him, and there was no anger in his eyes and no frustration in his voice except when he talked about Master Kingston and how he'd treated Chase.

His head was hurting, and it wasn't from the beating. He didn't know what to think anymore. His whole world had been turned around for the second time in his life, and he had no one to turn to for advice or help. He knew that, at his age, he should have been more self-sufficient, but he had no idea how to go about it.

Would he be allowed to leave? Could Master Kingston make him go back to the manor? He always said that Chase cost a lot of money to take care of, so would he have to go back because he couldn't repay him?

Chase could feel tears forming behind his eyes again. He felt so lost and alone, and he had no idea how to change it.

He looked up as he heard a key turn in the lock and breathed a sigh of relief when Devon came in the room carrying a tray full of food. Their gazes caught for a second, and he saw Devon smile sadly at him as he saw the tears in Chase's eyes.

He watched as Devon quickly set the tray on the dresser and then walked over to kneel down beside him. With gentle hands he smoothed Chase's hair back and wiped the tears from his lashes.

"It's okay, Chase. I'm going to make sure it gets better from here. You can trust me." Chase couldn't find any trace of a lie in those mesmerizing eyes. "You don't have to believe me now, but I hope you will one day."

He didn't know what to say, so he was just honest. "Me too."

They smiled at each other for a moment, and then Devon stood up. "Now, let's get some food into you. Dr. Jones was concerned about your weight, and I wanna be able to tell her that you've been eating when she comes to check on you. That woman scares the hell out of me!"

Chase almost giggled at the thought of this man being scared of anybody. He didn't think Devon had ever been scared of anyone in his life!

"Don't look at me that way, sweet boy. I'm scared of plenty of things, and I'm not afraid to admit it... and that woman is one of them!"

Chase just shook his head and smiled. Devon looked at him. "Do you want to try sitting up to eat?"

He thought about it and then nodded. "Yes, please." He let Devon help him sit back against a mountain of cool, soft pillows. It was sore on his back, but it settled to a dull throb after a few minutes. He took a deep breath and relaxed as Devon fussed over him, making sure he was comfortable and pulling the blankets up to make sure he was warm.

He hadn't been so well cared for since he was at home with his momma.

Devon got the tray and brought it to sit beside Chase. He arranged it so that it was over Chase's knees and then encouraged him to dig in. The food was awesome. The grilled cheese was crispy on the outside and warm and gooey in the middle. The soup was fragrant and comforting, so he ate as much as he could, as he wanted to please the man sitting with him.

After eating about half, however, he was too full to go on. "That was really good, but I don't think I can eat any more." He couldn't look the other man in the eyes. He didn't want to see the disappointment in them. But Devon just kissed him on the temple and took the tray back over to the dresser. He gave Chase another pill and a drink of water to go with it and then helped him get settled back on his stomach.

Chase watched as Devon turned off the lights and stripped off his hoodie before sliding back into the bed, under the covers this time.

"Is this okay?" Devon's voice was quiet and calm. Chase just nodded and reached out with his hand, smiling when Devon took it in his own. He was a little worried that he was getting too used to these comforting touches. He wondered if Devon would let him cuddle with him again.

"Go back to sleep, Chase." Devon massaged Chase's wrist with his thumb, distracting him from the ache in his back while he waited for the pill to take effect. "We'll talk some more when you wake up."

"M'kay...." He drifted off to sleep with the sound of Devon's breathing in his ear and the first feeling of safety he'd had in long time.

Five

THE NEXT twenty-four hours went by quietly. Chase slept as much as he could, ate a little when Devon encouraged him, and they chatted about nothing. Devon was using the conversation to figure out where Chase was mentally and emotionally, and he was getting more furious with Kingston the more he learned.

Chase had been almost totally isolated. He'd been given books to read and occasionally allowed to watch a movie, but there had been no TV, no Internet, nothing that allowed him any contact with the outside world.

The few times he'd been allowed out of the mansion had been under heavy guard, and he'd never been allowed to talk to strangers in the clubs they'd been to. It was like time had stood still for the last seven years, and Chase had a lot to catch up on.

Doctor Jones had been to see him and declared him fit enough to have a bath or a shower and to move living quarters, so Devon started making arrangements for them to travel to his house. But first he needed to talk to Chase.

When he came out of the bathroom to see Chase watching a *True Blood* marathon on HBO, he couldn't help but smile. There was no guile in that face, nothing calculating or sly. He was just an open book, letting Devon see every emotion that flitted across his expression.

"Have you watched this, Devon? It's hilarious… and some of these guys are really hot!" Chase was becoming a little more free when he spoke to Devon now, and he had the feeling that once the younger man was comfortable, he'd be a real chatterbox.

"No I haven't, but if you think it's that good, maybe I'll give it a look." Devon walked over and sat on the side of the bed to look at Chase. He'd lost some of the haunted look he'd been carrying, and he was moving better. "I need to talk to you about something."

Chase quickly shut the TV off and sat up at attention, looking scared. "I have to go back, don't I?" All the animation left his face, and his head sagged between his shoulders.

Devon pushed Chase's hair back so that he could see his face.

"I told you that you wouldn't have to go back, and I meant it. You'll find I always keep my promises, sweet boy." He was rewarded by a small smile, and he continued. "What I want to talk to you about is whether or not you want to move over to my house for a while."

Chase's head came up, his eyes wide with shock. "What...?"

"I want to know if you want to come and stay at my house or if you want to go somewhere else." He looked around and grinned. "The recovery room is okay but not really meant to stay in for too long."

He gently took the other man's hand to keep his attention. "I'm not asking anything from you, just offering a place to stay where you can recover in peace and feel safe. No one will come for you there, and being in my home offers you... protection."

He stroked Chase's wrist, trying to stave off the panic he could see blooming in his eyes. "I need protection?"

Devon considered how much to tell him. There'd been some information filtering through the community that had him a little worried. Apparently Kingston wasn't willing to let go of Chase without a fight. It was Chase's life, and he had a right to know. Devon would go to the cops if he thought it would do any good, but Kingston had powerful connections, and he wasn't sure it would help.

"Kingston's been making noises about getting you back, and he's not above using physical means to do it. There are too many people coming and going from the club all the time, and I know some of them are his. My house has a security system and some trusted staff to watch over you when I have to spend time at the club."

He could see Chase trying hard to not let the fear overwhelm him. The boy was a lot stronger than he gave himself credit for.

"And besides, I have to get home. My dogs are driving the housekeeper crazy because they miss me…. I'm the only one they listen to. Everyone else spoils them rotten and lets them do whatever they want."

Chase perked up. "You have dogs?"

Devon laughed. "Yeah, three of them, they seem to have taken over my life. Max is a little terrier/Chihuahua cross who rules the roost and Havoc and Cammy. They're husky/wolf pups that I found abandoned by the side of the road when I was in Alaska a few years ago. They're terrified of Max."

He let the fondness he felt for his animal friends show on his face. Chase needed to be able to see that there was no threat to him as far as Devon was concerned.

"I had dogs once. I left them with my family when I ran away." He looked up at Devon. "Do you think they missed me?"

He looked so sad, Devon couldn't help it. He gathered the younger man into his arms and held him close, mindful of his injuries.

"I'm sure they did, Chase. Dogs know who loves them, and I bet they loved you just as much." He rocked Chase for a while, letting him get control over himself again, then pulling back to look into his face.

"Now, what do you think? Do you want to come to my house? Or do you want me to find somewhere else for you to go? I bet Dr. Jones would let you…."

"*No!*" Chase looked horrified by his outburst, but he kept speaking. "I wanna go to your house. Dr. Jones is nice and all, but… she scares me." He sighed and looked down at his feet. "Everyone scares me… except you."

Devon knew how hard it was for Chase to admit that to him, so he kept quiet and just let him talk.

"If you really don't mind me being there, I'd like to go to your house. I know I'm a big burden, but I swear, Devon, one day I'll find a way to pay you back for everything."

"I really don't mind you being there, Chase. And don't worry about paying me back for anything. It's not like having you there is really going to cost me much." He wanted to ask about the burden comment, but he wanted to wait until they were at his house, where Chase could be comfortable and feel safe, before he started asking more questions.

"Okay, I'm going to go and find you something to wear and we'll leave. I'll let Andy and Joe know what's going on, and don't worry, it's only early afternoon, so the club's empty at the moment. No one's going to see you, okay?"

Chase nodded, still subdued, and Devon couldn't help but press a kiss to his forehead. "It's going to be okay, sweetheart. You'll see."

He gave Chase's hand one more squeeze and stood up. He went out the door and tracked Andy down in the main room, going through the liquor cabinets.

"Problem, Andy?" Devon could see the tense set to his friend's shoulders, and when he turned to look at him, the fury in his eyes was evident.

"Yeah, sorry, Dev, but I think that your former manager was either an idiot or a criminal." He sighed and ran his hand over his face. "There are some pretty big discrepancies between the books and what's actually in stock." He looked up at Devon, the frustration showing plainly. "Don't worry, though. We'll get it figured out."

Devon nodded. "I have faith in you guys. You know that. I knew some things weren't adding up a while ago and should have tackled it then, but I was so busy I let it slide." He clapped Andy on the shoulder. "Sorry you're getting stuck cleaning up the mess."

Andy grinned. "No worries, boss, we've got your back." He looked at his clipboard before looking at Devon curiously. "So, what's up?"

"I'm taking Chase out of here today. I'm gonna take him to my house." He waited for the questions to start.

"Your house? Are you out of your fucking mind? If you take him there, it's going to be like declaring war on Kingston. You know he wants that poor boy back, and I'm pretty sure he's willing to go to any lengths to get him."

"I realize that, Andy, but what else am I supposed to do? Dump him somewhere and hope he doesn't get found?"

"Send him back to his folks, put him in a shelter, anything." Andy took a breath, trying to control himself. "Look, Dev, I know you feel bad for the kid… so do I! But he's not your problem, and I don't want you getting hurt over him."

"I gave him my word, Andy. I said he'd never have to go back, not ever. No one deserves to be treated the way he was, and I won't let it happen again. You can either support me on this or not, but this is how it's gonna be!"

The two men glared at each other for a few moments before Andy backed down. "All right, calm down. You know that no matter what I'll do what I can to help. You're family to me, and you know it." That famous Smith grin stole over his face again. "Besides, Kingston's been bugging me for a while now. Might be good to poke him a little."

Devon sighed in relief. "Thanks, man, I appreciate it. Just… we're gonna have to be careful. I'm not scared of the bastard, but he does have some interesting *friends*."

Joe walked up, catching just enough of the conversation. He slung an arm around Andy's neck and smiled at Devon. "So do you, sweets, and don't forget it!"

Dev groaned. "Devon, not fucking sweets, at least where my staff might hear you. How's anyone supposed to take me seriously if they catch you calling me sweets?"

The other two just snorted. "Sorry, *Sir*, I forgot you're such a big bad Dom and all." Andy choked the words out through his laughter, and Devon punched him in the arm.

"Asshole!" There was no heat behind it, only fondness. "Either of you know where I can find something for Chase to wear out of here? He might feel a little more comfortable in something besides a robe that's almost too short."

Joe nodded and headed for the door. "Yeah, I have some sweats and a T-shirt in my duffle that should work. Pants might be a little short, but they'll do, I think."

"Thanks, Joe." He turned back to Andy. "I'm staying home with him for a couple of days to make sure he's comfortable around Kayley and Justin. While I'm there, I'm going to start the investigation into his family. I don't believe a damned thing Kingston says, but it is possible that they wouldn't have welcomed Chase back once they found out he was gay."

Andy nodded. "Probably a good idea. There's no point in getting his hopes up for nothing. Kid's been through enough already."

"If you need me or you hear anything I need to know, make sure you call." He tried to think of anything else he needed to tell his new manager. "Oh, and have Dani take over my training sessions for the time being. She's been asking to make a little more money lately, and here's her chance. And let the clients know in advance in case they want to postpone."

"You got it, Boss." The other man chuckled. "Should I keep this under wraps for now? You know she'll bust your balls for this."

Devon sighed. "Nah, it's okay. Might as well get it over with. Tell her she can call me later." He looked at Joe as he came in and handed him some clothes. "Thanks, guys. I appreciate you jumping in with both feet to take care of this place for me."

They both nodded, and he turned to go. He was stopped by a gentle hand on his arm, and he turned to see Joe looking at him. "It's not your fault, Dev. Whatever happened between you and Kingston, what he's done to this kid isn't your fault. The bastard made his own decisions, and it has nothing to do with you."

Devon smiled sadly and patted Joe's hand before pulling away. "It's not quite that simple, and you know it. But I appreciate the vote of confidence." He left them standing there, watching him with concern as he walked back to Chase.

When he unlocked the door and went in, Chase was sitting where he left him, obviously lost in thought, and Devon was struck again by how young he looked. It made him so angry to think of all he'd missed out on by being held prisoner in that godforsaken manor.

Making a decision, he sat down beside the younger man. Chase looked up at him through his lashes, and he smiled down at him. "Chase, do you want to go to the police? What Kingston did to you was against the law, and he deserves to be punished for it." It was against his better judgment, but he'd do it if Chase needed to.

There was fear and confusion in those hazel eyes, and Chase was shaking his head before Devon could even finish. "No, please, Sir. I can't go to the police. They won't believe me, and then he'll be able to find me." He looked down at the floor, his slender frame shaking in terror.

"I'll just go… somewhere. I won't bother you anymore. You won't ever see me! I just… can't go back there. I'd rather be dead." His voice was flat and without hope. It was heartbreaking to hear. He bent over and wrapped his arms around himself, rocking back and forth like a child.

Devon moved immediately to hold him, wincing when Chase flinched from his touch. "Chase, you aren't going anywhere right now but my house. You're going to play with my dogs and eat Kayley's cooking and sit in my hot tub. You're going to watch every episode of *True Blood* and whatever the fuck else strikes your fancy, and you're going to get better."

Chase was still bent over but slowly relaxed into Devon's lap, letting his head be petted.

"And when you're ready, we'll figure out what you want to do and where you want to go, okay?"

The younger man sniffed and nodded and then took a deep breath. He sat up and smiled timidly at Devon. He pointed at the clothes beside Devon on the bed. "Are those for me?"

Devon nodded and passed them over. Chase stood and dropped the robe from his shoulders so he could slowly slip into the sweats. They were a little short, as anticipated, but they'd do for now. They were gonna have to do some shopping for Chase at some point.

The T-shirt fit okay, as Joe was a little broader than Chase at the moment. But Devon could see that a steady diet of good food and a little exercise were going to have Chase filling out in no time.

As he dressed, Devon gathered up his wallet and phone, stuffing them into the pocket of his hoodie, and then grabbed his keys. "Come on. Let's go to my office. I think there's some flip-flops there you can use." He looked at Chase carefully. "What about the jeans and boots you were wearing when you came in?

"Burn 'em." For perhaps the first time, there was steel behind Chase's words, and Devon approved.

They got the shoes from the office, and Devon fired off a quick text, asking Andy to keep anyone in the place out of the way for the next couple of minutes while he got Chase out to the car. The young man had been subjected to enough scrutiny as it was.

They made it to the staff parking lot without seeing anyone, but he was pretty sure they were being watched discreetly. Andy didn't trust Kingston to leave them alone, and so he would be making sure they were safe.

Devon could see Chase's surprise when they walked over to a beautifully restored blue '69 Dodge Charger. "Hey, this is like in that show… from the '80s…. *The Dukes of Hazzard*! I like this color better than the orange, though."

Devon laughed. "Yeah, the good old General Lee. But my baby's better. It can drive for more than a mile without falling apart."

Chase loved cars; it was obvious. He was so careful opening the door and getting in it made Devon chuckle. "Just get in the car, dude. You aren't going to hurt it. The dogs ride in here all the time."

The younger man looked at him like he'd lost his mind as he carefully settled his sore back into the passenger seat. "Shit, Chase, do you want to lie down in the backseat? I forgot about you having to sit."

Chase shook his head. "Nah, I'm okay." He grinned at Devon, and it was a beautiful thing to see. "Besides, this car is too cool for that."

"Well, that's true." Devon climbed in and started the engine. The rumble made him smile every time. "Are you ready to meet my dogs?"

Chase nodded with enthusiasm, and they took off on the drive to Devon's house. They chatted a little about sports, Chase wanting to know how the Texas teams were doing, and Devon was amazed at how much better he was getting already.

It wasn't long before they were pulling into the driveway at Devon's house, and he could tell it was another surprise. It was a Craftsman-style home on a big, private lot, and it was something that had been restored as well.

"Devon, this house is amazing!" And Devon knew it was. Most people who came to his house the first time were completely floored. They seemed to expect some glass-and-steel industrial loft. Because he was a Dom—and a good one—they seemed to think his house would be cold and unwelcoming, and nothing could be further from the truth. Of course, there was a playroom in the basement.

"Thanks. I've put a lot of work into it, and it makes me proud."

"You should be!" Chase gingerly got out of the car and wobbled a little, so Devon hurried around to steady him.

"Okay?" He looked up at Chase and realized it was the first time he was standing straight up in Devon's presence. He had to be three inches taller than Devon.

Chase nodded but let himself lean on Devon a little.

"Come on. Let's get you in the house."

Dev led him to the door and was just reaching for his keys when it was flung open by a pretty blond with a scowl on her face. "About time you got here. These mutts are making me crazy. First it was moping because you weren't here and now bouncing all over trying to get out of the kitchen to get to the door!"

Devon could hear them whining and barking behind the closed door to the mudroom, and he smiled. "How come you locked them out?"

"Uh, so they wouldn't trample your guest, here?" She smiled sweetly at Chase and then went back to glaring at Devon. "I'm sure the poor boy isn't up to being mauled the first second in the door."

Devon hung his head at the chastisement. "Sorry, Kayley, I should have thought."

She smacked him with the dish towel in her hand.

"Don't give me any of that bullshit, Devon. You get this boy upstairs and get him cleaned up. By the time you're done, I should have lunch ready. You've got about an hour."

She gently touched Chase's arm. "Don't you worry, sweetie. Devon's a bit of an idiot sometimes, but he'll take real good care of you, okay?" She looked over at Devon with a fond smile, and he could see that it helped Chase relax a little.

"Yeah, I know."

Devon squeezed Chase's shoulder. "Just give me a second to say hi to the brats, and then I'll take you up."

Chase nodded, and Devon and Kayley went to the kitchen together. He opened the door to the mudroom, kneeling down to accept doggy kisses and love. Max was right in his face, and that was probably why he missed Cammy sneaking by him into the house.

When he was done with the other two, he went looking for his girl, and when he found her, it almost broke his heart. She was sitting in front of Chase, who had lowered himself to sit on the steps to the upper level. She had her big head on his lap, and he was leaned over, face buried in her fur, and he was talking to her.

Devon couldn't hear what he was saying, but that was all right. As far as he was concerned, it was between Chase and Cammy. He watched them for a few more minutes and then cleared his throat to announce his presence.

Chase's head bobbed up, his face flushing with the embarrassment of being caught talking to the dog, and he pushed himself up quickly.

Devon just walked over and crouched down by Cammy, letting her kiss him hello and giving her a good scratch. "This is Chase, Cammy. He's gonna be hanging around here for a while. That okay with you?"

The big dog huffed her agreement, and Devon continued talking to her. "We're gonna take good care of him, aren't we, baby?"

Chase stared at them in amazement as she woofed softly and went over to sit by Chase, leaning her body against his knees. "Does she really understand you?"

Devon could hear the awe in Chase's voice. "I'd like to think so." He walked up to Chase. "Come on. Let's go get you cleaned up."

They both moved toward the stairs, the dog at their heels. Devon turned to her. "We're going up to have a bath, Cammy. You want one too?"

Chase snorted with laughter when Cammy sneezed and shook her head and took off for the kitchen.

Dev just grinned. "That's my girl. She'll stick with you through thick and thin, but mention a bath and she'll run for cover every time."

He started up the stairs, Chase right behind him, and headed for the guest room. When he opened the door and let Chase in, he was surprised at Chase's reluctance to enter the room.

"What's the matter, Chase?" He was worried that it was bringing back bad memories for the younger man.

"Is this your room?"

Devon tried to read the expression on the other man's face but couldn't.

"No, my room is down the hall."

"Oh...." His voice was soft and filled with something... something Devon couldn't place.

"Come on. The bathroom's through here." He opened the door to the en suite, smiling because he knew the bathroom was one of the best rooms in the house.

"What'll it be, Chase? Bath or shower?"

Chase looked around, eyes widening at the huge claw-footed tub that dominated the other end of the room. "I can have a bath in that?" He looked like a kid in a candy store.

Devon smiled at him indulgently. "Yep, in fact it's probably a good idea. The warm water will help relax some of those sore muscles in your back." He walked over and started the water running.

"Please, Devon... not too hot, okay?"

Chase wouldn't look at him as he asked, and Devon felt another flush of anger as he realized why Chase made the request.

"You can have it however you want, baby. It's to make you feel better, not worse." He always knew that Kingston was a cruel bastard, but having it confirmed like this was sickening.

Chase nodded and stood beside the tub. He slipped off his clothes and folded them neatly and placed them on the counter. "Um, could you help me with these bandages please?"

"Yeah, no problem. They should be able to stay off now." Devon carefully peeled the bandages away from Chase's back, pleased that all the wounds seemed to be healing properly. "There, all done."

Chase smiled and reached down to check the water temperature before climbing carefully into the tub. The sigh he gave as the warm water surrounded him was its own reward.

"Now, don't fall asleep and drown. I'm going to see if I can find you some pajama pants. I know you just put those on, but you were dirty when you did."

Chase nodded, his eyes sliding shut, and Devon left the room. He remembered that his friend Stephen had left some clothes behind the last time he'd stayed, and he found them in the dresser.

Stephen was a big guy, and he knew the pajamas he found would fit Chase perfectly. There was a white muscle shirt there too, so he added it to the pile. Underwear might be a problem, but then he remembered the new ones he'd just bought a few weeks ago, still sitting unopened in his closet.

He darted down the hall, grabbed a package, and went back to the guest room. After dropping everything on the bed, he went back to the bathroom, knocking and waiting for Chase's quiet "Come in" before entering.

"How are you making out?" He could see Chase was trying to wash his hair, but it obviously hurt to reach his arms that far over his head.

"I want my hair clean, but…." He shrugged, wincing as he did.

Devon walked closer. "Can I help?" Chase nodded, and he knelt beside the tub. Chase ducked down into the water and got his hair wet, then sat back up. Devon grabbed the shampoo and lathered the younger man's hair.

As he scrubbed, he did his level best to ignore the fact that Chase was naked… and wet… and apparently enjoying having his hair washed. It was an impossible task, though. The groans of appreciation falling from Chase's lips had Devon's dick twitching in his jeans.

When he looked into the water, he discovered that Chase was indeed proportional. He was beautiful.

Of course, now that he was looking, he saw more scars from the abuse that Chase had been subjected to, and it made him feel sick. How could anyone look at this young man and want to hurt him? It would be like beating a puppy!

He didn't realize he'd closed his eyes until he heard Chase gasp, and they popped open.

"I'm sorry, Sir." Chase was hunched over and trying to hide from Devon's gaze.

"What? Why? You didn't do anything." He was confused. What could the younger man have possibly have done to apologize for?

He was back to not meeting Devon's eyes. "I'm not supposed to... I'm not allowed...." He didn't seem to know how to finish the sentence, but Devon figured it out.

"You weren't allowed to get hard?" His tone was incredulous. A teenage boy got hard when you looked at them funny, for fuck's sake. He pushed on Chase's shoulders gently, wanting him to relax again.

"No, Master said it was up to him to enjoy it, not me. It took me a long time to learn. I was... locked up in a cock cage for a long time." Chase shivered, remembering his "lessons."

"How long?" Devon knew he shouldn't ask, probably didn't want to know the answer, but he couldn't help himself.

Chase scrunched up his face as he tried to think. "I don't know, a year, maybe more?"

Devon was at a loss for words. And then Chase continued.

"He wanted it so that, no matter what he did, I wouldn't get hard. And it worked, mostly. But sometimes... sometimes I couldn't help it. It didn't feel good... but it made me come anyway." Those big eyes looked up at Devon, full of confusion and self-loathing, and he was about two seconds away from grabbing a gun and hunting Kingston down like the fucking animal he was.

But that wouldn't help Chase right then, so he settled for washing his hair. He knew what kind of methods the kid had been subjected to. All very effective Dominant strategies that brought a lot of pleasure when used correctly but were nothing short of torture when they were abused.

"His rules don't apply to you, Chase. Your body is your own, and no one can take that from you. Not anymore."

He could feel Chase relaxing under his fingers as he scrubbed. He leaned down to whisper in his ear. "And I think it's kind of hot that my washing your hair gets you all worked up."

Chase's erection, which had flagged from fear, roared back to life. "Oh God, Devon." His hand moved toward his cock and then stopped. Devon whispered some more.

"It's okay to touch yourself, Chase. I don't mind, and if I'm making you uncomfortable, I'll leave you alone for a while."

"No! Don't… just stay… please." Chase's voice was cracked and low, sending shivers down Devon's spine.

"Okay, baby, shhh, I'm not going anywhere." Devon kept up the soothing touches on Chase's scalp, breathing softly in the younger man's ear. "You're so beautiful, Chase. Soft and sweet, even after all you've been through."

He kept talking, smiling to himself in approval when Chase started to stroke himself. "So fucking hard, aren't you, sweetheart? That's good, baby, let yourself go."

He never moved to touch Chase anywhere else, not wanting to frighten him and needing to build trust between them. He kept cooing encouraging words in Chase's ear, feeling the tension grow as he neared his orgasm.

It didn't take long. A few more strokes and Chase threw his head back, his release clouding the water while he moaned Devon's name quietly. It made him want to hear Chase screaming it.

His own dick was rock hard, pressed painfully against the cold porcelain on the outside of the tub, but he ignored it. As Chase relaxed, one hand crept up to grab Devon's hand, and he let their fingers tangle together.

"Thank you." The young man's voice was shy and sweet. "That's the first time in over a year I've come from feeling good."

"Oh, baby." Devon just held his hand for a bit, letting them both calm down a little. "Come on. Let's get you standing so I can rinse you off. If you aren't ready when Kayley brings up lunch, I'm gonna be in so much trouble."

They got Chase to his feet, and Dev used the handheld attachment to rinse the soap out of his hair. Devon grabbed one of the fluffy towels off the shelf by the tub and passed it to Chase. He helped him step out of the tub and then let him dry himself.

Devon led him back to the bedroom, opened the package of underwear, and passed him a pair. Chase dropped the towel he'd slung around his hips onto the bed and slipped them on. It was obvious he had absolutely no sense of self-awareness when it came to his body, nor any expectation of privacy.

Once he had the clothes on, Devon grabbed the towel and rubbed it over Chase's still dripping hair, chuckling fondly at him.

"Come on. Let's get you into bed. Kayley will be up shortly. You can eat, and then I'll give you your meds." Chase yawned, the bath and the orgasm catching up with him and tiring him out. "And then I'd suggest a nap."

Chase nodded and settled back against the pillows. His dark eyes never left Devon as he moved around the room, tidying and waiting for Kayley.

"Thank you, Devon... for everything, I mean. I... I didn't know that people would be kind for no reason. I mean, I used to know, but I think I forgot."

Devon walked over, sat on the edge of the bed, and took Chase's hand. "I hope I can help you remember."

Chase smiled. It was small but there. "I think you might."

Six

KAYLEY BROUGHT up a delicious lunch of homemade stew and fresh cornbread and Chase ate almost all of it, to Devon and Kayley's delight.

She'd stayed and chatted with them for a little while, catching Devon up with all the things going on at the house and getting a little gossip from the club. When she saw that Chase was just about asleep, she gathered up the remains of their lunch and headed back downstairs.

"I'm going to go do some paperwork in my office, okay? It's just down the hall, so you can call me if you need anything." Devon waited for Chase to nod and turned to leave, stopping at the younger man's soft call. He turned back and waited patiently for him to speak.

"Would you stay, please? Just until I'm asleep?" Chase's face was red with embarrassment, but Devon was so impressed that he'd managed to ask for something for himself that he couldn't say no.

He walked back over and sat on the edge of the bed, taking Chase's hand and smiling tenderly at him. "Of course I can. Just close your eyes and relax. Nothing bad will happen here. I promise."

Chase sighed and turned carefully onto his side, curling toward Devon and snuggling under the covers. He smiled up at Dev sleepily and then let his eyes flutter shut.

He was out in a matter of minutes, but Devon sat there for a while, enjoying the chance to just look at him and making sure he was sleeping without nightmares before leaving him alone.

He slipped quietly out of the room, leaving the door open a little, and went to his office two doors down. He walked in, rounded the desk, and sat down heavily in his leather chair.

For the first time in a long time, Devon was unsure of what to do. In the bedroom down the hall, the answer to all of Devon's dreams slept soundly, hopefully finally feeling safe enough to relax and rest without nightmares.

The last two nights, the young man had whimpered and shook, and Devon could only imagine the horrors disturbing his sleep. He'd stroked his hair and hugged him close, telling Chase to hush when he'd tried to apologize for waking him.

They hadn't talked about it much, as Chase seemed ashamed of his fear, and that broke Devon's heart even more. If anyone had earned the right to be afraid, it was Chase.

But in spite of it all, the younger man retained his sweet, kindhearted nature. When he let himself forget for a while, he was quick to laugh and eager to please, and Devon found both traits equally attractive.

He was happy that Chase no longer cringed when Devon got close to him, and it even seemed like his presence made Chase feel safer than being alone.

The problem for Devon was simple. He wanted to protect Chase. He wanted to take care of him and keep him from coming to any kind of harm, mental or physical. He wanted to help Chase get back on his feet and find out where he belonged.

But he also wanted Chase to belong to him. He wanted to see Chase spread out on his bed, all that golden skin against snow-white sheets. He wanted Chase on his knees, a thin leather collar around his neck and begging Devon to let him suck him.

He knew that Chase was a natural sub, soaking up praise and kindness like a sponge. He was also easily intimidated, and therein lay the problem. Chase responded to Devon without hesitation, and while he appreciated it, he wasn't sure of the reason behind it.

Was it because he wanted to obey or because he'd been trained to? And because Devon knew that those training methods had involved cruelty and a lack of emotional connection of any kind, he wasn't sure that Chase was even capable of saying no to a Dom if he wanted to.

Devon rested his head in his hands and wondered if it was too early to have a stiff drink.

There was a knock on his office door, and he looked up sharply to find Kayley standing there. He flinched inwardly. He knew this had been coming.

"Something you need, Kayley?" He tried, but couldn't quite look her in the eye.

"No, just checking on you… and bringing you this!" She pulled out the glass she'd been hiding behind her back and walked in to set it on his desk. "I figured you could use a drink about now." She winked at him knowingly and settled into the chair across from him.

He picked up the glass and sniffed it, smiling appreciatively at finding his favorite Scotch. He smiled at her thankfully and downed the liquor in one shot. He grimaced at the burn as he swallowed and then sat the glass down.

"So, you want to tell me how you're doing? Or do I need to wait for Danielle to come over and beat it out of you?" She smiled at him, softening the words.

"I'm fine, Kayley, just tired." And that wasn't just an evasion either. Between being awakened by Chase's nightmares and worrying about where to go from here, he hadn't slept much.

"Well that much is obvious. You look like shit." She spoke with a familiarity that told of long years of friendship. "But unless I'm very much mistaken, that handsome young man is getting to you in more ways than one." She raised her eyebrow at him.

He looked her in the eye, debating how much to say. He sighed and briefly wished for another drink. "He's just so young, Kay, despite everything he's been through. He's been locked away from the world and tortured, and it makes me so fucking pissed off!" His voice had been rising, but a quick look toward the door by Kayley had him reining himself in.

"And you like him?" There was no mockery in her voice, just concern.

He stood and turned to face the window, wrapping his arms around himself. "Like isn't quite the word. He's sweet and innocent and beautiful. It's like the depravity he was subjected to didn't really touch his soul, and it makes me admire his strength."

"Is it true he was Kingston's sub?" Her tone was neutral, but Devon heard the concern.

"He wasn't his sub, he was his fucking hostage. He played on his insecurities and kept him away from almost all other people." Devon started pacing his office in an effort to keep from yelling. "I'm pretty sure he lied to Chase about his parents, although I have Jax looking into it to make sure, and I feel so fucking guilty about it all!" He knew his head of security wouldn't let him down. Jax took his job very seriously.

Kayley stood up and walked over to wrap her arms around Devon. He resisted at first but finally gave in, letting her comfort him. "What that bastard did, Dev, it wasn't your fault. He's sick in the worst way, and nothing you did or didn't do can change that."

He didn't argue with her, but she knew he wasn't agreeing either. They all had their crosses to bear, and Kingston was Devon's.

Once he'd calmed down, she let him go and looked up at him. "So when are you going to admit it?"

He shifted uncomfortably and looked away. "Admit what?"

"Admit that you want him." She said it quietly, without judgment, and he looked back at her gratefully.

"I can't... I mean, why on earth would Chase ever want to have anything to do with my lifestyle ever again? It's been nothing but cruel to him, and I'm betting that as soon as he realizes he's really free, he'll be headed home like a shot!"

"Because he doesn't know about you and how you live your life, that's why. He doesn't know that a Dom's job isn't about hurting innocent boys, but taking care of consenting men who are looking for something they can't find anywhere else."

She laughed out loud at his pout. "Come on Dev, you're the most caring person I know. You took in me and my dad when we were living on the streets and gave us jobs and a home and helped us remember that we're worth something. You're always there for Joe and Andy, especially after Andy's family disowned him when he came out."

She walked around the room. "Almost everyone who works at the club has been rescued by you one way or another!" Devon couldn't help smiling at her as she paced and raved. "You got Jayden into that drug rehab program, and three years later it's still sticking, and you literally saved Danielle's life by getting her away from her abusive fuckwad of a husband."

She whirled on him, and he thought she was gorgeous when she got passionate like this. "You don't just show that you're a Dom in the club, doing scenes that make people almost faint with pleasure, you show it in everything you do. You've proven you don't always have to be the boss, but you do always need to care about what happens to others!"

Walking up to him, she cradled his face in her hands. "No matter what Kingston does, he will never be what you are, because he only thinks of himself and his own pleasure, and you only know how to put others first."

She smiled up at him. "Give him the chance to find himself and to get to know you. You might be surprised at what you both discover." She leaned up to kiss him on the cheek, and at that moment Chase appeared in the doorway.

He looked from one to the other and then blanched. "Oh God… I'm so sorry." He disappeared from the doorway before Devon could say anything.

"Well, looks like we discovered something already." Kayley patted him on the cheek. "I think you'd better go and explain to Chase about my fiancé and the wedding you're going to be throwing for me and Justin next month."

She pushed him toward the door, smirking like she knew something he didn't. "Go on now. This is the perfect time to get to that 'getting to know each other' thing I mentioned."

"What do you mean, we've discovered something? What are you talking about?" He wasn't sure why Chase would care whether or not Kayley was his girlfriend, but he let himself be pushed out the door anyway. Devon had a feeling he would always take any chance he got to spend more time with him.

He looked back at her once, blushing a little at the wink she gave him, and walked down to Chase's door.

It was closed, so he knocked and was startled when it opened immediately. He looked up into Chase's face and was dismayed to see that his eyes were red rimmed and full of fear.

Devon cupped Chase's face in his hand. "Hey, what's wrong?"

"I'm sorry, Sir. I didn't mean to." Chase took a shuddering breath before continuing. "I just woke up... and got scared, so I thought I'd find you...." He trailed off, shrugging helplessly.

Devon smiled up at him gently and put his arm around Chase's shoulders, leading him to the bed. He urged him to sit down and then sat beside him, taking his hand.

"You didn't do anything, Chase. I was talking to Kayley, and she was helping me figure some things out. I'm sorry you woke up afraid, and you're welcome to come and find me anytime that happens. I won't be mad."

Devon grinned and bumped his shoulder into Chase's. "Oh, and she told me to tell you that you have to come to her wedding."

Chase looked at him, a totally stricken expression on his face. "You're getting married, Sir?" The question was so quiet that Dev almost couldn't hear him.

"Nope, it's still illegal in this state, but Kayley is. She and Justin are getting married right here, in fact, out in the backyard." He sat and waited for his news to sink in. It didn't escape his notice that whenever Chase got upset or nervous he called Devon Sir.

"Oh...." Chase seemed to relax against Devon's side, and it made Dev smile. Maybe Devon wasn't the only one getting attached.

"Yeah... oh! I thought maybe you would have picked up on the fact that we play for the same team when I admitted to finding you hot in the tub." He looked at Chase, raising his eyebrow.

Chase blushed furiously. "It's none of my business, anyhow. You're a Dom. You can do anything you want."

Devon looked at him sternly. "Being a Dom does not give me free rein to *do anything I want*. I know that's how Kingston acted, but honestly, Chase, the man is out of his mind." He took a deep breath to calm himself. He didn't want to scare him.

"What he did to you wasn't dominance, it was slavery and torture, and I'll make sure he won't do it to anyone ever again."

He looked at Chase, and the younger man nodded, smiling shyly at him.

"I wouldn't have enjoyed myself with you like I did in the bathroom today if I was with anyone else. I know you don't have any reason to believe me, but it's true. I believe in love and loyalty, and I don't believe in cheating… even as tempting as you are."

Chase looked up from where he'd been studying his hands and avoiding Devon's gaze. "How can you say that?"

"How can I say what? That you're attractive? Because you are!"

Chase stood up and walked to the bathroom door before turning around and walking back. "I'm not! I'm ugly and stupid and weak. How could someone like you possibly find me attractive?"

Devon rose from the bed to block Chase's path. He lifted both hands to frame Chase's face, forcing him to meet his gaze. "You're beautiful, Chase. Tall and sleek, with gorgeous hair and innocent eyes. I can see why that monster was attracted to you in the first place. Your sweetness just shines from you, even after everything."

He reached up to wipe at the tears slowly falling from those mesmerizing eyes. "You aren't stupid or weak either. You were scared and alone, and you were taken advantage of by someone with no morals or scruples. By the time you realized what was going on, you were trapped. I'm awed by the fact that you managed to survive with your mind and spirit intact. Most people would have crumbled and lost themselves forever."

Chase was sobbing openly now, and before Devon could grab him, he crumpled to his knees. "If I'm so great, why doesn't anyone want me? Not my parents, not him… they all just threw me away! I know that's why he took me there, to your club. He wanted me to fail. He left me there to be beaten and tossed out like I was garbage!"

Without even realizing it, Chase had fallen into position, arms crossed behind his back, hands grabbing his elbows, curled over on himself, waiting for blows to fall, and it broke Devon's heart. He fell to his own knees and pulled Chase into his lap. He gently pried Chase's hands from the bruising grip he had had on his own arms and rubbed up and down his back.

The younger man curled up as small as he could, burrowing into the comfort Devon was offering him. Devon could feel his shirt grow wet with hot tears, and he had never felt more useless in his life.

"It's okay, baby, you cry if you gotta. You've more than earned the right." He brought one hand up to stroke Chase's silky hair and rocked him gently. "But you need to listen to me, okay?" He could feel the small nod against his chest, so he continued.

"You're not garbage. I know, because I've seen people who deserved to be called that, people with no compassion or goodness in them, who only think of themselves and never give to others. And that's not you, Chase."

"How do you know?" Chase's voice was meek, and it made Dev smile.

"When you left your parents' house, did you take anything besides your clothes? Did you take money? Games? Anything?"

Chase shook his head, and Devon smiled.

"When you lived with Kingston, did you ever ask him to buy you things or do things for you?"

Chase shook his head again.

"And are you angry at me for what happened to you in my club?" Devon was sure he knew the answer but wanted to see what Chase would say.

Chase sat up and looked at Devon. "Of course not! It wasn't your fault, and you've been nothing but nice to me. Why would I be angry at you?" He looked genuinely confused, and Devon was captivated again by the other man's earnestness.

"A lot of people would be, Chase. They wouldn't care about whose fault it was."

"That's just stupid."

"You're right, it is." He kept petting Chase's hair, just enjoying snuggling with him.

"I'm sorry for yelling at you, Devon." He looked thoroughly ashamed of himself, so Devon poked him in the ribs, making him laugh.

"Stop apologizing. You have a lot to be angry about."

"You know I'm not really beautiful, right? I mean, I'm covered in scars and I'm too skinny and my nose is too big for my face and—"

Devon cut him off with a finger to his lips. "Stop it, Chase. You're beautiful. You have silky hair that feels good under my fingers and eyes that I get lost in when you're talking to me. And your nose is fine. Once you put a few pounds on, everything will balance out perfectly.

"As for your scars, well, I think they just show how strong you are." He reached down and under Chase's shirt, mapping the scars on his back with his fingers.

They sat there quietly for a few minutes. Devon was in no hurry to go anywhere, and he was disappointed when Chase started to get up.

"I'd better get up. I must be squishing you."

Devon let him up and then got up himself. "It was fine. I didn't mind." He was sure he was blushing as much as Chase was. "You want to go down and watch a movie? We can snuggle with the babies and eat things that are bad for us. What do you think?"

"That would be awesome! Can I go clean up first?" Chase nodded toward the bathroom.

Devon grinned and pulled off his damp T-shirt. He used a dry spot to clean off Chase's face a little more and then gave him a little push toward the bathroom. "Yeah, I'd better go and find a clean shirt. I'll meet you at the top of the stairs in five, okay?"

Chase grinned in agreement, and Devon didn't miss the long, hungry look the younger man gave his naked torso before he went into the bathroom.

Devon smirked as he left the room. That look had been pure lust. Maybe Chase wasn't clinging to him just out of gratitude after all. It was worth finding out.

$\mathcal{S}$even

THEY MET at the top of the stairs, and Devon led the way down to the kitchen. He kept his pace slow to make sure Chase didn't jar himself too much. He was moving a bit better, but Devon didn't want to push it.

"So what would you like, Chase? Kayley keeps the cupboards pretty well stocked. Anything you want, just ask. If it's here, it's yours."

He walked over and opened the huge walk-in pantry, motioning Chase to follow him. "In here we have chips, pretzels, cookies... God, the woman goes nuts in the snack aisle." He walked over and opened the fridge, peering inside.

"There's soda's in here. Not sure you should be having beer with the meds you're on... and I think there's ice cream in the freezer...." Devon trailed off and looked up when Chase let out a small noise that could only be described as a squeak.

Chase's eyes were wide and pleading. "You have ice cream?" It was almost a reverent whisper, and Devon knew he was all kinds of screwed. Saying no to that face would be pretty much impossible.

"Let me check, but yeah, I think so." He opened the freezer door and found three different kinds. "We have mint chocolate chip, rocky road, and maple walnut. What do you want?"

He could see the indecision in Chase's face and smirked. "Triple sundae it is." He grabbed all three flavors and took them to the counter.

He pulled two big bowls out of the cupboard and a couple of spoons out of a drawer.

Digging around in another drawer, he found an ice cream scoop and got to work. He looked up at Chase again for a minute. "There's whipped cream and caramel in the fridge if you want some."

"Okay!" Chase scooted over quickly as his back would allow and grabbed the stuff out of the fridge, and Dev smiled as Chase got distracted by the bananas in the hanging basket over the counter. Chase seemed to be debating with himself, one hand reaching toward them and then pulling back. Just as Dev was going to say something, Chase's hand darted out and grabbed one, and Dev looked down at the ice cream so he wouldn't be caught watching.

"Is this okay?" Chase stood there, holding out the banana and looked so worried it broke Devon's heart a little.

He nodded and smiled. "It's perfect." He finished scooping out the frozen treat and put the scoop in the sink. "Would you mind putting these back in the freezer while I do the rest?"

Chase looked startled at being asked instead of ordered, but quickly recovered and smiled and nodded. "Sure, no problem."

Dev opened the banana and started slicing it with a knife he grabbed from the block on the counter. He put half in Chase's bowl and then shrugged. "Might as well." He sliced up the rest and added that to Chase's bowl too. He grabbed the whipped cream, topped both bowls, and then drizzled on the caramel. He was pretty sure there was no way Chase was going to be able to eat it all, but Devon was gonna make sure he tried.

"There, these are about perfect!" He handed Chase his bowl and was promptly confused when Chase frowned. "What's wrong?"

"You didn't have bananas."

"I don't like bananas unless they're baked into chocolate-chip banana bread."

"Oh... I'm sorry, I didn't know."

Devon sighed in exasperation. "Do you like bananas, Chase?"

Chase nodded. "Yeah."

"Then eat them and don't worry about it. You don't have to like and dislike the same things as me."

He watched as Chase stopped, closed his eyes, and took a deep breath. When he opened them, he smiled timidly. "Yeah, okay."

Devon smiled and slowly rubbed his knuckles over Chase's cheek. "Come on, let's eat this before we let the dogs in, or we won't get any."

He waited until Chase nodded and then turned and led the way to the living room. He set his bowl down on the coffee table and got Chase situated on the couch, covering him with a blanket because he seemed to like snuggling under them.

He walked to the DVD cabinet and started looking around. "Any preferences?"

Chase blushed and shook his head. "You know it's all new to me."

Devon nodded and smiled. He grabbed his copy of *The Fast and the Furious* and held it up. "You like fast cars, chase scenes, and hot guys?"

"Uh, yeah?" Chase was a little overwhelmed, Devon could tell, so he just put the movie in and went to sit beside him, snagging his bowl of ice cream as he went by.

He grabbed the remote, turned on his ridiculously complicated home theater system, and got the movie started. They watched in silence for a while, both intent on eating their ice cream, but Devon soon found himself watching Chase more than the movie.

The other man was obviously enraptured by what he was eating, and it was entrancing for Devon to see. "When was the last time you had ice cream, Chase?" His own voice startled him. He hadn't meant to ask.

Chase smiled. "A few nights before I left home. My mom made me a big banana split as a reward for bringing up my English grade." He chuckled a little. "Writing essays wasn't my favorite school activity."

Devon smirked. "Yeah, me neither. School wasn't my favorite activity."

"Oh, I liked school. Loved science and math and stuff. And I was pretty good at sports. Played some basketball for a while, and I was pretty good."

"Hmm, you play basketball? Are you sure you're tall enough?" Devon couldn't help but tease him, and he was rewarded with another blush.

"Cut it out, Dev…." God, could he be any more adorable?

"Sorry, sweet boy, you're just too easy to tease." Devon bumped his shoulder into Chase's, happy when the other man didn't flinch or pull away.

They finished their ice cream, and Devon took the bowls back to the kitchen and put them in the dishwasher. Devon walked to the back door, opened it, and whistled for the dogs. He was surprised when the first one in the door was Cammy. Usually Max beat the other two easily. He waited for Max and Havoc and then made his way back to the living room.

The reason for Cammy's hurry was evident. She was sitting between Chase's feet, her head in his lap, and sucking up attention for all she was worth.

"I think I'm jealous." He smiled at Chase but was dismayed to see him frown and try to push Cammy away.

"I'm sorry." Chase hung his head, his long hair falling in front of his face, hiding him from view.

Devon walked over and sat beside him, reaching out to pet Cammy, who refused to be pushed away from Chase. "First of all, I was teasing. I know you're not used to that, and I don't blame you for being cautious, but I can't help it. You're adorable, especially when you blush, so I'll admit to trying to make it happen as often as possible."

Chase's head popped up, his mouth hanging open in surprise.

"And second of all, I was jealous of Cammy, not you." Devon sat there grinning, waiting to see Chase's reaction. He wasn't disappointed.

He wasn't sure he'd ever seen anyone's face so red, and that was sweet enough, but the look of hope that was there almost took Devon's breath away. He patted Chase on the shoulder.

"Come on. Let's finish the movie, okay?" He didn't move, just relaxed against the back of the couch, spread his arms across the back, and waited. After a minute, Chase relaxed too. He collapsed against the cushion and sort of tucked himself under Devon's arm before letting his head fall back.

Max tired himself out chasing his tail and jumped up on the couch to snuggle in on the other side of Devon, while Havoc collapsed at their feet, his big head pillowed on Devon's foot. Cammy mirrored him on the floor on Chase's side, lying against his legs and promptly falling asleep.

Devon couldn't remember the last time he'd been so relaxed and comfortable.

When the movie was over, Devon flipped to the television and found some scary movie to watch. It didn't occur to him that Chase wouldn't have any experience with those kinds of movies until he felt him jump at his side.

"You want me to change it?" He wrapped his arm around Chase's shoulder and smiled when he shook his head. The younger man just snuggled further into Devon's side, laying his head on his chest and curling his feet up onto the couch beside him.

The big hazel eyes looked up at Devon. "Is this okay?" He looked small and vulnerable, and Dev fell a little further.

"It's perfect." He knew Chase would be getting sleepy again soon and would need his meds as well, but for now he was content with how things were.

Devon lost himself in the movie for a while, his hand drifting up to rub the back of Chase's neck. Eventually he noticed that the other man's breathing was starting to even out, and knew he had to get him up to bed before he fell asleep.

"Come on, Chase, time for bed." He shook him gently and smiled as he yawned and stretched.

"Okay, Dev." Sleepy Chase was even more beautiful. "I'm really tired."

"Let's go. I'll give you your meds and tuck you in." He took Chase's hand and pulled him toward the stairs, shutting off the lights as he went. It was a little early for bed, but Devon hadn't slept in his own room for a few days, and the stress of everything had worn him out.

It was dark in the hallway, and Chase seemed jittery. "You all right?"

Chase swallowed nervously but nodded. "Yeah, I'm fine." They walked into the room Chase was using, and he relaxed a little when Devon turned on the small lamp on the dresser.

He gave Chase a gentle push toward the bathroom and then straightened the bed while waiting for the other man to brush his teeth and finish getting ready. When he came back out, Devon tucked him under the covers and then reached for the bottles of pills. He shook them out into his palm and passed them to Chase.

There was a pitcher of water on the nightstand, and Devon poured some and passed it to him. Once the pills were gone, Devon stood and went to turn out the lamp.

"Could…." Chase swallowed noisily before continuing. "Could you leave it on, please?" Devon could see he was embarrassed, but he knew Chase probably had reason to be scared of the dark.

"Yep, no problem." He walked to the bed and sat down on the edge. "I'm going to be just down the hall. If you need anything, just call me or come and get me, okay? No matter what, I won't be mad if you need me. It's what I'm here for."

Chase nodded and then slid down from where he'd been propped up against the headboard and curled onto his side, his arms wrapped around one of the soft pillows on the bed. "Okay, I will."

His eyes slipped closed, eyelashes fluttering delicately against his cheeks as he quickly faded off to sleep.

Devon leaned in and kissed his temple before straightening up and heading for his room. When he got there, he walked to the patio doors that led to the second floor balcony and opened them.

After the beautiful, unusually warm day they'd had, he wasn't surprised to see the clouds rolling in. There'd probably be a storm tonight, and that was fine by him. He always slept better when it was cooler.

He leaned against the railing and sighed. Chase was getting to him, and he knew it. There was still the question of his lifestyle, though. He'd been living and working as a Dom since he was twenty years old, and he didn't think he was ready to give it up. And giving it up for Chase would be virtually impossible. When he looked at that beautiful man, he saw the perfect sub.

And it wasn't something that Kingston had forced upon him. That kind of submission wasn't true submission. It wasn't something you could force or take. True submission was given freely and something to be cherished.

Chase's innocent and gentle nature was God-given, and Kingston had tried to corrupt it. It was kind of funny to Devon how many Doms never realized that the sub was always the strongest one of the relationship. The very existence of the bond between them depended on the sub allowing it to happen.

Devon knew that someone's submission was a gift that gave as much to the sub as it did to their Master. And it was something he wanted desperately with Chase.

With one last look at the lightning he could see starting up in the distance, he turned and went back into his bedroom. It was time he got some sleep before he did something foolish... like go crawl into Chase's bed.

DEVON WOKE with a start. He could hear the storm raging outside and smiled. He loved a good thunderstorm.

Rolling over and sitting up, he looked around for whatever woke him. It took a second for his eyes to adjust, but he finally spotted Chase sitting on the floor against the wall by the door, arms locked around a pillow he was hugging.

A bright flash of lightning lit up the room and was followed almost immediately by a huge clap of thunder. Devon saw Chase jerk, and a quiet whimper fell from his lips. He was terrified.

"Chase." Devon spoke quietly. "Are you okay, sweetheart?"

Chase shook his head, unable to speak, and Devon knew what he had to do. He flicked back the covers on the side closest to Chase and scooted back a little, giving him some room. "Do you want to sleep here?"

If he hadn't looked so scared, it would have been almost funny the way Chase scrambled off the floor and over to the bed as quickly as he could. He practically dove under the covers, still hugging the pillow and curling up as small as he could.

Devon lay down, turning on his side to face Chase, and pulled the covers over them. Reaching out, he gently pulled the pillow out of Chase's arms and threw it on the floor. "C'mere, baby."

He lifted his arm and pulled the other man close to him, letting him wrap his long arms around Devon's waist and hang on tight. Their legs tangled together under the sheets, and it took a few minutes for Chase to stop trembling.

"Have you always been afraid of storms?" Devon rubbed his hand over Chase's neck, soothing him.

"Yeah, since I was a kid." Their faces were so close that they were breathing each other's air. "When I lived with him…." Chase took a deep breath. "He used to lock me in the sunroom when it stormed. The roof and three of the walls were glass."

Devon pulled Chase closer, letting their foreheads touch.

"He'd chain me to the floor and leave me there, naked and alone." The confusion in his voice was evident. "After the first few times, he didn't even stay to watch, just left me there and went to bed."

Dev kissed Chase's cheek, not surprised at the salty taste of tears he found there. "I'm so sorry, Chase."

"In the morning when the sun came up, sometimes he'd forget I was there. It would be so hot, and after freezing all night it was unbearable." His hands gripped tight to Devon's back, like he was afraid he'd leave him there if he let go.

"Eventually, one of the servants who liked me would walk by and go and remind him so that he'd let me out. When he did, he was always mad, like I'd done something wrong."

Devon tucked a strand of hair behind his ear. "It wasn't your fault, baby. He was mad at himself. Forgetting about your sub is a Dom's biggest failure."

"I just don't understand. What made him like that? Why did he need… I don't know, to own me? What's he so angry about?"

Devon sighed. He knew Chase deserved the truth, but how would he feel afterward? He gently brushed his lips across Chase's, smiling when the other man sighed into the kiss. He memorized the taste and feel of them. It might be the only chance he ever got.

He pulled back and looked at the dim outline of Chase in the dark. He was so amazing. And it was time to tell him what he needed to know.

"Me, Chase… he's mad at me."

Eight

DEVON WATCHED as confusion clouded Chase's face. He hated to have to tell him this. It might change everything.

"What do you mean he's mad at you? What does he think you did?" He could feel Chase trying to snuggle in closer, even though there was no possible way.

"When I was eighteen, I was just getting into the Dom/sub scene. Everything I'd heard about it fascinated and excited me. I've been out since I was fifteen, and my parents didn't take it well. So I packed up as much as I could carry and came here, determined to find a life for myself."

Chase nodded, his hair brushing against Devon's forehead, making him smile.

"I found a club and started hanging out there. I watched for a long time, trying to figure out what it was that I wanted. Once I knew I wanted to be a Dom, I approached one of the Masters at the club."

A flash of lightning illuminated Chase's face, and Devon could see the astonishment there. "You just went and talked to him? A Master?"

"Chase, most Masters aren't like Kingston. They know they're there for a purpose, and they aren't mean or cruel for no reason."

"But they wouldn't talk to a sub…." The uncertainty in Chase's voice was so sad.

Devon brushed Chase's hair back from his face. "Sweetheart, Doms can't exist without subs. There would be no point to being a Master if you didn't have someone to take care of. It's all about trust and respect for the rules and boundaries... or it should be." Devon couldn't help the bitterness that crept into his voice.

"It's what I thought I was getting with Ma... Kingston. It's what I wanted. I thought it would make me feel safe." Devon loved the honesty that the dark brought out in Chase.

"So you wanted a Dom? It wasn't a concept that he pushed on you?" Now that was a piece of information that made Devon happier than it had any right to.

The younger man nodded. "Yeah, I'd done some research before I left home... watched a few things. I liked how the idea of it made me feel." Chase snuggled his face into Devon's neck. "I thought it would make me feel safe and loved, and it did... for the first month or so."

"What happened?" Devon knew he was deflecting for a bit but felt the answers were important.

"Someone touched me... a friend of his grabbed my ass. He laughed about it at first, so I thought it was okay." Chase took a deep breath before continuing. "But that night he took me to his playroom...." Chase shuddered.

Devon ran his hands up and down Chase's back, hoping to soothe him a little. "What did he do to you?"

Tears were running off Chase's face, and his chest hitched in little sobs as he finished his story.

"He tied me up, and there were so many ropes. He tied me to a bench so I could barely move, and then he gagged me."

Devon listened with growing horror. Chase had been so young!

"The ropes were so tight and rough, and they cut into my skin when I moved.... I tried not to move, Devon.... I tried to be good, but it hurt so bad." His voice was cracked and raw, and it ripped at Devon like barbed wire.

"How did he hurt you, Chase?" Devon held him as tightly as he could, feeling the other man's tears pool on his chest before running down onto the sheets below.

"The cane... he always used the cane." Chase was sobbing so hard he couldn't breathe, and Devon knew he needed him to calm down.

"Oh, baby, I'm so sorry he did that to you." Devon knew from experience that the bamboo cane Kingston favored was flexible and strong. It could inflict severe damage without any lasting scars. It would bruise and leave horrid welts, but Devon knew it wasn't the cause of the myriad of scars that crisscrossed Chase's ass cheeks and thighs, which meant there was another instrument of torture that Kingston used on the other man.

Devon cradled Chase against him, whispering how sorry he was that he'd been hurt and promising him it would never happen again. He let him cry it out and was gratified when he finally calmed down.

"Afterward, he felt bad... he always did at the beginning when he hurt me. He said it was my fault, though, first because I let someone touch me and then because I didn't tell him to stop."

Devon could feel him pull back a little and look up at him. "How was I supposed to stop those things? I didn't know he was going to touch me! And I tried to tell him to stop... I screamed at the top of my lungs around the gag, but he didn't listen!"

Devon felt such a terrifying anger building in him. "None of it was your fault, Chase. It wasn't up to you to control his friend's behavior, it was up to him. And subs who are gagged need to be given a signal of some sort to be their safeword. It wouldn't have mattered, though. He would have kept beating on you anyhow.... I should know."

Chase was quiet for a moment. "How?"

Devon knew it was time. "The Master I talked to at the club told me that before he would train me to be a Dom, I had to spend six months as a sub. He said I had to know what it felt like to have someone have that kind of control over me so that I could understand my responsibilities."

"You were a sub?" The disbelief in Chase's voice was almost comical.

"For a little while. I went and found someone who I thought would be a good match. He was smart and handsome and had been a Dom for a few years. I checked around and didn't get any bad reports about him, and so I signed the contract. All it proves is that I didn't know shit back then."

"Kingston?" Devon felt Chase tense up when he nodded, and he'd been expecting it, but when Chase spoke, he was surprised.

"What did the bastard do to you?" Chase was struggling to get up, obviously furious with the thought of someone hurting Devon.

"Relax, sweetheart, it was a long time ago." He waited until he felt Chase sink back into his arms and then continued.

"It was fine for the first couple of months. We talked a lot, and I had been up front with him about what I wanted and why I was doing it, and he seemed okay with it. But as time went on, he got more and more aggressive. It turns out he didn't want just the six-month contract. He'd decided he wanted a more permanent arrangement."

Chase shook his head, tickling Devon's jaw with his hair. "But you're not a sub. Anyone can see that."

Devon chuckled a little. "You have to understand, back then I was a lot… prettier than I am now. I looked like the perfect little twink, all delicate with cock-sucking lips." Devon lifted his hands and did air quotes for the words "cock sucking," even though Chase couldn't really see it.

"But you're right, I'm not a sub. I played my part and learned a lot mostly what not to do—but it wasn't true submission, and Kingston knew it."

He smiled as Chase started rubbing small circles on Devon's chest, trying to comfort him. The younger man was so much sweeter than he'd even realized.

"What happened?" Chase's voice was hesitant, like he was scared of the answer.

"He decided that my problem wasn't that I was a Dom but that he hadn't truly dominated me yet. He figured the solution to that was to tie me to a bondage horse and beat the ever-loving shit out of me."

"Oh no…." Chase was horrified. Devon could tell by his voice. He started pressing small, soft kisses to the underside of Devon's jaw. It was very distracting.

"He started with the cane. No warm-up, no working up to it, nothing. He beat me black and blue with it and left me there, tied up and battered, for hours. He'd just started in with the flogger when Andy came to the door."

"That's your friend at the club?"

Devon nodded. "Yeah, my best friend since I was twelve. When Kingston told him I'd gone away for the weekend, Andy knew he was lying. I would have told him if I was going anywhere. He left but didn't go far. He got a hold of our other friend, Joe, and the Master I'd spoken to. His name's Jax, and he's not someone you want to piss off."

"What did they do?" Chase couldn't get any closer to Devon without climbing inside of him.

"They came back, and Kingston had to let them in. Jax was a very well-known Dom back then, and he was the one who held our contract, and he took his responsibility seriously."

Devon chuckled a little. It was easy now... back then it had been terrifying. "Jax took one look at what Kingston had done to me and punched him so hard it broke his jaw. The only reason Andy didn't kill him was because Joe made him think about me, because I was a fucking mess."

Devon moved his fingers down to where one of the scars wrapped around his ribs and curled under a nipple. The man had been a very enthusiastic flogger. "God only knows what would have happened if they hadn't shown up. I think he might have killed me trying to get what he wanted."

"Jesus Christ, Devon... it makes me want to kill *him*." Chase's voice was strong and full of passion.

Devon laughed out loud and hugged him tight. "God, sweetheart, you're something else."

Chase pulled back, startled. "Is that a bad thing?" He sounded so worried, and Devon hated that sound in his voice. He kissed him gently before pushing his head back to lie on his chest.

"No, Chase, it's not bad. You're so good and so sweet. After all the horrible years you spent with him and all the things he did to you, you're angrier over what he did to me."

Devon could feel the heat coming off Chase's face and knew he was blushing. "You're nice to me. He shouldn't have done that to you." Chase was quiet for a few minutes, obviously taking it all in. "I don't understand why you think it's your fault, though. You didn't do anything."

"Well, I kind of did. It took me six weeks to recover. I had two cracked ribs and some pulled muscles in my shoulder from trying to get free. Once I was better, I found him in a club...." He trailed off briefly, lost in the memories.

"You know, he has a few problems, the first one being he doesn't understand that size doesn't mean shit. I was a lot smaller back then, but I walked up to him and laid him flat. I was nice, though. I hit him in the chest and broke a couple of ribs instead of hitting him in his still healing jaw." He couldn't help smiling a little at the image in his head of Kingston gasping on the floor.

"Then I tore up the contract in front of him and all his friends, the whole time talking about how he didn't know the first thing about being a Dom. I walked out, leaving him lying on the floor, and never looked back. It should have been the end of it."

"But it wasn't?"

Devon was pretty sure Chase already knew the answer to that. "Nope. It took me a while to figure out that he was stalking me. The only place I was safe was at the club with Jax. Kingston had been blackballed for his behavior and didn't dare set foot in the place. I got messages too. Notes left on my car... e-mails, all of them detailing what he wanted to do to me once I came to my senses and realized that I was just a sub with delusions of grandeur. He still believes it as far as I know."

"He really is crazy... it's not just about me." Chase sounded as though he couldn't decide if he was relieved or even more scared.

"It's very little about you, I think. You were just a pawn that I was probably supposed to find out about a whole lot sooner than I did. He disappeared for a while about a year after it all happened. I'd heard that his father got sick of his whack-job son embarrassing his family and shipped him out of the country for a year, but then he came back."

Devon kept stroking Chase's skin, taking comfort from the simple touch. "I kept waiting for him to come after me again, but he didn't, and I thought maybe he'd smartened up, but I think that was when he found you."

He couldn't help but pull Chase closer, as if he could somehow protect him from the horrors he'd suffered.

"We heard rumors once in a while, about him keeping someone at the Manor, but by then there were so many about him that it was just dismissed. I never thought he would be so stupid."

Devon turned on the bedside lamp, then tipped Chase's chin up so he could look in his eyes. "I really am so sorry, Chase. He's still trying to get to me after all this time, and he used you to do it. There's part of me that wishes I'd let Andy kill him when he wanted to… or that I'd had the guts to do it myself so you never would have had to suffer through so much pain."

Chase touched a tear that had escaped Devon's eye with a shaking hand. "You're crying… for me?"

Devon nodded. "For you… for the boy you were… for all you lost and everything he took from you. And that's the saddest thing of all. He's never learned that this life is about giving, not taking."

Chase looked at him, seeming to search for something in his face. He must have found it, because he leaned up and pressed his lips to Devon's, his hand resting on the older man's chest over his heart.

Devon was too startled to react for a moment, but when Chase gasped and opened his mouth, Devon took the invitation and slipped his tongue into Chase's mouth.

He brought one hand to curl around Chase's cheek, tilting his head gently so he could better explore. The little pleading sounds Chase made tugged at Devon's heart and made his cock twitch at the same time.

When Chase slowly lay back on the pillow, he pulled Devon along with him, opening his legs so that Devon could fit between them and then lifting them to wrap around his waist.

Devon pulled back a little and groaned when Chase slid one arm around his neck and one around his shoulders, pulling them flush together. The first startling brush of cock against cock with nothing but thin cotton separating them was heavenly.

Chase looked up at him, smiling shyly. "I like this."

Devon smiled down at him. "Me too, as it happens."

Chase shook his head a little. "No, I mean I like *this*!" He almost looked embarrassed by his little statement, and Devon finally got it.

"You like me over you... me holding you down?" He carefully unwound Chase's arms and then slid his hands up, catching his wrists. Going slowly and giving Chase time to object if he wanted to, he lifted them up and pressed them to the pillow over Chase's head.

Chase's breath hitched, but this time with excitement. Devon could see the want and need in his eyes, and the lack of fear made it even better. He wrapped Chase's fingers around one of the metal bars that made up the head of the bed. "Keep them there."

Chase nodded. "Yes, Sir." The easy compliance made Devon even harder, but he knew it wasn't time for that yet. He framed Chase's face with his hands, holding him like he was something precious, hoping that Chase would realize how serious he was.

"We aren't in a scene, baby. You're not healed enough on the outside or on the inside for something like that. When you've had some time to figure things out and when I'm sure you're capable of making your own decisions, if you still want to, we'll talk."

He watched as some of the animation faded from Chase's face and he started to let go of the bar. Devon leaned in and kissed him before pulling back and looking him in the eyes.

"This isn't a rejection, Chase... far from it." He ground his cock down against Chase's, causing them both to moan. "You can feel I want you, and I have a feeling that isn't going to change anytime soon, but you've been through so much and you were kept isolated for so long, I need to make sure that it's really something you want, not just what's familiar to you."

"He said I wasn't worthy of a collar...."

"Oh, baby...." Devon leaned in, sucking a bruise into the soft skin under Chase's jaw. "Any Master would be blessed to have you. If I took you to the club now, I'd have to put a collar on you just to keep them all from fighting to get you."

Chase pressed his neck against Devon's mouth, moaning for more. "But you need to choose if you want this... when you're ready."

"Then what are we doing here, then?" Chase's voice already sounded fucked out. Devon loved it.

"We're enjoying each other. Making each other feel good." He turned Chase's head and sucked on the sensitive skin under his ear. Chase moaned, long and low. "Don't you feel good?"

"Oh… oh God… feels so fucking good."

Devon smiled. He was going to have bruises on his hips from Chase trying to pull him closer with his legs, but he didn't care. All that mattered was that Chase knew he was wanted and cared for.

All the sexual experiences he'd had so far had been tainted by Kingston's madness. Devon wanted to show him that sex should be something positive, that it didn't have to be about pain and denial.

He moved his hands down Chase's neck to his chest. He let Chase rub them together however he wanted as he used his fingers on one nipple and his mouth on the other.

"Devon… I can't hold… oh…. *Oh!*" Chase cried out as Devon gently bit down on his nipple. He arched his back and Devon could feel Chase's cock twitch against his own as he came.

Chase was panting as he collapsed back on the bed, hands still wrapped tightly around the headboard. When Chase relaxed his legs, Devon sat back on his heels and stuck his hand down his pajama pants. It wasn't going to take long. He was already on edge and looking at the beautiful young man lying there on his bed looking sated and happy just brought him closer.

He stroked himself quick and hard. Then he heard Chase's voice. He looked up at him and smiled when the younger man spoke.

"Can I… I wanna see." Devon was totally lost as to how someone could look so debauched and so shy at the same time. He nodded and pushed his pants down around his thighs. He started stroking again, his other hand going down to rest on one of Chase's legs.

Chase let go of the headboard, and Devon almost protested, but just whined when the other man started running his hands over his own chest. He watched as Chase pinched his own nipples curiously, a small gasp letting Devon know he liked the feeling.

"Chase… fuck… so gorgeous." Devon was so close. He swiped over the head of his dick with every stroke, and his hips kept bucking into his hand.

"Come for me, Devon… let me see…." The plea in Chase's voice was the last straw. He felt his balls tighten, and he moaned as he came all over Chase's stomach and chest and his own fist.

When the aftershocks stopped and he could move again, he leaned over Chase and kissed him, plundering his mouth and hopefully leaving no doubt in the younger man's mind as to whether or not Devon wanted him.

"You okay, sweetheart?" Devon wiped his hand on his pajamas and used his clean hand to brush the hair back from Chase's eyes.

Chase nodded. Between the meds and the orgasm he was pretty much unconscious, and it made Devon smile. A distant flash of lightning lit the room, and although his eyes had slipped closed, Chase still flinched. "Guess you're sleeping here, then."

"Is that okay?" Chase's voice was quiet and unsure.

"It's perfect. You stay here. I'm just going to clean up a little and get something to clean you up with." Devon slipped off the bed and finished removing his clothing, then walked naked to the bathroom.

He cleaned himself quickly and brought a warm cloth and a towel for Chase. He managed to get the soiled underwear and sleep pants off of him and cleaned him up as best he could. He debated trying to get some kind of clothing on him and then gave up. He was too tired to try, and it wasn't like they hadn't slept together with Chase naked before.

He pulled on a pair of boxers and crawled back into bed. He'd settled into the warmth that Chase had made under the covers, and almost immediately, Chase turned over and snuggled into Devon's side.

Devon pulled him close and relaxed into the feeling. It was a really complicated situation they were in, but for the moment, he let it all go and just enjoyed being there with Chase. He figured they both deserved it.

Nine

DEVON WOKE up the next morning wrapped around Chase. They were lying on their sides, facing each other, with Chase a little farther down in the bed. He had his arms around Devon's waist and his head tucked under Devon's chin.

Devon had one arm under Chase's neck, pillowing it, and one arm slung across his hips. Their legs were so tangled together it was hard to tell where one ended and another began, and Chase's morning wood was rubbing up against the inside of Devon's thigh, making his own twitch in response.

Devon sighed and pressed a soft kiss to the crown of Chase's head and started trying to dislodge himself from the other man without waking him up. When he finally managed to get free, he tucked the covers around Chase and headed for the bathroom. He stopped when he heard his name.

"Devon?" Sleepy Chase was pretty much the most adorable thing Devon had ever seen.

He walked back to the bed and slid his hand into Chase's hair to pet him gently. "Go back to sleep, sweetheart. It's early."

Chase peered up at him with a pout. "Where you going?"

Devon smiled when Chase pushed into his touch. "I have some work to get caught up on in my office." He ran his fingers down Chase's face and curled his hand around his jaw before leaning in and kissing him chastely on the lips. "I'll be there for a bit. Go back to sleep, and I'll wake you in a while for breakfast, okay?"

Chase smiled sleepily and let his eyes flutter shut, his long eyelashes fanning over his cheeks.

When he was sure Chase had faded back to sleep, Devon got up and continued his journey to the bathroom. He decided he might as well take his shower now, so he stopped to grab a fresh pair of boxers from his underwear drawer along the way.

As he stepped in front of the mirror to brush his teeth, Devon noticed a couple of little bruises under his jaw where Chase had sucked a little overenthusiastically the night before. The memories flooding back had him hard as steel in seconds.

When he was done with his teeth, he turned the water on, and once it was hot enough, climbed into the shower. The water felt good on his skin, and he relaxed into the spray.

He washed his hair first and relished the feeling of the suds sliding down his body. When he'd rinsed all the shampoo out, he grabbed his bodywash.

As he soaped up his chest and stomach, every pass over his nipples sent pleasurable shocks right to his cock, and he couldn't resist. He slipped his hand down to stroke himself, letting the images of Chase naked and writhing below him flood through his mind.

The man was positively wanton when he was aroused, responding to the slightest touch. Kingston had been a complete idiot to not take the opportunity to have a real relationship with Chase.

He remembered the needy little whimpers that fell from Chase's lush mouth when he came and how easily he'd just given over control of everything to Devon.

Devon could feel the tingle in his balls that signaled his orgasm was about to overtake him. He let himself remember the way the younger man had smelled as he'd pressed up against him and how he'd come without Devon ever touching his cock.

He knew some men had really sensitive nipples, and it appeared that Chase was one of them. It made Devon want to try all sorts of things to see how many times he could make him come.

He could feel his balls start to draw up close to his body, and he knew he was already screwed when the thought that finally pushed him over the edge into bliss was how it felt to wake up tangled up with the beautiful young man.

He bit his lip to keep from crying out too loudly and disturbing Chase as he erupted all over his own stomach and the wet tiles in front of him. He stroked himself through it, taking a moment to make sure he wasn't going to embarrass himself by falling over.

Once his legs were a little steadier, he rinsed off the evidence of his passion and turned off the water. He got out of the shower, dried off, and almost decided to forgo shaving, but Chase seemed to have an affinity for rubbing up against Devon's face, and he didn't want any more marks on the poor man's skin at the moment.

He finished the chore quickly and slipped into his underwear before padding back into the bedroom. Chase was still sound asleep, but he'd been moving around, as the sheet and blanket covering him had slipped down to his waist, revealing still-bruised skin and scars.

Devon's jaw tightened, and he walked over to grab a pair of jeans and a white button-down from the closet. He pulled them on quietly, and with one last look at the man who was quickly stealing his heart, he slipped out the door, leaving it ajar so he could hear Chase if he called out.

He entered his office and woke up his computer to check his e-mail. He saw one from Jax and clicked on it. It was the information he'd requested on Chase's family. He skimmed it quickly and replied, giving Jax the go-ahead to speak to Chase's family. He wasn't taking any chances with them until he knew what kind of a reception the younger man would get.

The second one that interested him was the one from Lisa Jones. He saw that she'd sent the list of therapists he asked for, and she had noted which ones she thought would be the best. Finding someone who had an understanding of the Dom/sub community was essential so that Chase wouldn't face any prejudice about it.

He decided that he would offer Chase the choice of talking to a man or a woman, whatever made him feel more comfortable. He'd do anything in his power to help Chase, even if it meant Chase being away from him to heal.

At that thought, Devon propped his elbows on his desk and held his head in his hands. He knew it was true. He'd do whatever Chase needed to recover, even if it meant letting him go. He wasn't sure it wouldn't break his heart at this point, but he was determined.

Sitting up, he sent his thanks to Lisa and then looked at a few other pressing matters. He had a tendency to get lost in his work and wasn't surprised when he looked up and saw that a couple of hours had passed.

He got up from his desk and snuck quietly down the hall to check on Chase. He was still sleeping, so Devon left him and slipped down the stairs. He let the dogs out and decided his first order of business was coffee. Kayley didn't usually come in till the afternoon, as she used her mornings to run errands and spend some time with her dad.

Once the coffee was started, he started work on breakfast. During one of their talks at the club, Chase had mentioned loving pancakes, and they just happened to be Devon's breakfast specialty. He started some bacon cooking and then began mixing up the batter. He turned the radio on quietly and just let himself get lost in preparing the meal.

When he was done, he put everything he needed on trays, one for him and one for Chase, and smiled. It felt good to have someone to take care of for once that wasn't all about the stuff that went on at the club.

He carried Chase's tray up first, stopping in the guest room to grab Chase's meds. When he entered his bedroom, Chase was just beginning to stir. He set the tray on the dresser and walked over to the bed.

He leaned down and kissed Chase on the shoulder, and the other man hummed his approval. Devon smiled. "Mornin', Sunshine, you up for some pancakes?"

Chase's eyes popped open, and a sleepy grin spread over his face. "Really? You have pancakes?"

Devon nodded. "I made pancakes... and bacon!"

Chase sat up and hugged Devon. "You made me breakfast? Really?"

Devon couldn't help but chuckle at Chase's childish enthusiasm. "Yes, I really did. You wanna eat now?"

Chase nodded but then ducked his head and blushed. "I have to go to the bathroom first."

"Go for it. The door is right there." He pointed to where the en suite was. "I'm just going to go down and get the other tray, okay?"

Chase nodded, threw back the covers, and scampered toward the bathroom door, completely unabashed about the fact he was naked. Devon took a moment to appreciate the beauty in front of him before heading quickly downstairs for the other tray.

When he got back up the stairs, Chase was just coming out of the bathroom, and Devon smiled when a blush rose over his cheeks.

"Sorry, Devon. I keep forgetting I shouldn't be walking around naked all the time."

Devon chuckled and leered appreciatively. "Don't apologize on my account. Not like I'm complaining about the view." He watched as the blush deepened but was happy when Chase smiled shyly. "Now, get back into bed, please."

Chase scrambled to obey, and once he was settled against the headboard, Devon set the tray in his lap. When he lifted the cover on the plate, Chase practically beamed. "You made me blueberry pancakes!"

Devon walked back to the dresser and retrieved the other tray, balancing it carefully as he sat beside Chase on the bed. "Yep, you told me they were your favorites." He took the cover off of his plate and then put both his and Chase's on the nightstand. "Eat up, sweetheart, and then you can have your meds."

Chase nodded and grabbed his fork. He poured a little of the syrup Devon had put on the tray over the fluffy stack and then dug in.

His moans of appreciation were almost pornographic, and Devon was in serious danger of his dick pushing his tray right off his lap. He tried to ignore his discomfort and got down to eating his breakfast.

They ate quietly, Devon asking Chase a few questions about his childhood, games he liked and movies he'd enjoyed. When they were done, Devon put the trays on the dresser and brought Chase his meds. Once those were taken care of, Devon decided to approach Chase about the therapy Devon thought he needed.

"Chase, I want to talk to you about something." He watched as Chase froze. He wished he wouldn't always assume the worst, but he could understand why he did.

"Did I do something wrong?" The fear in his eyes told Devon that this was the right thing to do. He reached out and put his arm around Chase, pulling him close.

"No, baby, you didn't. I just want to suggest something to you." He stroked Chase's back and held him close. "I asked Dr. Jones to help me find you someone to talk to… someone who can help you figure some stuff out."

Chase stiffened in his arms, but Devon had been expecting it. He didn't let go, but made sure that Chase didn't feel he was being held against his will. He'd had enough of that, Devon was sure.

"No, Devon, please… I don't want to." Chase stopped trying to pull away and curled in on himself, shaking in fear. "I can talk to you, right? Can't that be enough?"

Devon shook his head. "No, baby. It's not enough. You need someone who isn't so closely tied to the community to talk to. Someone who you trust that you can talk to about what happened to you and help you make sense of the feelings you're having about everything you went through."

Chase looked up at him. "I trust you, Devon."

Devon's heart broke a little at the pain in Chase's eyes. "I know you do, Chase, and that means so much to me." He leaned in and pressed a kiss to the other man's temple. "But, baby, you've been lost from the world for a long time, and I don't know how to make sure that you find your way back the best way possible."

"Other people scare me, Devon. I don't know how to talk to them." Chase was laying half in Devon's lap, hiding his face against the older man's stomach.

Devon ran his hands through Chase's hair. "Well, that's one of the things I wanted to talk to you about. Do you think you'd be more comfortable talking to a man or a woman?"

Chase blushed. "Devon, I can't talk to a woman. I can't tell her what he did… it would disgust her."

"We can find you a man, then. And I'll take you there and stay in the waiting room the whole time. You'll never be left there alone." He just kept petting Chase, letting the man find comfort in the touch. "And the people Dr. Jones suggested are all familiar with our community, so they are going to understand and not judge you."

"But what if they want me to tell? What if they tell someone? The Master will be so mad, Devon... he'll kill me." He was shaking in fear, and it made Devon so angry. Kingston was going to pay for what he'd done.

"He's not your Master anymore, Chase. He never really was, because he didn't do the one thing that is a Master's most important job... he didn't take care of you." He pulled Chase up so he was resting against his chest, his face buried in Devon's neck.

"And he won't kill you. He won't be able to get anywhere near you. I'm looking after you for now, and I know how to do my job properly." He rocked Chase slowly.

"And besides, the doctor can't tell anyone what you tell him, not even me. It's against the law, and he could get in big trouble if he did. If you were still in danger it might be different, but you're safe now."

Chase looked up at him from under his bangs. "Really? He can't tell what I say... he can't tell anyone the things that happened to me?"

It wasn't difficult to imagine Chase as a child right then. He had no idea how things worked out in the world, and the fact that he had trusted the first person who'd been kind to him was both a blessing and a curse.

"Really, he honestly can't. What you say stays between the two of you." He kissed Chase's cheek. "I hope that you'll continue to talk to me too. I want you to know that you can tell me anything, and I will always be willing to listen to what you have to say, even if it's hard... even if it's scary, okay?"

"I'm scared, Devon... and I'm tired of being scared." When he looked up at Devon again, fat tears were rolling down his face, and Devon thumbed them away.

"I know, baby. I was scared for a long time too, after what he did to me. But talking to someone helped me, and I know it'll help you too."

Chase seemed to be considering his words before nodding. "Okay, I'll talk to someone if you want me to."

Devon really wished it was something Chase would do for himself, but for the moment, he'd take what he could get. The important thing was that Chase would be getting help.

They sat quietly for a little while, relaxing and letting themselves drift. After a bit, Chase gave one last sniff and then sat up. "I need a shower. I'm...." He bit his lip and looked down at his lap before continuing. "I'm still a little sticky from last night."

Devon smiled and kissed him gently. "I'm going to find you a robe. Why don't you head back to the guest room and shower there? There's more underwear for you there, and I asked Kayley to pick you up some clothes while she was out doing errands this morning."

"I can't walk back there naked!" He sounded so scandalized it made Devon chuckle.

"In case you haven't noticed, Chase, I've seen you naked... a lot. And no one else is here." He took pity on Chase's embarrassment. "Here, let me get you a towel to wrap around you."

But before he could get up, Chase grinned up at him, threw the sheet back, and slid off the bed to his feet. "Nah, it's okay. You're right... nothing you haven't seen before, right?"

With that he walked to the door, stopping once to look over his shoulder and smirk at Devon's gaping expression. "See yah later!" And with that he slipped out the door and was gone.

Devon grinned and shook his head. The more confidence Chase started to find, the more Dev realized he was going to be a real handful.

He couldn't wait for that to happen.

Ten

THEY SPENT the next few days like that, Devon working from home and Chase getting used to having some freedom. Kayley had picked Chase up some sweats and T-shirts and warm hoodies, because he always seemed to be cold unless he was cuddled up with Devon.

Chase healed quickly, at least physically, and he was eating much better, thanks to Kayley and Devon plying him with all his favorite foods. He'd put on a few pounds by the time Dr. Jones came to visit a few days later, and she was pleased by the fact that Chase called her by name instead of Mistress. He flinched a little when she patted him on the shoulder, but otherwise he seemed to be pretty comfortable around her.

Devon had made the therapist's appointment for the following week after slipping out for a couple of hours to meet him one afternoon while Chase was napping. The younger man was getting better at being alone at the house with Kayley, but he was still much happier when Devon was around.

Devon had learned that Chase talked to him best while they were snuggled up on the couch with the dogs watching a movie or when they went to bed at night.

For the moment he'd given up trying to make Chase sleep in the guest room. He'd go willingly enough, usually falling asleep quickly, but he'd often wake a few hours later, crying and shaking in terror. He'd tried to hide it from Devon, saying he didn't want to annoy him all the time, but when it was really bad, he'd slip out of bed and pad down the hall and into Devon's room.

After waking up to Chase sleeping propped up against the wall in his room twice in three days, Devon had just started tucking him into his own bed.

They hadn't gone past kissing and touching because Devon was determined to wait until he was confident of Chase's ability to make his own decisions, but he couldn't deny that waking up with the younger man curled up in his arms was the best thing that had ever happened to him.

After three days of working from home, Devon knew he needed to go into the club, at least for a while. There were some things he needed to discuss with Andy and Joe, and Dani had been demanding to talk to him via texts and e-mails for days. The fact that she stayed away from the house showed she understood what was going on and that Chase probably didn't need the stress of a yelling match between his favorite person and a strange woman.

Kayley had been bringing Justin by the house so that Chase could get used to him being around, and the fact that the man was quiet and easygoing helped Chase accept him.

Devon had arranged for Kayley and Justin to stay at the house with Chase while he went into work the first night. He wasn't so much concerned with his physical safety as he was his mental health.

He spent the afternoon on the back porch with Chase, sitting on the swing and holding his hand as he explained that he had to go to work but that he'd be back before morning. Cammy would be allowed to keep Chase company in Devon's room until he got home, and he promised to not be any longer than he had to be.

Chase looked up at him with big, concerned eyes. "What if he shows up there? What if he hurts you?"

Devon put his arm around Chase's shoulders and held him close. "He won't come to the club; he's not quite that stupid. Right now he's waiting to see what you're going to do."

Chase eyes widened. "Me? Why?"

Devon smiled at him. "Because what he did to you was illegal. He's waiting for a visit from the cops, and the fact that they haven't shown up yet is probably puzzling him."

Chase shook his head. "I can't, Devon. I know I should, just to stop him from hurting anyone else, but...." He trailed off, obviously not sure how to defend himself, but Devon shook his head.

"Don't you worry, baby, he's not going to get his hands on anyone else." A thought occurred to him. "Unless... was there anyone else there, Chase? Someone we need to go and help?"

Chase shook his head again. "No, there isn't. If there was, I'd have told you... I wouldn't leave anyone there suffering." He was shaking a little, and Devon rubbed his back to soothe him.

"I know, Chase. I just had to make sure." He rocked him slowly, letting the other man calm a little. "In any case, Andy will be escorting me to and from my car, against my wishes... by the way, and all the security has been trained on how to deal with him if he does show up." He kissed Chase on the temple.

"And I want you to know that you're safe here. The gates will be locked, and I have a friend on the police force that's willing to make a few extra passes by the house. There's a security system that has a direct feed from the house to the club, so if something happens, I'll be alerted as well as the police."

He stroked Chase's head. "How are you feeling about it all?"

Chase shrugged. "Okay, I guess. I'm glad that Kayley and Justin are going to be here because they're really nice, but are they going to be offended if I don't talk to them much?"

Devon shook his head. "No, baby, you just do what you want to, okay? You're free to roam where you want to in the house or the yard. Just don't leave, okay? Not until I deal with Kingston."

Chase nodded and smiled at him.

Devon took a deep breath and then stood up. He grabbed Chase's hand and pulled him up as well. "Come on, I need to show you something."

He led Chase into the house and then through the kitchen and down the hall. At the end there was another door that Chase had never been through, although Devon had seen him eyeing it with interest.

"I want to show you this room because I don't want you finding it by accident and being scared." He pushed the door open and flipped a light switch, illuminating the stairwell that led to his basement.

"You don't ever have to go down here, Chase. It's my playroom, and I didn't want you stumbling upon it. I'm pretty sure mine is nothing like Kingston's, but it still might seem a little scary, okay?" He held Chase's hand and waited.

Chase was a little pale, but at least he wasn't running away screaming. He took a few more breaths and then turned to Devon. "Can I look at it?"

Devon nodded and tried to let go of Chase's hand so he could investigate, but the other man pulled him along down the stairs.

The lights were all on, and so the room was well lit, leaving everything on display.

There was a beautiful wooden cabinet on one wall that housed all his tools. Dildos, different kinds of cuffs, clamps, blindfolds, and gags, as well as floggers and soft silk ropes used to tie people up without hurting them. It was definitely a treasure chest.

On another wall was a St. Andrews Cross, and in the corner was a beautifully appointed bondage bed. There was a kneeling bench and a Berkley Horse as well. None of it looked all that scary there in the bright light, but Devon knew that in Chase's eyes, it could all look terrifying.

He watched as the younger man wandered around, examining everything quietly and never letting go of Devon's hand. He saw a faint smirk cross his face when Chase spotted the swing hanging from the corner and breathed a small sigh of relief that the other man didn't seem to be traumatized by what he saw.

"It's not like his room." Chase's voice was soft and unsure. "His had cement floors and walls, and it was always dark unless he had a spotlight on." He looked around at the smooth hardwood that Devon had laid on the floor and the cream-colored walls that had hooks and hardware attached at various places.

"It was always cold, and I hated every minute I spent there." He tucked himself a little closer to Devon at the memory. "But this is room is warm, seems safe and comfortable." He looked up at Devon. "Thank you for showing me. It helps to know that it doesn't have to be like that."

Devon took him in his arms and hugged him. "You're welcome. If there's anything you need to ask or want explained then you can always come to me, okay?"

Chase nodded and then looked at the cabinet. He looked to Devon for permission, and at his nod, he walked over and opened it. His eyes widened as he took in the array of toys on display.

He ran his fingers tentatively over some of them, stopping to pay particular attention to a couple of sets of nipple clamps. Devon smiled inwardly. As sensitive as Chase's nipples were, it didn't surprise him that the other man would be interested in those.

Chase looked at a few more things before closing the cabinet and turning back to Devon. "Okay, I'm good now."

Devon nodded and leaned in to kiss him softly before pulling back. "Come on, I have to get going. Andy will tear me a new one if I'm late."

Chase smiled and headed for the stairs, still hanging on to Devon's hand. When they reached the top, he closed the door and smiled shyly at Devon. "You'd better get to work. Don't want all your friends thinking I'm a bad influence on you."

Devon could see he was trying hard to be brave about him leaving, so he didn't call Chase on the tiny tremors he could see.

"Yeah, you're right, I should. The sooner I go, the sooner I get home." He hugged him tightly for a moment and then kissed him on the forehead before heading for the front door. He turned back for a second.

"You have my cell number if you need me, right? And Andy's?" Dev had given Chase a cell phone to keep with him at all times so they could reach each other if they needed to.

Chase nodded, and Devon smiled again. He quickly and efficiently put his boots on and went out the door, reluctantly leaving Chase behind.

He would have liked to have taken the younger man with him, but it just wasn't a good idea. He didn't know how Chase would react to being in the place where he was beaten and abandoned, and the chance that Kingston could show up himself or send others to do his dirty work was too great. Once the asshole was dealt with, then it would be safe to take Chase to work with him if he wanted to go.

It was harder than it should have been to drive away and go back to the other place he called home, but once he was on his way, he started to feel better.

The drive didn't take long, and when he stopped at the last stop sign before reaching the club, he sent Andy the text he promised so that security could be waiting to accompany him from the parking lot into the club.

When he pulled into his parking space, he was unsurprised to find Andy standing there, along with Jax and another member of their security team, Scott.

Jax Logan was forty-six years old and probably one of the scariest men Devon had ever met. He was also one of the kindest to the people he considered family. Devon counted himself lucky to be among them.

Scott Keller was tall, well built, and one half of a security team that probably knew as much about personal protection as the secret service. His partner, Mike Nickels, was almost certainly certifiably crazy. He was also devoted and talented, and Devon was smart enough to know they had probably saved his life on more than one occasion.

Mike was presumably around, probably skulking in a dark corner somewhere, trying to look for whoever might be looking for Devon or Chase.

Devon stepped out of the car and smiled at Andy and Tom. "Howdy, fellas! Are y'all looking for me?"

Andy grinned and stepped in to give him a hug before releasing him to shake both Jax's and Scott's hands.

Jax's deep voice broke the good-natured silence. "I made sure that Justin was up to date on all the security procedures, and Mike made sure that the feed from the security cameras at the house will be available on the computer in your office. Your boy is about as safe as he can be at the moment."

Devon nodded. "And you're sure this is necessary? Kingston will really go after him?"

Jax sighed and ran his hand over his hair. "You took him in and offered him safe haven. He's going to take it as a personal affront. He's always considered you his, and now he wants Chase too. I'm not sure if he wants to keep him or just get him away from you. Are you sure we shouldn't go to the cops?"

Devon knew that Jax was insinuating that if Kingston didn't want to keep Chase, the younger man would probably disappear and never be heard from again. Kingston had access to the resources to make it happen.

Devon looked Jax in the eye and growled. "He's not getting anywhere near Chase." He looked around at the other two men, catching each of their gazes before moving to the next. "Are we clear? We both know that Kingston's father will not let his son be charged with anything. All that will happen is that we will end up in shit up to our ears. He's too fucking powerful."

All three men nodded, and Devon moved past them and headed for the back door of the club, the other three following quickly. He looked over his shoulder at Tom. "Tell Mike to come in from wherever he has himself stashed, please."

The tall man nodded and made a quick hand sign before resuming walking.

The club was just getting ready to open. He walked through to his office and checked the security feed before heading for the bar. Joe was there, going over things, and he looked up and smiled at Devon's approach.

Devon smiled back. "So, gentlemen, did we get the distribution issues worked out?" They didn't serve a lot of alcohol in the club... drinking and their lifestyle didn't mix very well. They discouraged subs from drinking, period, as it was imperative that their consent was never in question.

And dominating someone while under the influence of alcohol could lead to the Dom losing track of what their sub needed and where the limits were.

However, there were some drinks available to guests who were just there to observe, and those beverages were always top quality.

"That douche you fired made a real mess of things with some of your suppliers, but I think we managed to smooth most of it over." Andy smirked at Devon. "Of course, we had to offer a couple of them some free services, but I think you'll be okay with it. They didn't demand anything too outrageous." He passed Devon his clipboard, and Devon chuckled as he read the request of the man who supplied their champagne.

Devon looked up at Andy and raised an eyebrow. "He wants to be the one in the schoolgirl uniform?"

Andy just shrugged. "What can I say? I think he's gonna look good in the skirt. He certainly has the legs for it."

It never failed to impress Devon how the guy he'd always thought was so straight-laced in high school had become so accepting of the kinks and fetishes of the rest of the world.

"All right, then. Let me know who he wants to be his headmistress."

Andy shook his head. "Headmaster...."

"Headmaster...." He looked through the rest of the papers and then handed the clipboard back to his friend. "Anything else that needs my attention at the moment?"

"I do!" They all looked up, and Devon smiled as Danielle Rimmer walked in the room.

"Hello, beautiful!" Devon shared a glance with Andy and Joe before walking to meet the gorgeous redhead. "Guess it's time for the inquisition, huh?"

She smacked him on the arm before pulling him into a big hug. "You okay there, sport?"

Devon squeezed her tightly before releasing her and taking her hand. "Let's go do this in the office, hot stuff. I'd rather not be reamed out in front of the entire place."

She giggled at him. "I know, big boy, you'd rather do the reaming!"

She followed him into the office, stopping to grab a couple of bottles of cold, sparkling water on her way.

Once the door was closed and they were seated, him behind his desk and her in front of it, he sighed and looked at her. "Go ahead, ask away."

She looked at him for a moment, searching his face for something before she spoke.

"Do you have any idea what you're doing? Or are you just flying by the seat of your pants on this one?" She smiled as she said it, letting him know she wasn't judging him.

Devon rubbed the back of his neck. "I'm trying to save someone's life and maybe my own as well."

"It's that important... he's that important?" There was no teasing in her voice now. "You've never taken a sub on for more than six months and lately you've contented yourself with the subs that come into the club. I guess I thought you weren't really into a relationship of any kind."

Devon looked at his computer monitor and saw the front of his house. He could see Chase there, sitting on the porch with the dogs, and it all looked so right to him.

"I've been looking for someone special and he might have just been dropped right into my lap. I think he could be my everything, and I might have to let him go to save him."

Eleven

CHASE WATCHED Devon walk out the door, smiling as best he could before turning back and heading for the stairs.

He knew that the older man had to go back to work, but Chase had been spoiled the last little while, having all of Devon's attention to himself. It was the kind of attention Chase had always dreamed of, the single-minded focus without the cruelty he'd grown used to at the mansion.

It wasn't the only attention he wanted from Devon, though. The tour of the playroom reminded Chase of why he was interested in the Dom/sub lifestyle in the first place. All those amazing toys looked a lot less scary in the warmth of Devon's basement than they'd ever looked in his old Master's dungeon.

He found himself drawn back to the closed door but turned away at the last moment. He couldn't go down there by himself… could he?

He walked into the kitchen and found Justin and Kayley in there together. He liked Kayley a lot. She was really kind and made really good cookies. Justin seemed like a nice guy, but Chase was still a little nervous around him. He was used to people either ignoring him or taunting him cruelly, and while he knew in his head that it was different here, it was still going to take some getting used to.

"Hey, Chase, how are you, sweetie?" Kayley's bright smile made him feel a little better.

"I'm okay." He blushed and looked down at his feet before continuing. "Are there any more of those cookies from the other day… the ones with the little chocolate candies in them?"

Kayley chuckled and pointed at the cookie jar on the counter. "Help yourself, big guy, but don't spoil your dinner. I'm making barbecued chicken and garlic mashed potatoes. And those rolls you like to go with it."

Chase grinned. "I can't wait." He looked at Justin to make sure he wasn't getting mad. "You're an awesome cook, ma'am."

Kayley ruffled his hair. "Thanks, sweetheart. Just remember, my name's Kayley. When you call me ma'am, you make me feel old." She smiled to make sure he knew she wasn't mad.

Chase blushed a little harder and nodded. He darted to the cookie jar and grabbed a couple before heading out to the porch.

He sat on the swing and smiled when Cammy came over and put her huge head on his knee.

"Sorry, girl, these aren't good for you. Chocolate is bad for puppies." He reached up to the window ledge and grabbed the treat can that Devon kept there. He shook out one for all three dogs, and the other two came running at the familiar sound.

He sat and relaxed for a while, enjoying the animals' company. He found himself getting sleepy, sitting there in the shade, so he took the throw off the back of the swing and curled up under the blanket and let himself drift off. He was feeling better after almost a week, but he was still tired. Dr. Jones said it had something to do with him being underweight. It's no wonder everyone was trying to feed him all the time.

When he woke up a little while later it was to Justin shaking him gently.

"Hey, buddy, it's time to get washed up for dinner." Chase knew he probably looked a little scared, but Justin was kind enough to not mention it.

Chase yawned and nodded. He got off the swing and stretched before making his way to the kitchen, followed by the three dogs. He stopped to fill their food bowls, a job he'd gladly taken over because their gratitude always made him smile.

He made his way to the small bathroom in the hall and then joined Kayley and Justin in the kitchen to eat at the counter with them. He didn't say much, but he did manage to ask a few questions when they started talking about the wedding. Kayley was more than happy to tell Chase all the details, and it was obvious she was proud of what she had managed to organize.

When they were finished, Kayley asked if Chase wanted to join them in the small TV room to watch a movie, but he wasn't in the mood. He thanked them and left them to their cuddlefest.

He headed for the stairs but was once again drawn by the closed door to the playroom. He went to it again, wondering what Devon would say if he went down there. The other man had told him he could go anywhere, and he didn't specifically say he couldn't go in the playroom, just that he wouldn't make him go down there.

He looked around to make sure no one was watching him and then opened the door quickly and flicked on the light. When it was bright enough, he closed the door quietly and padded down the stairs.

He knew why he was there. The things in the cabinet had fascinated him. Metal and leather and rubber, all crafted together to make something beautiful.

He went and opened the doors and pulled out the first drawer. It had an amazing array of dildos and butt plugs, some of which Chase had never seen the likes of before. He picked some of them up, testing their weight and imagining how it would feel to have them inside him, holding him open and getting him ready for his Master to fuck him… for Devon to fuck him.

There was one that was almost as big around as Devon's cock and just long enough that Chase knew, if he was walking around wearing it, it would press against his prostate every time he sat or had to do something like climb stairs. He ran his hand over it reverently before laying it back in its spot.

It was the next drawer that really fascinated him, though. When he pulled it out, he was delighted by the different styles of nipple clamps he could see. His nipples were very sensitive and had always been a source of great pleasure for him, so he enjoyed all kinds of nipple play. It was probably why Kingston had never used them on him after the first couple of months—he might have enjoyed it.

He picked up a set that could be adjusted for tightness and held them up. They were connected by a slender chain that had more weight to it than it looked. He could imagine what it would feel like to walk around with that chain swinging back and forth and brushing against his skin.

He slid his hand up under his shirt, brushing it against his nipple, and sighed. It felt so good, and it seemed so decadent after not being allowed to feel pleasure for so long.

He tucked his shirt under his armpits and then opened the clamp. His nipples were already hard at the thought of how it was going to feel, and when he closed it on himself, the slight pinch of pleasure/pain almost had him coming in his sweats. He attached the other one and then walked to the full-length mirror that was mounted on one wall.

It looked hot. The clamps weren't too tight, and the pressure felt amazing. When he let the shirt drop, the brush of the fabric over the chain had him hissing in pleasure.

He walked around the room, examining all the different toys Devon possessed and imagining how they would feel.

The big bed was amazing, but he thought Devon's looked better. He wanted to climb up to the Dom's room and lie there with the nipple clamps on and play with his cock and his ass until he came. He sighed. Actually, he wanted Devon to do it for him.

He walked back to the cabinet, closed it tightly, and then snuck upstairs. He peeked out to make sure the coast was clear and then turned off the light and let the door snick shut softly behind him.

He let the dogs in and then went up the stairs to Devon's room and closed the door behind him.

Chase climbed onto the bed and slipped his shirt off. He felt so bad and so good at the same time, it was almost overwhelming. Bad because he was playing with Devon's toys without his permission and good because he knew Devon wouldn't be angry at him for it.

Bringing both hands up, he explored the hardened nubs and pebbled flesh. Every touch to his pinched nipples had his cock twitching against his stomach, and the soft weight of the sweatpants he was wearing was like sandpaper on his oversensitive flesh.

He was sure Devon wouldn't be home for hours, so he impatiently pushed off his pants and lay there naked.

He felt a little leftover trickle of fear as he reached down and stroked himself but tried to ignore it. Instead he remembered Devon's voice as he'd whispered in his ear that day in the bath, telling him that feeling good was okay, that he deserved it.

He'd let the warm voice and the intimate tickle of Devon's breath on his neck push him over the edge that day, and remembering it almost did the same thing. He slowed his hand, wanting to prolong the pleasure a bit more.

He wanted so much for Devon to be here for this, but as time went on, he could understand better where the man was coming from. He never rejected Chase, just let him know he needed to give the younger man time to heal and figure out who he was and where he needed to be.

But God, he wanted Devon in every way possible. His fingers sped up again as he thought about the nights he'd spent curled up against the older man, wishing that Devon would just fuck him into the mattress and give them what they both wanted.

With his free hand, he tugged on the chain that connected his nipples, arching his back against the sheets with the pressure and pleasure.

In his mind he could see Devon, his green eyes crinkled at the corners as he looked down at Chase with approval and pride. He could hear Devon telling him to stroke faster, tug harder on the chain, so he did.

He could feel the tingle start in his balls, the sign that he was so close to coming, needing only a little more to get himself there. He gave the chain a good yank, smiling in bliss as the clamps pulled free and the blood rushed back into the aching flesh.

He brushed one finger over a nipple, and Chase cried out and came, Devon's name falling from his lips. He stroked himself through it, trying to prolong his orgasm as much as possible. Thick ropes of come landed on his stomach and chest. The heat of it felt almost searing on his nipples, causing his cock to twitch in desperate aftershocks.

When his hand became too much, he let it fall to the bed, the other one still resting on his chest. He knew he should go to the bathroom and clean himself up, but he was exhausted.

He decided to rest a while before crawling into the shower. The last thought he had before he faded off to sleep was that at least Devon wouldn't be home for hours.

HE WOKE to the feeling of being watched. He opened his eyes, instinctively seeking out what had woken him, and smiled softly when green eyes met his.

Devon was lying on the bed beside him, facing him and smiling back at him. When Chase reached up to touch that smile, he froze when he realized that the nipple clamps were still clutched in his hand. He was torn between horror and embarrassment, but Devon just reached out and took them and threw them onto the bedside table.

Chase closed his eyes and waited for Devon to leave the bed and was startled to feel a gentle touch to one nipple from a warm cloth. His eyes flew open.

"I saw that you messed yourself up a little. Is it okay if I clean you off?" Devon's voice was soft and deep, like he was turned on by what he saw but didn't want to scare Chase.

Chase nodded and relaxed as Devon wiped the dried come from his skin. It didn't take him long, and when he was finished, he got off the bed and tossed the cloth in the hamper before grabbing Chase's meds from the dresser. He passed Chase the pills, frowning when the younger man passed them back.

"I don't need them, Devon. I'm not hurting much anymore, and I don't like the way they make me feel." He looked up into Devon's face, hoping he wasn't mad. "I don't like feeling out of control that way, like it's not my choice."

He was surprised when the older man smiled. "So you don't mind not being in control when it is your choice?"

Chase thought about it for a moment before shaking his head. "No, if I'm letting it happen, then it's okay."

Devon leaned down and kissed him, letting it deepen for a moment before pulling back and smiling at him. "Good to know."

Chase watched as Devon stood up, stripped quickly down to his underwear, and then climbed into bed. When he was settled on his side again, Chase inched closer.

He reached out and tentatively put his hand on Devon's where it lay between them. "You're not mad at me? Or disgusted?"

Dev smiled and turned his hand over so that their palms met. "No, baby, I'm not mad. I told you that you could go anywhere and that included the playroom. I also told you it was okay to make yourself feel good, and I meant it."

Chase smiled, and he could feel the blush rise in his cheeks. "You don't think I'm weird for still liking some of that stuff?"

Devon chuckled. "Are you seriously asking me that? I'm pretty sure that's my kinky playroom down there you were exploring." He flicked a gentle finger over one nipple, causing Chase to hiss and his dick to twitch. "I would never think you're weird, Chase."

It felt so good to have Devon touching him. His whole body felt hot, and he just wanted to throw off the covers and lie there exposed for Devon to see how he was affecting him.

"Are they sore?" Chase looked up into Devon's face when the other man spoke.

He nodded. "A little." When Devon started to pull his hand back, Chase caught it in his. "Please don't stop." It didn't really hurt, just a dull, pleasant ache that he felt down deep inside.

Devon leaned in and kissed him and then pushed him onto his back. Chase was pleased when the blanket was tossed aside and he was left open to Devon's knowing gaze, like he could read his mind that this was what he wanted.

When Devon bent and put his mouth on Chase's chest, it felt like sparks crawling up his spine. Devon circled his tongue around the pebbled flesh and then over the sensitive nub, and Chase was rock hard in an instant.

Devon growled a little, and the vibrations made Chase hump the air, dying for some friction, but he wouldn't touch himself. He wanted Devon to do it... to make him come.

He must have said it out loud, because the next thing that registered was Devon whispering "Yes" into Chase's skin.

Devon moved, hovering over Chase and pinning his hips down with one leg. He mouthed his way across Chase's chest before pulling on the other nipple with his teeth and then soothing it with his tongue.

Chase wondered if someone could die from feeling so good. The moments of pleasure that Devon was giving him were helping to push away all the pain and misery he'd suffered at Kingston's hands.

Devon slid his hand down over Chase's abs and cupped his balls, rolling them slowly in his palm.

"Devon... oh God, please... I need...." Chase's breath caught in his throat when one long finger pressed into the sensitive skin behind his sac.

"I know what you need, sweetheart... let me give it to you." There was no arrogance in Devon's voice, just caring and confidence.

"Yes... anything...." Chase arched his back again, trying to get his body closer to Devon. He whined when the hand left his balls as Devon reached behind himself, but it died away when one slick finger slid between his ass cheeks and rubbed over his hole.

"So beautiful, Chase." Devon's voice and the hot breath across his chest made him shudder. "Walking in and seeing you naked in my bed, poor little nipples all red and swollen, the room smelling like sex."

Another swipe of Devon's tongue over his nipple had Chase whimpering, but it broke off into a gasp as the finger at his entrance sank in slowly and ever so gently.

"Devon...." Chase froze for a second, and Devon stopped and waited.

"Not gonna hurt you, baby. I just want to take care of you." Chase looked down at the words, his eyes seeking Devon's and finding nothing but honesty and desire there.

Chase relaxed and let his head fall back as he pressed down onto Devon's hand.

"Good boy, Chase... so gorgeous like this." Devon curled his finger, stroking gently, and Chase lit up from the inside. His hands flailed, looking for something to hang on to, and grabbed Devon's shoulder before letting go, scared of making the other man angry.

"You can touch me, Chase. Hang on to me, baby. I won't let you go." Devon spoke the words into Chase's skin as he rubbed against Chase's prostate, and Chase let his hand fall to Devon's shoulder again, letting the feel of it anchor him.

After that he couldn't focus on anything that wasn't Devon's mouth on his chest or his finger in his ass. When a second finger joined the first, he opened his legs wider and let the sensations overtake him.

He knew Devon was talking to him, whispering words of comfort and encouragement, but his brain couldn't really comprehend them. He knew the sounds he was making were loud, the moans and cries as the pleasure built under his skin.

Chase was desperate for release but couldn't seem to reach the summit until Devon pulled away from his chest for a moment and spoke in his ear.

"Let go, Chase." With those words, Devon ducked his head and bit down on Chase's nipple, and the perfect pressure and the stroke of Devon's fingers inside him had him coming, even as Devon's soft pink tongue licked away the sting.

When he came back to reality a few minutes later it was to Devon's fingers slipping gently out of him. He watched as the other man wiped his sticky fingers on the sheets and then pressed a soft kiss to the lovingly abused flesh on Chase's chest.

Chase could only look down at him, smiling shyly until the other man looked up. When he did, Chase's bliss faded to horror, and he started scrambling backward, desperate to get away. He didn't notice the edge of the bed until the world started to drop away from under him. Only Devon's lightning-quick reflexes stopped him from falling to the floor.

"Chase…. Chase, look at me." Devon's voice was soft, and he didn't sound angry….

"Sorry… so sorry, Master… didn't mean to…." Chase hated how weak and pathetic his voice sounded, but he couldn't help it.

Careful hands framed his face, and gentle but firm pressure had him looking into Devon's eyes. "Why are you sorry, Chase?"

Chase shook his head and closed his eyes, but Devon didn't let go. He waited, pressing small kisses onto Chase's face until he calmed down.

"Tell me, Chase."

He couldn't resist that voice. It was quiet and commanding, and it made Chase ache to obey.

"Your face." He swallowed, trying to get rid of the lump in his throat. "I got come on your face. And I...." He licked his lips before forcing himself to go on. "I marked you... bruised your shoulder...."

Devon frowned and reached up to touch his cheek, finding the splash of Chase's release drying there. He grabbed the edge of the sheet and wiped it off before smiling down at Chase.

"Damn, you really went off like a rocket, didn't you?" Using the sheet, he wiped Chase's stomach and chest as best he could, then pulled the sheet off the bed and tossed it onto the floor.

He pulled Chase into his arms, and Chase let him. "I won't punish you for losing control, Chase, especially when I'm the one who makes you... at least not in this room. In this room, I'm Devon and you're Chase, and there is no Master, okay?"

Chase nodded and then let his head sink down onto Devon chest. God, he was tired.

"As for the bruises, well... I really don't mind those either. They mean you trusted me enough to let yourself go and to make me your anchor while you did." Devon stopped for a minute and then cleared his throat. "I'm sorry if I pushed you too far, sweetheart. You were so beautiful I couldn't resist."

Chase's heart had been returning to its normal pace, but it sped up a little at those words. He shook his head.

"You didn't. It was really good, Dev." His tongue felt stupid in his mouth, like the orgasm had pulled all the words out of his head. He slid his arm across Devon's belly, looking down when it brushed against Devon's cock.

"You're still hard!" He twisted his head to look up.

"Yeah, it's okay."

Chase grinned as Devon shrugged. He slid down Devon's body until his mouth was level with the older man's cock. He stuck out his tongue and lapped at the wetness at the head through the cotton of his boxers, but stopped when Devon's hand grabbed his hair and tugged.

"You don't have to do that, Chase." The simple words made Chase's heart sing.

"I want to...." He licked his lips, savoring the taste of Devon there. "Let me, please?" He nuzzled his cheek against the hard length, desperate to get it in his mouth.

The other man held his gaze for a moment before relaxing his grip and nodding. He kept his fingers in Chase's hair, not holding or directing, just stroking as Chase grabbed the waistband of his underwear and pulled them down and off.

Chase sucked Devon into his mouth as far as he could, until his nose was pressed into soft, damp hair. He was surrounded by Devon, his taste and smell, and it made Chase's exhausted dick twitch.

He relaxed his throat and bobbed his head, swallowing reflexively around the hard length. He was in heaven. Chase loved giving head, and he was damned good at it.

He slurped up and down, letting saliva slick the way, encouraged by the low moans falling from Devon's lips and the way his fingers tightened in Chase's hair.

"Fuck, Chase... your mouth...." Whatever Devon was going to say was bitten off as Chase used one hand to play with his balls as he sucked on his cock.

Devon tasted so good, and Chase moaned around the cock in his mouth, making the other man shake.

He felt another, harder tug on his hair. "Gonna come, Chase."

The words were meant as a warning, but Chase just sucked harder, wanting everything Devon would let him have.

Chase felt Devon's balls draw up close to his body as he swelled further against Chase's tongue. He pulled back a little so he wouldn't choke and used his free hand to stroke the flesh his mouth couldn't reach.

"Chase!" Devon cried out as his cock jerked in Chase's mouth, and he arched his back as he came.

Chase swallowed as much as he could, not stopping the pressure of his lips and tongue until Devon whined and gently pushed him away, his cock too sensitive to take any more.

He rested his head on Devon's thigh, both of them getting their breath back, until Devon grabbed his arm and pulled him up.

He curled against Devon's chest, letting himself relax as Devon ran his fingers through his sweat-damp hair.

"You okay, sweetheart?" The question was followed by a kiss to the crown of his head.

He looked up and nodded, confused when Devon brushed his thumb against the side of his mouth.

He smirked as he showed it to Chase. "Now my come's on your face." The smirk died as Chase sucked the thumb into his mouth, licking it clean.

"It's how it should be." Chase almost didn't recognize his own voice as he spoke. "It's how I want it to be."

Devon cupped his cheek, his eyes searching for something in Chase's before pulling him in for a kiss. It was sweet and almost chaste compared to what they'd just shared.

"Go to sleep, Chase. We both could use the rest."

Chase nodded again and let himself relax. Devon wouldn't be pushed any more tonight, and Chase was too comfortable and sated to care.

He laid his head on Devon's chest and let the steady beat of the other man's heart lull him into a dreamless sleep.

Twelve

DEVON WOKE the next morning to the sound of his cell phone ringing. He reached for it on the nightstand, untangling himself from Chase enough to grab it.

"Like a freaking octopus." Devon mumbled as he answered the phone.

"Good morning to you too, sunshine." Jax's gruff voice rumbled through the phone.

Devon groaned. It was too early for this shit. "Why the hell are you calling me at ass o'clock in the morning after I was at the club half the night? And why are you even up? You were there half the night too!"

Chase stirred beside him, whimpering in his sleep, and Devon rubbed the back of Chase's neck. He snuffled adorably against Devon's chest and then settled back to sleep.

"Some of us had some work to do this morning." The older man sounded a little stressed, and it was unlike him. "Sorry, Devon, but I just got done talking to Chase's parents. You told me to call as soon as I had news."

Devon looked down at Chase and felt a twinge in his heart. He had a feeling he wasn't going to like what Jax had to say. He scrubbed his hand over his eyes and sighed. "Give me ten minutes and I'll call you back, okay?"

"Sure thing, son. I'll be waiting." The other man disconnected the phone, and Devon put his cell back on the night table and looked down at Chase again.

The younger man was starting to look healthy, but he still needed his sleep. Devon hated to wake him up, but he didn't want Chase waking up and finding Devon gone after last night. He didn't want him jumping to the wrong conclusions.

He leaned down and kissed the top of Chase's head, then pulled back a little. "Chase... sweetheart...?"

Chase groaned a little, and his eyes fluttered open. He tilted his head to look up at Devon. "Dev?" He was so sleepily befuddled, and it was more than a little adorable. "What's wrong?"

Devon smiled at him softly and pushed back the bangs that were hanging in Chase's eyes. "Nothing, don't worry. I just wanted to tell you that I have to make a few calls. I didn't want you waking up and finding me gone."

Chase turned his head and looked at the bedside clock. "It's early...."

Devon chuckled. "Yeah, it is. Go back to sleep. I'll come back when I'm done."

The other man snuffled and then snuggled back down into the bedding, pulling away from Devon's warmth with obvious reluctance. When he was settled, he looked up at Devon once more. Those sleepy puppy eyes were going to be Devon's undoing, he was sure of it. "Kiss?"

Devon grinned and leaned down to kiss him gently on the lips. It was just a soft brush, and Devon was pretty sure Chase had fallen back into sleep halfway through it, but when he pulled back there was a happy little smile on Chase's face, and that was enough.

He pulled the covers up a little more and then got out of bed. He grabbed his sleep pants from the floor, pulled them on, and snatched his phone from the night table. He slipped into a hoodie he picked up from the back of the chair by the door on his way out, only to discover it was Chase's. He took a deep breath, savoring the smell of Chase's soap and shampoo wafting up from the cotton.

He wandered down the hall and into his office and proceeded to make a quick pot of coffee from the emergency supplies he kept there. Once that was going, he flopped down in his chair and called Jax.

"Sorry about that, Jax. Just needed a little privacy." He winced a little as he said it, knowing his friend wouldn't be able to leave it alone.

"You sleeping with that boy, Devon?" He could hear worry and affection in Jax's voice, but no disapproval.

"Yes, but we haven't... we've only done a little exploring." He sighed and silently prayed that the coffee would hurry up and finish. "But you know how I feel about him."

It was Jax's turn to sigh. "Yeah, I know."

"So, what did they have to say?" He didn't really want to know, but he didn't have a choice.

"Well, like we suspected, Kingston never went to them. They've had no idea where he's been, and they miss him a lot."

"What did you use for a cover story?" He needed to know that no one was coming for Chase before he was ready.

"Told them I was a private investigator who did pro-bono work from time to time. Said I'd heard about the case and wanted to see if there was anything I could do to help." He took a deep breath. "I told them I'd heard about a white-slavery ring that took advantage of young gay runaways and wondered if Chase could have gotten caught up in that."

"And?" Devon knew this was important.

"They looked a little uncomfortable at first, but after they talked by themselves, they admitted that they'd wondered if maybe Chase was gay before he ran away. I asked them how they felt about that... if maybe Chase had left because he was worried about their reaction. They said that it was possible, but if that's what had happened, they wished he'd talked to them. They said they never would have turned away from him for being gay. They loved him too much."

"So I guess there's really no choice, is there? He's gotta know, and so do they." He could feel his gut churning. Giving up Chase was going to be the hardest thing he'd ever done.

"I'm sorry, son. I think it's the right thing to do. They deserve their chance to be a family again."

Devon pulled his bare feet up into his chair and wrapped his arms around his legs. "Yeah, I know." He leaned his forehead on his knees for a moment before straightening up.

"I want to talk to them first. They need to know what he's been through so they can help him. I know it's his story to tell, but he's not in any shape to do it."

Jax hummed his agreement. "Yeah, I think that's a good idea. If they can't deal with it, then there's no sense in him going back there. It'll just do him more harm than good."

Devon felt like he couldn't breathe. "Can you set up an appointment with them as soon as possible? It's a short flight, and I can be there whenever."

"Yeah, I'll let you know." Jax seemed to hesitate and then spoke again. "He might come back to you, Dev. I'm sure you mean a lot to him."

"Jax, I love you and I appreciate that you're trying to make me feel better, but we both know there's no way he's gonna choose this life over a normal one with his family. It's what he deserves after everything he's been through." Devon had never been in love before. He'd avoided it at all costs, but Chase had crawled right in under his defenses, and he was falling fast.

"I'm going to go now, Jax. Call me as soon as you have a time for the meeting." He needed to get off the phone and have some time to think.

"Sure thing, Dev."

And then he was gone and Devon was alone in his office with his breaking heart. He wondered what it said about him that there was a small, hidden part of him that had hoped Chase's folks hadn't wanted him back.

He had to get himself together enough so that Chase didn't know something was wrong. With his luck, Chase would think it was something he did and blame himself.

Taking a deep breath, he pushed out of his chair and out of the office. When he walked into the bedroom, Chase was still fast asleep, the covers having pulled down enough that the broad expanse of his back was visible.

In the sunlight shining through the curtains, he could see every scar on the other man's back standing out in sharp relief, and it made him ache to go back in time and prevent them all from happening.

He crossed to the bed and settled himself carefully on the edge, not wanting to wake Chase. His face was so relaxed and young in his sleep, projecting an innocence that had been torn away from him in the worst way possible.

He reached down to trace some of the larger marks with gentle fingers, causing the younger man to stir, but he settled back into sleep with a murmured "Shhhh" from Devon. The fact that Chase found enough strength in himself to trust someone so instinctively was nothing short of a miracle.

He knew he should leave Chase to rest and get some work done, but he couldn't seem to pull himself away from the warmth and comfort he'd found. When Chase shifted and suddenly turned over, shifting closer to him and laying his head in Devon's lap, the urge to do anything else abandoned him completely.

He gave in and petted Chase's silky soft hair, smiling when the other man sighed and pushed into the touch like a cat.

"Hmmm." Chase snuggled closer. "Everything okay, Dev?" His voice was soft and sleepy, and it tugged at everything Devon was.

"Yeah, baby, everything's fine. Go back to sleep." He kept up his petting, and Chase made a few breathy little sounds that reminded Devon of a puppy.

"M'kay." He wrapped both hands around Devon's leg like he was hugging a teddy bear and let himself drift again.

Devon watched him sleep, letting himself enjoy something that he soon would be denied.

"Don't worry, Chase." The words were barely a whisper, but they were a fierce promise. "Gonna take care of you the best way I know how."

He leaned in and pressed a kiss to Chase's brow and grieved for something he'd never had but wanted desperately.

NINE DAYS later, Devon stood on the front step of a modest home on the outskirts of San Antonio, more nervous than he'd been in years. Jax had been by a couple of hours earlier and told Chase's parents that they'd found him and that his boss would be coming by to speak to them in a little while.

Devon wasn't sure how he was going to get them to understand that this all needed to move slowly. Chase's first visit to the therapist four days earlier had been devastating for the young man, and Devon had spent two days coddling Chase like he'd had to in the beginning. After the second day, he'd finally calmed down enough to tell Devon some of the things he'd talked about but Devon didn't press him for all the details.

Now he was going into this perfect family home to tell them all the horrible things that had been done to their loved one and hoped they could get past it enough to be what Chase needed.

He took a deep breath and raised his hand to knock when the door was suddenly pulled open. He looked into the eyes of Chase's mother, eyes so like Chase's that it was impossible to mistake her for anyone else.

"I'm sorry if I startled you, but you've been standing out here a while, and I just couldn't wait any more." Her voice only wobbled a little as she spoke, but her anxiety was obvious.

He gave her a little smile and offered his hand. "I'm Devon West, ma'am. It's good to meet you."

She shook his hand, her grip firm and sure, and he hoped she'd be as cordial when the meeting was over. "Liz Mackenzie. Thank you for coming, Mr. West. I can't wait to see Chase." She looked over his shoulder in confusion. "Isn't he here with you?"

He opened his mouth to respond when a man appeared beside her. Chase's father looked at him with a little more suspicion than his wife had, but he was quick to offer his hand as well.

Once the introductions were done, he found himself invited into the living room and offered a drink. He really needed one, but he declined. He needed the Mackenzies to take what he said to heart, and he wanted them to know he would do his best by Chase.

He was introduced to Chase's brother, and then they were all sitting and staring at him, waiting for answers.

"We've sent our daughter off to her friends for a few hours. I'm not sure what you want to talk to us about, but I was worried it wouldn't be appropriate for her to hear." Colin Mackenzie was doing his best to be patient, Devon could tell, but that patience was nearing an end.

"You're right, it wouldn't be." He looked around at the anxious faces and began his explanation.

"Seven years ago, Chase figured out he was gay and ran away from home. From what I could get from him, he didn't want to hurt or embarrass you in your church or your community, so he left. I think he was afraid of being rejected as well, so he never gave you the chance to do it." He took a breath, trying to decide where to go from there. There was no way around the truth, so he decided to just say it.

"When he arrived in the city, he was picked up by a man who seemed to be kind and told Chase he would take care of him, and for a while he did. But he manipulated Chase and took advantage of his innocence." He winced as he spoke, knowing this was going to hurt them.

"He convinced Chase that he had talked to you and that you had told him you never wanted him to come back—" He was cut off by a pained gasp from Chase's mother.

"No one ever came to talk to us… we would have demanded he come home immediately! He's my baby. I never wanted…." Her voice was rising, and Devon held up his hand, stalling her in her tracks. He carefully took her hand and looked into her eyes.

"I know he never came. He's a miserable bastard who hurt Chase badly. None of this is your fault. I know it, and Chase will too." He stopped and waited for her to calm down before continuing. Chase's father and brother were vibrating in anger, and he hoped they would let him finish before giving in to their emotions.

He told them the whole story, about Chase being held hostage all those years, treated worse than a slave, molested and beaten. He told them about Chase being left behind in his club and how he'd taken care of him, letting him heal physically and mentally.

When he was finished, he looked at them and waited.

His mother spoke first. "I still don't understand why he's not here with you now. I want to see him!" She was getting angry, and Devon was a convenient target.

"Because I had to tell you his story first." He summoned all the love he had for Chase and looked them in the eye, one by one. "I had to tell you what happened to him and make sure that bringing him back here was going to help him, not hurt him."

"What the fuck are you talking about, West?" Colin was furious. "He's my son! Of course he needs to come back here! Why wouldn't he?" The man started to get off the couch but was stalled by his son.

Devon looked up at Tom Mackenzie. The man was a doctor, one who spent most of his time in the ER of a big hospital. If anyone understood, it would be him.

"I need to make sure that you'll be able to deal with everything he's been through without making him feel like any of it was his fault." Devon's voice didn't waver, and he could see the other man looking at him with respect.

Tom nodded, but his father exploded in anger once more. "Who in the hell do you think you are? He's our family, not yours! What right do you have to see him and we don't? You're no better than the filth that kept him from us all this time!"

Devon hung his head. He knew that once Chase was back here, he'd never get to see him again. The family wouldn't allow it.

The quiet voice of Chase's mother broke in. "He's in love with Chase...." She turned to Devon and looked up at him. "Aren't you, Devon?"

He took a deep breath and nodded. "Yes, ma'am, I think I am. But being with me right now isn't what's best for him... and it could be dangerous. The man who kept him has a grudge against me. He wanted to own me, and when he couldn't, he went out and found someone he could own... someone who wasn't capable of saying no to him like I was."

The guilt he felt was almost overwhelming. "You will never know how much I regret that Chase was that person."

Colin spoke again. "Has he been arrested? The bastard should be rotting in jail!"

Devon shook his head. "No, sir, he isn't. Chase won't go to the police. He's still too afraid. And the man's father is someone you don't want to mess around with lightly."

"I don't give a shit! I'll go and kill him myself! Now tell me his name!" The man's face was red, and Devon was worried he was going to have a heart attack.

"No, I won't. This man is dangerous and a little crazy. He also has a lot of power and money at his disposal, and he wouldn't hesitate to crush any of you to get what he wants." He stood up and looked Chase's father in the eye, letting him see the truth of his words.

"He's going to pay for what he did, Mr. Mackenzie, and he's not going to be able to do it to anyone else. You have my word." His anger and resentment towards Kingston and his love for Chase fought for dominance inside him. He let his determination to keep Chase safe show in his eyes. He didn't become one of the best Doms in the city by not being able to show confidence in his own abilities.

The older man looked at Devon, his eyes unreadable, until he slowly nodded. "I believe you." Colin took a deep breath, trying to calm himself. "What are you going to do?"

Devon shook his head. "I think it's for the best for everyone if I keep that to myself for now." When Chase's brother tried to interrupt him, he held up his hand. "No, the less you know the better it is for you."

He let the implications sink in.

Liz broke the silence. "When can I see my son, Mr. West?"

"Please, ma'am, call me Devon. I'm going to be flying home as soon as I leave here. Chase thinks I'm at the club doing paperwork. I've been trying to leave him alone a little more lately so he can regain some of his independence, but he had his first therapy session the other day, and it kind of knocked him back a little."

Chase's brother nodded. Devon hoped he could count on the other man for a little backup.

"I'm going to tell him about you… that I came to see you and that you want to see him. I'm not going to push him, though. If he's not ready to talk to you, I'm hoping you'll give him some space. If he is? I'll have tickets waiting for you at the airport as soon as you can get away." He waited for the objections and wasn't disappointed.

"I want to see my baby, Devon. He needs to know we still love him!" Liz's voice was getting shrill, and Colin seemed ready to back her up. Tom chose that moment to speak.

"Mom, Devon's right. Chase has been forced into too much over the last seven years, and now he needs to be the one making the decisions." He walked over and put his hands on his mother's shoulders. "He's being taken care of. You said it yourself. Devon loves him and knows him better than us at this point."

Tom looked at Devon. "I trust you to do what's best for him. If you think we should wait, then we'll wait until he's ready." Tom hugged his mother for a moment and shared a look with his father before continuing. "Can I make one suggestion, though?"

Devon nodded. "Of course."

"Mom should write a letter for you to give him. She can tell him we love him and that we trust you to take care of him. She can give him our phone number and let him know that, as soon as he's ready, we want to hear from him. What do you think?"

Devon smiled at him. "I think it's an awesome idea. I'll give it to him after I tell him I've spoken to you." He reached up and rubbed the back of his neck. "He's probably going to be upset with me because I didn't tell him I was coming here, but I had to be sure it wouldn't cause him more pain."

Colin spoke up. "You said he was home alone... isn't that kind of dangerous if that man is running free?"

Devon shook his head. "No, he's not alone. My housekeeper and her boyfriend are there keeping him company, and my security guys are keeping a close eye on the place. He's as safe as I can make him."

He turned to Liz. "If you can go ahead and write that letter, I'd like to get going. Chase has been a little clingy the last couple of days, and for some reason he feels better when I'm around."

Liz grinned shyly at him. "For some reason, huh? I wonder why? Couldn't have anything to do with all the kindness you've shown him after years of pain and anguish?"

Devon tried to smile back at her, but the reminder of the fact that Chase was more grateful than anything else hurt a little.

As if sensing his thoughts, Liz hugged him and then patted his shoulder. "I know this is hard on you, so thank you so much for returning him to us."

Devon just shrugged. "It was the right thing to do."

Liz nodded and turned to the desk in the corner of the room. "I'm going to get that written. Excuse me, please."

Devon watched her go before turning back to the other two men. "I know there are things that you want to ask, so go ahead."

Colin spoke first. "What is it that you do exactly, Devon?" The suspicion was back in his voice.

"I run a club. It's a place for people to explore things about themselves that is safe and completely lacking in any sort of derision or judgment." He stopped and let that sink in.

It was Tom's turn. "And that lets you make a living?" There was no condemnation in his voice, just curiosity.

"It's a very popular club." He wasn't bragging, just telling the truth.

"Chase wasn't very safe there, now was he?" Colin was starting to get angry again, and Devon couldn't blame him.

"No, he wasn't. Two of the people who were responsible for what happened are no longer employed by me. One will never work in my city again. I hired people who turned out to be untrustworthy, and that has been rectified. The two men in charge now have made some changes to make sure nothing like that can happen again." He never wanted to see that in his club again. Mindless brutality had no place in his world.

He turned and paced a few steps before going on. "As for the man who's truly responsible... well, let's just say plans are in the works that will lead to him being stripped of his money and power so that he can never hurt anyone like this again."

"I can't begin to understand what it is that you're involved in, Devon, but I can see that you truly mean what you say. Chase's in good hands now. Just... send him home to us soon, okay?" Colin's plea shattered what was left of Devon's splintering heart. This was where Chase needed to be.

"Yes, sir, as soon as I can." He meant it with all his broken heart.

AN HOUR later, Devon had said his good-byes and was on a plane heading back to New Orleans and Chase. He couldn't wait to get back to the younger man but knew their time together was limited. It was time for Chase to get his life back, and this was just another step in the journey.

Devon had things he needed to get done… the most important was making sure that Kingston was put out of commission for good. Chase needed to be safe, and the only way that would happen was if Kingston could never touch him—or some other innocent boy—ever again.

When he and his friends were done, James Kingston's reign of idiocy in New Orleans would be finished, and Devon would be able to stop looking over his shoulder.

Maybe then he would be able to figure out if he had a place in Chase's future.

Thirteen

WHEN DEVON got home, he could hear laughter from the backyard and went to investigate. He couldn't stop the grin at seeing Chase flat on his back, being licked to death by three dogs.

He was giggling like a kid, and something about the scene stole Devon's breath away for more than one reason. It was awesome to see the younger man acting so free and happy, but it also drove home the fact that Devon's time for enjoying this was very limited.

Chase and the dogs spotted him at the same time. The dogs came running, tackling him and letting him know they missed him.

The man they'd been mauling stood more slowly, his grin turning a little shy as he walked over and accepted a hug from Devon.

"How are you doing today?" Devon brushed the hair from Chase's eyes, needing to see those expressive hazel windows to Chase's soul.

Chase dipped his head down to nuzzle into Devon's neck before murmuring against the older man's skin. "I'm okay. Had fun making cookies with Kayley this morning."

Devon played with Chase's hair, stroking it softly and relishing the way it made the younger man seem to melt against him. "Good." He gave Chase's ear a little tug. "You better have left some for me."

Chase chuckled and nodded. "I didn't eat them all… yet."

Devon loved how Chase had become comfortable enough to joke around and tease him. He'd come a long way in the last little while, and

Devon hoped that the news about his parents didn't set him back too far.

Devon put his arm around Chase's shoulders and led him to the porch. He settled him on the swing and sat down beside him before taking his hand.

"I have to talk to you about something, Chase, and I'm really hoping you won't be too angry with me about it." He stroked his thumb over Chase's wrist as he debated what to say first.

"I don't think I can be mad at you, Devon. I don't think you'd ever do anything to upset me on purpose." The trust in Chase's voice had Devon wishing he could avoid this all together, but he couldn't.

Devon sighed and pressed a kiss to Chase's knuckles before speaking. "I went and saw your parents today."

The young man's jaw dropped, and he visibly shrank back against the swing and away from Devon.

"Why would you do that? I told you they didn't want me. Master—" Chase paled and swallowed before continuing. "—Kingston went and saw them." He turned his head to look out over the yard. "They think I'm garbage they can just throw away...."

Devon reached up, stroking Chase's cheek, hating it when the other man flinched at his touch.

"They don't think that, Chase. Like everything else, Kingston lied." Chase turned quickly to look at Devon, his gaze searching.

"He never went to your parents, and they've never stopped looking for you. They love you and miss you and want you to come home." Devon hoped the pain in his heart wasn't leaking into his voice.

Chase shook his head, eyes darting away once again. "No, they won't... not now. When they find out what I did... what I let him do... they'll never want to see me."

Devon moved closer, even as Chase tried to move away. "First of all, you didn't let him do anything. He took everything from you, and there wasn't anything you could do about it." He put his arm around Chase's shoulder, tucking him in close to his side. "And second of all, I told them everything. Not all the details, of course, that's yours to tell who you want... but enough so that they could decide if they could deal with it or not."

Chase pulled into himself further, his distress making him shake against Devon. "Why would you tell them that?" He was crying into Devon's shoulder, and it was breaking Devon's heart all over again. He stroked the younger man's hair, hoping Chase could forgive him eventually.

"I had to, sweetheart. I needed to be sure that you being with them wasn't something that was going to hurt you more. If they couldn't deal with having a gay son or the horrible things that had been forced upon you, then you would have never known I talked to them." He kissed the top of Chase's head, wishing so much that he could take all his pain away.

"I'm sorry that I went behind your back, but I care about you too much to let anyone hurt you ever again, even if they are your family." He held Chase against him, never stopping his soothing touches.

Chase shook his head, not speaking, even crying silently. His arms were pulled in tight against his chest, but both of his hands were twisted into the front of Devon's shirt as though holding on to Devon might keep him from falling apart.

Devon rocked him gently, letting him cry out his pain and grief until the silent sobbing faded into soft hiccuping breaths.

"You should have let them think I was dead… it would have been better for all of us." Chase's quiet voice was filled with self-loathing as he pulled himself away from Devon onto his feet. When he was standing, he looked down at Devon with a defiance that the older man could see he wasn't really feeling. "I told you before, if you don't want me here, I'll go. You don't have to pawn me off to more people who don't really want me."

He turned and ran into the house, slamming the door on the way in. Devon sighed and scrubbed his hands over his face, looking up quickly when the door opened. He was disappointed but not surprised when he saw Kayley standing there.

"What did you do?" Kayley's eyes flashed with anger as she looked at him, her foot tapping impatiently.

Devon stood up and headed for the door, huffing impatiently when Kayley blocked his way. "I went and talked to his parents. They love him and miss him and want him back, even after I told them the horrible things he's been through." He looked down at her and waited, daring her to tell him he'd been wrong.

"Oh, Devon...." She trailed off and took a step closer so she could wrap her arms around him and hug him tightly. "I'm sorry, sweetie. I know how much you care about him." She pulled back and looked up at him, biting her lower lip and obviously considering her words before speaking again. "Maybe you should let him decide what he wants to do? It's his life, after all."

Devon hugged her for a moment before stepping toward the door again. "He needs to see them. He needs people around him who love him, and being here...." He broke off, swallowing around the lump in his throat. "It could be very dangerous for him. I want him as far away from Kingston as possible until that fucking monster is taken care of."

Kayley nodded, her worried eyes mirroring Devon's. "You should be talking to him."

Devon gave her a small smile. "That's where I was going when I was detained by his guard dog."

She smacked him on the arm before pushing him through the door. "Get your pretty ass upstairs."

Devon nodded and headed through the kitchen. He could hear dresser drawers slamming as he headed up the stairs two at a time. When he walked through the open door of Chase's room, there were clothes piled up all over the bed, and Chase was standing beside it, looking down at everything, his chest heaving, with his hands clenched into fists at his sides.

He slowly turned his head to look at Devon, and the older man crossed the room quickly, catching Chase as he collapsed to his knees.

He fell forward, his head colliding painfully against Devon's shoulder. "I was going to pack my stuff and go...." He took another heartbreaking, shuddering breath. "And then I realized I don't have any stuff. Everything that's there...." He gestured vaguely to the pile of clothing on the bed. "Everything belongs to you." He looked up into Devon's eyes. "Even me."

Devon's eyes widened. "Chase, I...."

The other man cut him off. "You don't want me... not to keep, anyway. I know that." The pain radiating through those hazel eyes took Devon's breath away. "But I'm not going back to them either. I can't go be their burden—the fucking freak that can't take care of himself. They don't deserve to deal with my bullshit."

Chase hauled himself to his feet and headed for the door before Devon could stop him. "I may not be able to get a real job, but there's one thing I'm fucking good at, and that'll make me lots of money."

It took a second for the pieces to connect in Devon's brain, but when they did, he was up and on his feet with a growl. He caught Chase two steps outside the bedroom and pulled him back, pushing the younger man face down over the bed and holding him there with a hand on the back of his neck.

He leaned in to speak in Chase's ear. "You're not a fucking whore." He could feel Chase tremble beneath his touch, but the younger man didn't fight the hold. He ran a comforting hand down Chase's back and then reached for his own belt.

He unbuckled it and pulled it free, quickly looping it around Chase's wrists, and then pushed all the clothing off the bed and onto the floor before urging him farther up so he could tie his wrists to the headboard.

He pulled Chase's hips up and helped him get his knees under him before pulling down the back of his sweats and boxers just enough to get to bare skin.

He petted Chase's back, soothing him before he spoke. "You're not garbage." He punctuated his words with a firm swat to Chase's ass.

"You aren't worthless." Another loud slap that pulled an almost inaudible moan from Chase.

"You didn't deserve what happened to you." He pulled his hand back, and he smirked when Chase's ass lifted a little, almost pushing into the next blow. "You're not bad because you're gay."

Another smack and Chase was whimpering, but he wasn't asking Devon to stop. "There's nothing wrong or demeaning about being a sub."

Devon made sure to not overlap the blows too much. The point wasn't to damage Chase, just to make sure he understood what Devon was saying. Still, the cheeks of his ass were starting to glow prettily, and it made the Dom in Devon smug with pride.

"I don't want you to go… I need you to go. So you can be safe." One more slap of Devon's hand and Chase was whining pitifully, but he still rocked back into the next one.

"You will never talk like that about yourself again. Do you understand me, Chase?" He spanked Chase again, this one a little harder, causing the other man to cry out. He didn't answer Devon, shaking his head stubbornly, so Devon gave him two more in quick succession, watching as Chase finally broke and spoke.

"Yes, Devon, I understand." His voice almost came out a whine, and his breath hitched as he spoke, but Devon was satisfied that he meant what he said. He undid the belt from the bed, but Chase protested quietly when Devon tried to free his hands, so he left them tied together.

He rubbed his hand over the heated skin of Chase's ass, smiling as Chase pushed back into the touch. When he was sure he hadn't really hurt or scared the younger man, he pulled him into his arms.

Chase hissed as the oversensitive skin came into contact with the blankets, but then he smiled sleepily and settled into Devon's embrace.

Devon pushed the hair back from Chase's eyes. "You okay, sweetheart?"

Chase nodded gently before forcing himself to speak. "I'm fine, Dev." He bit his bottom lip, looking down before continuing. "I'm sorry I acted like that. You didn't deserve it."

Devon smiled and stroked Chase's face. "You're allowed to be angry over the things that have happened to you. You just aren't allowed to do anything to hurt yourself." Chase nuzzled closer, and his soft breath raised goose bumps on Devon's skin.

"Your family loves you. That's the important part. They deserve the chance to know you again, and you deserve the chance to be a part of their family again. I'm not sending you away to punish you. I wouldn't do that." He could feel Chase relaxing against him, more and more.

"M'kay." Chase mumbled it against Devon's chest. "I trust you...." The words trailed off as Chase drifted to sleep.

Devon sat there quietly, looking up when Kayley peeked in on them, smiling as she saw Chase curled up in Devon's embrace. She opened her mouth to speak, but he shook his head, mouthing the word "later" at her. She nodded and ducked out.

Devon settled back against the headboard and prepared himself to wait for Chase's nap to be over. They still had a lot more to talk about, and he was sure it wasn't going to get any easier. It was necessary, but he didn't have to like it—neither of them did.

DEVON MUST have drifted off, because he awoke with a start a little while later. He looked at the clock on the bedside table and saw that almost two hours had passed. He lifted the hand not currently trapped under Chase and wiped the sleep from his eyes. Apparently snuggling with Chase made him sleepy.

He snorted quietly. He'd never been one much for cuddling with his lovers. Even the few men (and even fewer women) who'd been invited to his bed when he was younger usually left after the sex was finished, sent off with a pat on the ass and a false promise of a call later.

Devon liked his personal space, but for Chase, it seemed like he was willing to break more than one rule. Waking up every morning and finding himself being used as Chase's personal teddy bear was something he was quickly becoming used to, and when he left, Devon was willing to bet he'd have a few sleepless nights… for more than one reason.

Chase stirred, and Devon rubbed his back encouragingly. "Hey, how are you feeling?"

Chase's eyes fluttered open, and he looked up from under his lashes at Devon. "I'm fine."

Devon searched his eyes but finally nodded. "Good." He ran his fingers through Chase's hair, letting the other man wake up more before trying to continue their conversation.

He knew the second that Chase was finally aware enough of his surroundings to realize that he was curled up in Devon's lap, his pants and underwear still pulled down, exposing his ass. When he started to blush and pull away, Devon put a hand under his chin and lifted it so that their eyes could meet.

"Don't pull away. It's nothing to be ashamed of." He held Chase's face steady until he could feel the younger man's body relax.

"I have something I want you to see before we talk any more about your parents."

There was a spark of defiance in Chase's eyes, and it made Devon happy to see it. The events of the afternoon were difficult to deal with, but they did prove that Chase was starting to heal psychologically. If he felt comfortable enough to lash out at Devon, that was a good thing, and he needed to make sure that the spanking hadn't set Chase back any.

After quickly freeing Chase's hands from the belt, Devon shifted enough so he could reach into his back pocket and pull out the letter from Chase's mom. He held it out to the younger man, who reached out with a shaking hand to take it.

"This is from your mom. It took me and your brother to convince her that rushing up here and surprising you wasn't the best thing for you, and Tom had an idea that maybe writing a letter was a good idea."

Chase was trembling against Devon and looking at the letter like it might explode.

"Do you want me to leave you alone while you read it?" He knew it needed to be Chase's choice, so he just sat and waited for him to decide, but Chase quickly grabbed his wrist.

"No, don't...." Chase took a deep breath before continuing. "I just... I need you here."

Devon smoothed his hand up and down Chase's back as he nodded. "Okay, I'm not going anywhere."

Chase blew out a breath. "Okay... good." He turned his eyes back to the letter in his hand. "You don't know what it says?"

Devon shook his head. "I haven't read it, but I have a pretty good idea." He kissed the top of Chase's head. "She loves you. No matter what, you're still her baby, and she wants to know that you're okay, and she wants you to know that you're loved, no matter what."

"But all the things I did." Chase cut himself off with a little hitch before continuing. "How can she still want me around? I'm... I'm dirty... broken...."

Devon wrapped both arms tightly around Chase. "You're not broken, baby. You're just a little bent. And the things that happened, that's on Kingston. His filth doesn't taint you."

He knew Chase didn't believe him, not really. But he was going to keep working on it, and now he hoped he had some help, in the form of Chase's family. Working with them was going to be difficult, but it was something that needed to be done.

Chase sat silently for a few minutes, letting Devon rub his back under his T-shirt and rock him, until he finally opened the letter and pulled out the single sheet of paper.

He turned a little in Devon's arms and leaned back against his chest so they could both see the paper. Devon tried desperately not to read it.

"It's okay, Dev… I want you to see what it says." Chase's voice made him smile before he turned his attention to the letter.

Dearest Chase:

Your friend Mr. West brought us the wonderful news today that you're alive and well. Baby boy, you have no idea how much that means to me. I've spent the last seven years looking for you, and I never stopped hoping that you'd find your way home one day.

I'm so sorry, baby, that you felt you had to run away instead of talking to your father and me. I always thought you knew that nothing could ever make us stop loving you, but looking back now I can see why you felt the way you did. It never occurred to me that we were hurting you and pushing you away when we were spouting off the nonsense that we'd been hearing at church. I didn't really have my own opinion on gays, just accepted what I was told. It was stupid and shortsighted of me.

Now I know better. I'm sorry that it took you leaving for me to pay attention to things I should have noticed. How you started avoiding the church functions that you used to love. How girls never seemed to catch your eye.

After you left I realized just how much you'd pulled away from us, and I'm sorry I was so blinded to it. I have no excuses, except to say that you were always such a good child I never worried about anything you did. Your older brother caused enough hoopla all the time, that my attention was usually on him, and when I thought of you it was usually to thank God for having one boy who knew how to behave!

Anyway, I know it's not the same because I've had so much time to think about it, but if I'd had the chance to talk to you about this then, I like to think that this is what I'd say.

I love you, Chase. Nothing you could ever do or say would ever change how I feel about you. You're my child, and it's my honor to be your mother, no matter who you are. I will do anything in my power to help you deal with the things you're feeling.

Mr. West has told us about some of the things that happened to you, and I want you to know that it doesn't matter. The things that were done to you aren't your fault. That despicable person took advantage of a lost, lonely boy, and that was something you had no control over, no matter how it feels to you.

It doesn't change the fact that we love you and need to see you as soon as you're ready. It seems like Mr. West is taking good care of you, and it makes me so happy that you have him right now. I can tell he cares about you a lot, and you deserve no less.

He said you're going to therapy and that you've come a long way in the time since he found you, and I'm so glad to hear it.

Do what you have to, baby. Find the things that you need to feel better, and your family will be here waiting when you're ready to come home.

Oh, by the way, our phone number is still the same, but I've given it to Mr. West in case you forgot. You can call me anytime, Chase. I can't wait to hear your voice again.

Love,

Momma

Devon could feel the tears prickling at the backs of his eyes. It was the perfect letter, and he could feel the sobs shaking Chase's body as he cried, but the tears were different this time.

This time, Chase cried not only for what he'd lost, but also for what he still had. Devon had a feeling he'd be seeing the Mackenzie family again sooner than he thought. It made him happy for Chase, but it also made him sad. He knew it was selfish of him, but he knew that this was the beginning of the end of his time with the younger man.

Devon could feel his phone vibrating in his pocket but ignored it for the moment. He knew it was Jax, calling about the plans they had for Kingston, but Chase needed him more at the moment.

"You okay, sweetheart?" Devon kept his voice soft, not wanting to break the moment.

"Yeah." The younger man stopped, swallowed loudly, and then continued. "I can't believe they still want me in their family."

Devon rubbed Chase's arms. "Well, they do. Trust me, I saw their faces. If it wasn't for your brother, they would have forced me to bring them to you. They've waited a long time for you to come home."

Chase was quiet for a moment, then spoke again. "Tom doesn't want me to come home?"

"Oh, he wants you home. But, he's a doctor, Chase. He's been working in the emergency room of Santa Rosa Hospital in San Antonio for the last four years. He probably understands as well as I do the kind of trauma you've been dealt takes time to heal." Devon had no doubt that Tom Mackenzie was a good doctor. He'd had Chase's brother investigated thoroughly. The man had almost as many disciplinary letters on his record as he did commendations. The man wasn't afraid to buck the system to do what was best for his patients. Devon liked that about him.

"What about Zoe?" Chase's voice was full of worry.

Devon shrugged. "Honestly, I don't know. She wasn't there. Your parents sent her off to a friend's house so they could talk to me."

Chase nodded. "Good. She doesn't need to know that stuff about me."

Devon smiled. "I happen to agree with you. But she's going to want to know some of it, Chase. She's seventeen, not seven. Don't brush her off and expect her to accept it."

"I know." Chase looked up at him again. "It's just hard to know what to say."

"Just tell her enough of the truth to satisfy her curiosity. I think you've earned a few passes to have people let stuff go." Devon looked down at him again. "How do you feel?"

Chase looked thoughtful for a moment before answering. "As good as can be expected, I guess. My ass is a little sore." He blushed as he said it, and it was an observation, not a complaint.

"Still?" He gave the younger man a little push so he had to roll onto his stomach. "Let me take a look."

Chase rolled his eyes but did as he was told. Devon gently ran his hand over the still reddened skin, but there were only a few welts left, and other than that, just a pleasantly attractive pink blush.

"You want some pain meds for it?" He grinned when Chase pushed back into the touch, moaning quietly.

"No, Sir. I kinda like it. Helps me focus a little."

Devon kept touching him softly as Chase almost purred under his hands. "I'm glad it helped you. I'm never gonna blow smoke up your ass, Chase. If I'm telling you something that I see in you, you'd better believe I'm telling you the truth."

Chase's face was as red as his ass, but his body kept begging for Devon to keep going. "I know. I'll try to do better."

Devon let his fingers wander a bit more, edging down as Chase spread his legs as much as the pants around his thighs would allow.

"Please, Dev...." Chase was trying to push back into the touches and hump the bed at the same time.

"No, not right now." Devon gave the soft skin a regretful pat and pulled his hand away. He leaned down and kissed Chase on the forehead before getting off the bed. "I'm sorry, but I have a few calls to make that can't wait any longer."

"But... but... look at me!" He pushed up into a full kneel, letting Devon see his erect cock. It was standing proud, almost touching his stomach, and it looked a little uncomfortable. Devon couldn't help but grin as he leaned down to whisper in Chase's ear.

"Why don't you go and have a nice warm shower. The hot water will make your ass sting a little, and you can jerk off remembering how my hand felt when I spanked you." Chase's cock twitched at Devon's words, so he gave it a couple of strokes.

Chase sucked in a breath, and his cock twitched again, precome sliding down and slicking the next few strokes of Devon's hand, before he pulled away regretfully and walked to the door. It took everything Devon had to ignore Chase's disappointed whine. He looked back, just once, for one parting shot.

"Be good and let me make my calls, and maybe later I'll let you suck my cock." Chase's groan followed him out of the room as he walked down the hall to his office and went in, closing the door after himself.

He pulled his phone out of his pocket and dialed Jax. When the other man answered, Devon was ready. "It's time to get this started. Tell me this is gonna work." And he waited with bated breath for Jax's reply.

Fourteen

THE MUSIC in the main room was thumping loudly, but it faded as Devon walked down the hallway toward the playrooms. He saw Dani coming toward him and smiled.

"What's going on, gorgeous?" He leaned in so the redhead could kiss him on the cheek.

"Mr. Smallwood, that's what." She grinned at him as she moved past him. "He's waiting for you in room one."

"Good. I'm just going to change and I'll be right there." He started walking and then stopped and turned around. "How long has he been there?"

Dani looked back over her shoulder. "About fifteen minutes. He should be almost ready."

He nodded at her. "Thanks."

"Uh, Dev?"

He swung back once more to look at her. "Yeah?"

"You sure you're not pushing him too hard?" She looked down at her feet before looking back up at him. "I know you're distracted right now—"

Devon cut her off. "Don't worry, Dani. If I had any doubts, I would have put him off or passed him on." He smiled so she'd know he wasn't angry at her. "I need to keep busy while we're waiting for things to… happen."

She took a deep breath and smiled back. "Okay. You know I trust you. I'm just worried about you."

He walked back to her and hugged her tightly. "I know you are, and I love you for it, but I've got it covered, okay?"

Dani nodded and then pulled away. "Okay, boss, you've got work to do." She gave him a push. "Quit being such a slacker, mister."

Devon chuckled and gave her a swat on the ass, grinning when she yelped. "And you quit being so bossy, *Mistress*."

She put her hands on her hips and glared at him. "Don't make me go and get my whip!"

He backed away, hands raised in surrender. "I'm going, I'm going!"

She giggled and then turned and strode off, and he knew she had her own client waiting.

He walked down to the dressing room door and went in. He stripped out of his street clothes and pulled on the black leather pants and tight black T-shirt that was waiting for him there. It was a uniform of sorts for him when he did a scene, along with the heavy black boots sitting in the corner. Black leather gloves completed the picture.

His clients expected a certain image, depending on what they needed from him.

This client was the CEO of a multimillion-dollar company. He was married and very much in love with his wife. He had three children he adored and had a reputation as an excellent employer and a fair businessman.

He was also a former alcoholic who had been moving on to even worse destructive habits and had almost lost his family over it. He'd made the decision to find a less self-harming way of dealing with his stress and had been directed to Devon and his club by a friend who was a regular patron.

The man had seemed surprised at the level of professionalism he'd found when he came in for his consultation and to negotiate his contract. He hadn't been expecting to be sent home after that first visit to think about everything he'd learned about the service that Devon and his associates provided and to make sure he was positive about what he wanted.

Devon had smiled when the man walked back through the door three days later for his first session. He'd chosen Devon for his first time, admitting he was old-fashioned enough that he didn't think he'd be able to completely surrender to a woman the way he would need to.

That admission had gotten him his first punishment… and his first reward.

When Devon was finished dressing, he walked down the hall to the room his client was waiting in. He walked in without knocking to find the man on his knees, hands behind his back, clasping his elbows, in perfect submissive position.

"Good evening, Miles." Devon walked over to stand in front of the kneeling man, smiling in approval as the man bent and touched his forehead to the floor before sitting back up and speaking.

"Good evening, Sir." He kept his eyes down, waiting for permission before seeking eye contact with Devon.

"You can look at me, Miles." He waited for the other man to raise his head before continuing. "I see you found the cuffs I left for you?"

The other man nodded. "Yes, thank you, Sir."

"Hmmm, looks like you remembered the lessons about manners you learned last time you were here." He walked around the man, taking in his physical appearance, looking for anything he'd need to be careful of.

"Yes, Sir, I did. I don't want to disappoint you that way again." Miles looked up at him, so obviously eager to please. Seeing him like this, you'd never know he could be completely ruthless in the boardroom when he needed to be.

It was kind of the point, really. The man needed a few hours to let go entirely. When the weight of his responsibilities got to be too much, instead of reaching for a bottle—or worse—he called and made an appointment with Devon.

When he was with his Dom, he could hand over the reins of responsibility to someone else and just let himself relax. Of course, it wasn't really as easy as that. He had to be coaxed into letting go because he was a man who was used to being in charge.

Devon reached down and ran his gloved fingers through Miles's hair. "I know you'll do your best." He felt the other man shiver under his hand. "Did you have any problems getting the cuffs on? Do you want me to check them?"

Miles shook his head. "No, no problems, but you can check them if it pleases you, Sir."

Devon stood back and motioned for the other man to get to his feet. "I have confidence in you." He walked over to stand beside the St. Andrew's cross that was on the wall across from the door. "Come here, Miles."

Miles walked to the cross and stood facing it, waiting for more instructions. He was naked except for the cuffs, as vulnerable and trusting as he'd ever been in his life. It wasn't about sex; it was about control… and giving it up.

Devon gave Miles's ass a hard smack, the sound of leather on skin sharp in the room. The other man hardly flinched, just sort of sighed in relief. "Closer."

Miles stepped closer to the cross and waited as Devon lifted first one of his arms and then the other, attaching the cuffs to the metal rings at the top of the X. Devon used his foot to push the other man's ankles farther apart before crouching to attach the cuffs on his legs to the cross as well.

"How does that feel? Are you comfortable?" If Miles was uncomfortable for this, it would distract him from focusing on what Devon was doing.

"Yes, Sir. It feels good." Miles's voice was calm and quiet, and he seemed completely at ease with where he was. It was a long way from the man who almost shook himself apart the first time he was in Devon's club.

"Okay." Devon walked over and picked up a wooden paddle from a table by the door. It looked like a large wooden hairbrush with fur attached to one side instead of bristles. "Tell me about your week, Miles. Anything happen that I need to know about?"

The other man shook his head—too quickly—and Devon gave him one more chance. "You sure? You look like you have something you want to tell me." He gave him a sharp slap with the wooden side of the paddle, right on the fleshiest part of his ass. "Use your words!"

"No, Sir!" Once again the answer was too quick, and this time there was a harsh breath that accompanied it.

Devon pulled his arm back and laid another stroke of the paddle over the first, and this time Miles flinched. The sound of wood against skin was shocking in the small, dark room.

"I'm disappointed in you, Miles." Devon let the paddle fall again, this time a little lower. "I thought we'd gotten over this lying bullshit."

When the paddle fell the next time, it was a little harder, but still just a warming stroke. The delicate skin was turning dark pink a lot quicker than Chase's had the day before.

"I'm not lying, Sir." The protest died out with the next smack of the paddle, this one catching the top of Miles's thigh, and he cried out.

Normally Devon would be insisting that the sub stay quiet as another measure of discipline and focus, but today he wanted Miles to talk, because it was what the man needed to do.

"You called and begged for a session as soon as possible. You said you couldn't wait for your regular appointment in two days. Mistress Danielle said you were quite insistent about it." He laid another two strokes to the tops of Miles's thighs, causing him to sob, before continuing. "Tell me again that you don't have a problem."

Miles keened deep in his throat, every slap of the paddle making his breath hitch higher, his cries get louder until he broke.

"I went to a bar... oh God, please, Sir... I went to a bar and sat down at a table and ordered myself a bottle of bourbon." As he spoke, Devon lessened the power of the strokes but didn't stop.

"Then what?" Devon had been worried about Miles after their last session. The man was being pushed to the breaking point by his job and a family crisis that involved his ailing mother. For a man who'd broken before, the breaking point was closer than for most.

"I looked at the bottle for an hour... even poured myself a glass—" As he spoke and let the shame and fear and desperation flow out of him, Miles seemed to relax into his bonds. "—then I walked out of there and called for an appointment."

His head hung loosely between his arms as tears and sweat dripped off his face, but the admission seemed to have lifted a weight off his shoulders. "I'm sorry for being so weak, Sir... I have no excuse."

Devon could hear the genuine remorse in the other man's voice, and he stopped the spanking. He turned the paddle over and used the side padded with rabbit fur to run soothing touches over Miles's back and shoulders.

"I've told you before, Miles, you're not weak." He was careful to keep the fur away from the redness on the other man's ass. As soft as it was, it would feel like sandpaper on the abused skin at the moment, and he didn't want him distracted. "You walked away and left it there without drinking any of it, yes?"

"Yes, Sir." Miles leaned his head on one arm, and Devon let him rest for a moment.

"Then you did what you were supposed to and called for help, right?" He knew repeating Miles's words back to him would help him hear what he had said and know it was important.

Miles took a deep breath, letting it shudder out before speaking again. "Yes, Sir."

The other man was in his late forties, reasonably fit, and probably appeared strong and capable to his employees and family, and he was both of those things.

But he was also scared and worried about the future of all those he cared about, and it was a heavy burden for anyone to carry on their own.

These sessions with Devon helped him let go of that burden and let himself rest, while at the same time, he found forgiveness within himself for the mistakes he'd made.

Devon ran his fingers through the older man's salt-and-pepper hair, letting him feel the approval from Devon at making the right choices in the end.

"Then you did the best you could do, Miles. That's all anyone can ask of you." Devon wasn't quite sure if the older man was ready to end the session or not. It seemed like he needed something more.

He turned the paddle over once more and smoothed the now cool wood over the reddened skin of Miles's ass and upper thighs, noting how he squirmed but didn't pull away.

"Are we done for today? Or do you need a little more?" He was pretty sure which it would be, but he needed Miles to realize it.

"Sir, I think—" The other man swallowed before continuing. "—I think I need more." His voice was quiet but sure. "May I have a drink of water first, though?"

Devon smiled gently at him. "Of course." He walked to the little table, brought back a bottle of water and twisted it open, then held it up to Miles's lips. He only let him have a little of the cool liquid, knowing that too much in his stomach might upset it.

After a few swallows, he pulled it back and was given an almost shy smile by the man. "Thank you, Sir."

A few months ago, before he found Chase, Miles's quiet submission would have stirred Devon's blood and made him crave a few hours with a sexually submissive young man. Now it just left him satisfied that he'd done what he could to help the man bound in front of him.

"Time to begin again." Devon made it a statement instead of a question and was rewarded with a shudder and a nod.

"Yes, Sir. Thank you, Sir."

Devon petted Miles's hair once more before moving back to the table. He put the wooden paddle down and picked up a wide leather one. It had a little give but would still deliver a stinging slap with every stroke. He didn't want to leave too many bruises, knowing the man spent a great deal of time sitting behind a desk.

The soreness would linger for about three days or so, giving Miles a point of focus and reminding him he had other alternatives to his former self-destructive behavior.

He walked back to the St. Andrew's cross and the sub, letting him see the leather paddle. Miles looked at it wide-eyed for a moment and then nodded.

Devon squeezed the other man's shoulder quickly before stepping back. "Let's make you fly, Miles."

WHEN HE stepped out of the recovery room forty-five minutes later, Devon was sweaty and tired. The session with Miles had taken a lot out of him, and he still had one more to go. After spending a few quiet minutes with Miles, he left the sub in the capable hands of the nurse that volunteered three nights a week in return for the use of a room for her and her boyfriend.

It never failed to amuse Devon to see the tiny little nurse with her hands around her football-player boyfriend's balls, making him beg for mercy.

He went quickly to his private bathroom and stripped. He jumped in the shower and cleaned up, knowing he didn't have a lot of time before his next appointment.

Once he was clean and dressed, he grabbed his cell phone and called Chase. He knew the younger man wouldn't go to sleep until he'd heard from Devon, and he needed his sleep.

When Chase answered the phone, his voice was adorably sleepy, and it made Devon wish desperately that he was home and in bed with Chase snuggled up beside him.

"Hmm... hey, Dev. How's your night going?"

Devon could picture him lying there, Cammy curled up next to him. She seemed to be taking her job of protecting Chase very seriously, and Devon could understand how she felt.

"It's going good. Just heading off to my second session of the night, and I wanted to see how you were doing."

Chase chuckled warmly. "You could have just looked at your security monitor. I know you have the whole place wired." There was no resentment at being watched in his voice, only amusement.

"I didn't want to be too creepy, and I like talking to you. It makes me smile." Devon wondered if he should be keeping things like that to himself, knowing Chase would be leaving, but he couldn't help it. He knew Chase was probably blushing adorably on the other end of the phone at that moment, and it made something warm expand in his chest.

"Dev...." Chase breathed his name like a prayer, and it took everything Devon had to not run out the door and drive home.

"I've gotta get back to work, sweetheart." Tearing himself away was getting harder and harder. "You get some sleep, and I'll be home soon. You need your rest before your therapy appointment tomorrow."

Chase sighed. "Okay. Just... be careful, please?"

Devon laughed. "Baby, I don't need to be careful. Andy and Joe are standing guard, and Jax is ready to rip someone's arm off. I'm as safe as I can be in here. Don't worry."

"I know. It's just...." Chase trailed off, seeming to be mulling over what to say.

"It's just what, Chase?" He kept his voice gentle. "You know you can tell me anything, right?" He heard a rustling sound and knew Chase was nodding.

"It's just that I need you to be okay. He can't hurt you because I'm too weak to stand up to him myself."

The younger man's genuine concern for Devon's well-being was heart wrenching to hear, but the self-depreciation was worse.

"You're not weak, Chase. You were just alone before. Now you're not. You have me and my family and yours as well, when you're ready for them. None of us are alone in this. Don't forget that, okay?" He could hear Chase's breathing calming over the phone.

"Okay." The phone crackled as Chase shifted. "Give me a hug when you get home?" The quiet pleading in his voice made him sound so much younger all of the sudden, and it made Devon want to rip Kingston to shreds all over again for ever daring to hurt the child Chase had been at sixteen.

"I will if I can get past Cammy. She loves you best, you know?" Devon heard Chase snicker.

"Nah, she's just following your lead and taking care of me." His voice was getting softer as he drifted toward sleep.

"Yeah, she's a good girl that way." He sat and listened to Chase breathe for a few minutes before speaking again. "Gotta go, darlin'. Hang up the phone so it doesn't go dead, okay?"

Chase huffed a quiet breath into the phone. "M'kay." Another deep breath... probably a yawn. "Night, Dev...."

"Night, Chase. Sweet dreams." He listened until the call ended and then put his phone away in his desk.

The certainty of having to let Chase go was ripping his heart out a little more every day, but he wouldn't change meeting him and falling in love for anything... even to get rid of the pain.

He straightened his back, pulling himself together mentally. It was time to get back to work, and it needed all his attention. After Chase was gone, it would be the only thing he had left.

WHEN DEVON walked into the playroom, he took one look at the man waiting there and knew something was wrong. The man leaning against the opposite wall didn't have a submissive bone in his body, and the file specifically said that's what he was there for.

Devon walked to stand against the side wall and looked the other man over. He was taller than Devon by about two inches and had a hard body that was shown off by a skintight T-shirt and jeans. His whole stance screamed aggression, and he wondered how the man had gotten past Scott and Mike without arousing suspicion.

"You mind telling me why you're really here, Mr. Jacobs?" Devon could see that his words startled the man.

"What makes you think that I'm not here for a session?" His voice was low and full of derision.

Devon snorted. "You're no more of a sub than I am."

The man grinned wickedly. "That's where you're wrong, pretty boy. According to Mr. Kingston, you're all sub... a sheep in wolf's clothing, he said."

"Kingston's fucking delusional and has been for a long time." He let every ounce of disgust and hatred he felt for the man's employer show in his face.

Jacobs shook his head, still smiling. "Funny, he says the same thing about you." He looked at Devon appraisingly. "He said you need a beating to remind you of your place."

Devon folded his arms and leaned against the wall. He raised one eyebrow. "I suppose he thinks you're the man to give it to me?"

The other man smirked. "Maybe."

Devon chuckled mirthlessly. "Seeing as how I beat him last time, at least he was smart enough to not come himself."

"You attacked a wounded man. I'm not wounded."

Devon knew that Jacobs's overconfidence would be his undoing. He was too brainwashed by Kingston to realize that Devon was any kind of threat.

"Mr. Kingston also said to tell you that you shouldn't worry about that useless sub you've taken such a shine to. He'll find a way to dispose of him properly for you." The evil leer on his face made it clear he was looking forward to that particular duty.

The mention of Chase made Devon see red, and he lunged off the wall toward the man without thinking about it. Jacobs had obviously been counting on Devon's reaction and used the distraction to straighten and pull the riding crop he'd been hiding from behind him.

He pulled it back and swung at Devon's face hard. Devon managed to get his arm up to block the hit, but the force carried it a bit, and he felt the bite of the leather on his cheek.

Being hit with his own crop pissed him off, though, and he got a hold of the guy's arm and twisted, using the other man's momentum to turn him around. Jacobs got in one more shot, bringing his elbow back into Devon's ribs, but the pain didn't even register.

The man was facedown on the floor, both arms pinned behind him, and he screamed when Devon leaned on them, almost popping both shoulders out of their sockets.

"You fucking go near Chase and I'll rip your balls off and feed them to you... and that's not a threat... it's a promise."

Devon was reaching for the crop, his anger all-consuming, when Andy and Scott broke into the room, closely followed by Mike. They pulled Devon off the other man and secured Jacobs with zip ties before hauling him out the door.

"Go ahead, pretty boy... call the fucking cops...." Jacobs cackled as he was hauled out. "I'll tell them I was trying to teach you fucking perverts a lesson!"

His voice faded as he was pulled down the hall. Devon straightened himself out and then looked at Andy.

"Drop him on Kingston's doorstep. No cops, you got it?" Devon felt warm wetness on his face and reached up to touch it. He pulled back his fingers to see blood on them and groaned.

"It's not so bad, Dev. It probably won't even scar." Andy was trying to make him feel better, but it wasn't working.

"I won't be able to hide it from Chase." When he moved to wipe the blood from his face, he hissed from the pain in his ribs. "Fuck!"

Andy looked at him, and Devon couldn't really decipher it. "That's your biggest worry, huh? What Chase's gonna think?"

Devon nodded. "Yeah, stupid kid will probably blame himself."

Andy stared at him thoughtfully. "Huh…."

Devon was getting irritated by his friend's weird behavior. "What do you mean, 'huh'? What the fuck?"

"It means…." Andy herded him toward the door. "It means that I never thought I would ever see you so hung up on one person. You never seemed to believe in love and shit."

Devon let himself be led down the hall to his office, unsurprised to see Jax waiting there with the medical kit. He pulled off his shirt when Jax gestured toward it and sat on the edge of his desk to let the older man get a look at his injuries.

He could feel Andy staring at him. "I guess I didn't… until I met Chase."

Andy nodded but didn't say anything more. He patted Devon on the shoulder and headed for the door. He turned back once.

"Gonna get back to work. Mike and Scott are dropping off the asshole, and I don't wanna leave Joe out there alone." He looked torn, but Devon just waved him off.

"Sounds good. I'll be fine." Devon looked his friend in the eye and waited for him to nod and leave before letting his eyes slide shut.

They popped open when Jax cleaned the cut on his face with an antiseptic wipe. "Jesus, Jax! Warn a guy, will you?"

Jax cocked an eyebrow at him. "I did warn you. I told you that doing sessions was a stupid idea until this was over." He put a small bandage on Devon's face and then started inspecting his ribs. "Will you at least stick to your regulars for the moment? You, Dani, Scott… the rest of the Doms… and none of the subs should be working right now. It's too dangerous for them."

Devon sucked in a pained breath as Jax probed his side but finally nodded his agreement. "Yeah… you're right. Gonna have to supplement their income somehow, though. It's not their fault they can't make tips that way, it's mine."

Jax looked up at him finally. "Nothing's broken. You're just bruised." He put a friendly hand on Devon's shoulder and gave it a squeeze. "You're a good man, Dev. None of this is your fault. Kingston is a crazy fucking bastard, and you have no control over his behavior."

Devon sighed and ran his fingers through his hair. "I have to protect Chase. None of this is his fault either, and right now he's incapable of protecting himself."

Devon's stomach turned at the thought of that freak Jacobs getting anywhere near Chase.

Jax gave him a gentle shake. "He's gonna be fine. You've made sure of that." He passed Devon his shirt. "You need to go home and rest. You want some meds?"

Devon shook his head. "No, I've got some at home and I've gotta drive." He pulled the shirt on and got to his feet. "I'll check in later, okay?"

Jax clapped him easily on the shoulder and pushed him toward the door. "Let's get you to your car."

He stopped Devon before they got to the door, looking at him intensely. "This is gonna work, Dev… and he's going to be out of your life forever."

Devon looked into Jax's eyes, looking for any signs of doubt, but there weren't any. "Okay… let's get it done. Chase's gonna have to go to his parents this weekend at the latest."

He shivered at the thought of making Chase go… but it was for the best.

It was going to be a long week.

Fifteen

DEVON WOKE up slowly to Chase straddling his hips, his long fingers very carefully tracing around the cut on Devon's cheek, his eyes big and glassy, and Devon held in a sigh.

"I'm okay, Chase." He brought his hands up to rest on Chase's thighs and rubbed them soothingly.

"Who did this to you?" His voice was tight and worried. He let his fingers trail gently down Devon's throat and across his collarbone, wincing as he delicately traced the bruises left on Devon's ribs.

He looked up, and his eyes caught Devon's. "Was it Kingston?"

Devon shook his head. "No, one of his friends." He caught Chase's hand, pulling it to his mouth and kissing the knuckles gently. "It won't happen again."

"He'll keep trying, though, won't he? He's never going to leave you alone... or me." Chase sounded so scared and defeated, and it was breaking Devon's heart. He took the younger man's wrist and pulled gently as he turned so that they lay side by side, sharing the same pillow.

"Yes, he'll keep trying... but it won't be forever." He pushed Chase's bangs off his forehead, loving the gentle smile the action got him. "We have a plan. All of us at the club."

Chase had met the men involved over the last few weeks. They had all come by the house at one point to talk to Devon, and they'd all been charmed by Chase's gentle personality and his quick smile.

"He's too dangerous to mess with, Devon." The fear in Chase's eyes was palpable, but Devon was coming to realize that it was fear for Devon, not himself, that was causing those shadows in his gaze. "We should just leave… get away for a while until he forgets about us."

He looked at Devon with such hope that for a moment Devon was tempted to agree with him. Packing Chase up and leaving the country for a while was very appealing, but he knew it would only be a temporary solution. When they got back, Kingston would still be there… and probably more determined than ever.

And it wasn't in Devon's nature to run. When you run, you're just asking to be chased.

"No, baby. Running's not an option. I don't wanna live like that, and I don't want that for you either." He leaned forward so their foreheads were touching.

"The plan's gonna work, and when it does, he'll be out of our lives forever." He brought his hand up to cup Chase's cheek. "But you're going to have to do something that I know you really don't want to do." He rubbed his thumb over Chase's cheek.

"I didn't want to push you, but I don't have a choice right now." Chase looked so frightened, and Devon hated that look on him. "It's not something horrible, Chase, just hard."

Chase swallowed, his eyes getting big and bright. "What is it?" He trembled under Devon's touch but didn't move away.

"I need you to go and stay with your family in Texas." Chase flinched but pushed closer to Devon.

"Dev, I don't…." Chase seemed to be forcing the words out. "I'm not ready to go back there. It's too soon." His voice was quiet and he sounded scared, and for a moment he looked like the sixteen-year-old he'd been when his world had been ripped apart. "I haven't even seen them in person yet."

Devon nodded and closed his eyes for a second, knowing he needed to be the strong one. "I know. If I could, I'd bring them here to see you first, but I don't want to draw Kingston's attention to them, and your family trooping through my door would definitely be noticed."

He took a deep breath and opened his eyes. "You and I are hitching a ride on a friend's plane to Corpus Christi tomorrow. Tom is gonna pick us up there and drive us to a place I rented for them. You're all gonna stay there until this is done."

Chase started pulling back, shaking his head. "No… no, I can't go there…." His voice cracked, cutting him off.

Devon took Chase's face in both his hands, stopping his attempt to flee. "Yes, you can." Devon let his strength come through in his voice. "You can and you will. I need to finally deal with Kingston, and I can't do that if I'm worrying about him getting to you."

Chase closed his eyes, and Devon knew it was his way of trying to shut Devon out. "Open your eyes, Chase!" He felt bad about being so stern, but he needed the younger man to listen to him.

"Your family needs to see you. Your mother needs to put her hands on you and know that you're still alive and not lost to her forever." Chase's eyes popped open at Devon's words. "Your father needs to see that you're not just a broken shell, and your big brother needs to know that you don't blame him for not knowing how to find you."

Tears fell unchecked down Chase's face, but Devon didn't dare let up. "And your beautiful little sister deserves the chance to know you, to learn to love the man you've become." He used his thumbs to wipe some of the tears away and kissed Chase on the forehead.

"You're not damaged or tainted or any of the other awful things that you have running around in your head. You survived something horrible and came out of it a good and decent human being. Not everyone can say that."

He loved the blush that stole over Chase's face. It meant he was hearing what Devon was saying.

"You're going to do this, Chase, so I can do what I have to without worrying that you're going to get caught in the crossfire." He looked into the other man's eyes, letting him see he had no doubt about the outcome of the coming fight.

"When it's done, we're both going to be free. You understand me?" He waited, letting go of Chase's face to give him room.

"Yes, Sir, I understand." The words told him Chase was taking him seriously; the tone told him it was Chase's respect for Devon as a person and as a Dom that would help him get through it.

Devon nodded and then pulled him close, tucking Chase's head under his chin. "Good... that's real good, baby." He rubbed his hand up and down Chase's back, smiling at the little shivers running through the younger man's body.

"You want me to stop? Is it too ticklish?" Devon had never met anyone with skin as sensitive as Chase's.

"No!" Chase shook his head to reinforce his words. He tucked himself close to Devon, one big hand splayed gently across the older man's chest, carefully not touching the bruise on his side. "I kinda like it. It feels nice."

"Good." Devon kissed the top of the younger man's head, as they snuggled together. It was going to be a long day, and maybe a little more rest would make things easier.

TOM MACKENZIE was a nervous wreck. In a few minutes his little brother that he hadn't seen for seven years was going to walk through the front door of the beautiful house they were hiding out in, and he didn't have a single clue what to do.

His parents were both trying to keep calm and failing miserably, and his little sister was bewildered by the whole situation, not that he could blame her. He was feeling a little lost and confused himself.

The whole family had come up with a story about an ill family member who needed their help in another state and they'd all arranged to have a couple of week's holidays. It had taken some doing, though. Zoe had been pulled out of school and arrangements were made for homework, and Tom had found himself being volunteered as a tutor and taskmaster to make sure her schoolwork didn't suffer. Zoe hadn't been pleased with being pulled away from her friends and boyfriend, especially as everyone was keeping her in the dark about a lot of the things Chase had gone through, and she knew it. But in the end, she agreed to go because she loved her brother.

His mom didn't work so she didn't have any problems, and both Tom and his dad had enough holidays accrued that no one complained too much about being left shorthanded. Tom felt bad about leaving the hospital in a bind but after not taking a vacation in over three years, he didn't feel too guilty.

He'd missed his brother fiercely, and he was so glad to have him back in their lives, but he was worried about how much of the bouncy, loving young man who'd disappeared remained in the man he'd become.

He'd talked to Devon a lot, but the man had insisted that Chase be allowed to tell them what he wanted them to know, and Tom had reluctantly agreed, knowing it could be important to his brother's recovery.

He was glad Devon wouldn't tell him the name of the man who had hurt Chase so badly. If he knew who he was, there was every chance that Tom would already be in New Orleans looking for him so he could kill him.

But Devon had promised that it was being taken care of, and he'd seen the anguish and anger in his eyes and believed him. It made him feel better to know that the man was going to face some kind of justice, and he had a feeling it was going to be more than proportional.

He heard a car pulling into the drive, and his heart almost stopped. It took everything he had to stay away from the door and wait for them to come in. He didn't want to overwhelm Chase, but he was desperate to see him.

Tom could hear the quiet murmur of voices, and then there was a quick knock on the screen door before it opened and Devon walked in. He held his breath as the other man turned and reached through the open door, and then he was pulling through a tall, handsome, younger man that he knew was his brother.

He looked so miserable standing there trying to hide behind Devon that Tom wanted to do anything he could to wipe that look off his face. His parents and sister appeared in the doorway from the living room. All of them seemed to be frozen there, and he knew it was up to him.

He took a couple of steps forward and smiled at the first man. "Hello, Devon."

Devon smiled back. "Hello, Tom, it's good to see you again."

Tom nodded. "Yeah, you too." He paused and finally turned his gaze to Chase. "Hello, little brother. I've missed you so much."

It felt like the whole world waited as Chase decided what to do.

His brother looked at Devon for guidance, and Tom was grateful when the older man smiled reassuringly at Chase and tugged him forward.

It wasn't until Chase finally spoke that the world seemed to breathe again.

"Hello, Tom." He looked back at Devon for a second before looking at Tom again. "I missed you too."

Tom heard a choked off sob and looked over as his mother finally found it in herself to move forward. She opened her arms as she walked toward him, tears running down her face, but with a smile that would have lit up any room.

Chase took a tentative step toward her and then another until at last, he was wrapped in her arms, both of them crying now, and Tom could hear his mother whispering.

"Oh, my sweet baby boy, I'm so sorry."

Chase shook his shaggy head and held her closer. "It's not your fault, Mama... really it's not."

She grabbed his face in both hands, pulling him down so she could kiss his forehead and look into his eyes. Tom noticed that, even though Chase was almost a head taller than his mother, he seemed almost small in her hands.

Tom watched as his father walked forward, reaching out to put his hand on Chase's shoulder, and he winced as Chase flinched away from the touch. His father pulled back his hand like he'd been stung, but then Devon moved forward and put his hand on the small of Chase's back. Chase looked at him, leaning into the touch before turning to smile at his father.

"Hello, Dad. It's so good to see you." He gave his father a wary hug, never moving far enough away from Devon for that contact to be lost.

Tom saw his sister standing alone, wringing her hands and looking sad, so he calmly walked over and put his arm around her shoulder, urging her gently forward and into Chase's line of sight.

Chase must have seen them moving, because he turned to face them both. When his eyes landed on Zoe's face, he smiled, and for the first time since he disappeared, Tom got to see the dimples that made up the majority of his memories of his brother, and he felt tears push at the backs of his eyes.

"Oh, Zoe Bean... look how beautiful you are." The delight in Chase's voice had his sister flinging herself at him, and Tom watched as the younger man wrapped her in his arms and lifted her off the ground, holding her tight.

Finally those hazel eyes turned back to Tom. "You got a shotgun, right, big brother? To keep the boys off her?"

Tom couldn't help it. He ground out a sound that was half chuckle and half sob before carefully pulling both his siblings into a giant hug.

They stayed like that for a few minutes, faces buried in each other's hair, murmuring "missed you" and "love you" and "don't ever disappear again."

When he finally lifted his head, he looked around the room and saw tears of happiness in the eyes of his parents and a smile on Devon's face.

As he looked closer, though, he could see the crushing sadness in the older man's deep green eyes as he looked at Chase, and he understood that when Devon left them in a day or so, he'd be leaving his heart behind.

DEVON WATCHED Chase's reunion with his family with decidedly mixed feelings.

He was so happy that the Mackenzies seemed to have welcomed Chase back with open arms and open hearts. He could see how much they'd missed the quiet young man, and he was glad to not see any judgment or condemnation in any of their eyes.

Most of his own family had pulled out of his life years ago, unable and unwilling to accept him being involved in the life that made him happy.

The exception was his little sister, Victoria, who continued to defy the rest of the West clan and came to visit him whenever she was home from college. She'd scoffed at their parents' insistence that continued association with him would lead her down the path to perdition, and she rolled her eyes when she told Dev about how their mom still prayed for his soul every Sunday at church.

"Don't you worry none, sweets." Vicki had picked up Andy's unfortunate obsession with using the hated nickname. "One day she's gonna wake up and realize that she lost you out of her life over her stupid worry about what people who don't even love her think, and I hope it breaks her cold, judgmental heart."

He always admonished her to be respectful, but inside he adored Vicki for the unwavering devotion she showed him.

Devon looked at Chase wrapped up in the hug with his brother and sister and tried to move slowly away to give them some time together, but Chase was paying better attention than Devon had given him credit for.

Chase's head came up, and he freed one hand to grab Devon's wrist and keep him close. The pleading in the young man's eyes stopped Devon's retreat, and he settled in to wait.

When Devon turned his gaze to Chase's brother, the amount of warmth and understanding he saw there overshadowed any gratitude, which he really didn't want anyhow.

Finally everyone pulled apart, and Liz managed to get them all into the sitting room. Chase sat by the arm of the couch and then pulled Devon down to sit beside him, effectively giving himself some space in a situation that was threatening to become overwhelming.

Colin smiled at his son and then turned to Devon.

"So, this plan that you have… it's going into action when?" The man was worried, and Devon couldn't blame him.

"It's already in play. The man who we're after is going to be very curious about where I am and what I've done with Chase. When I get back, I'm going to distract him by making myself appear vulnerable."

He glanced at Chase, squeezing his hand in reassurance when the younger man paled.

"Devon, we want this man to pay for what he did to our boy, but it's not worth you getting hurt." Devon was touched by Liz's display of concern on his behalf.

"Don't worry, ma'am. I won't ever be in any danger. My friends will have me in their sight at all times." He could feel Chase pushing closer to him and put his arm around him.

"It's all gonna go down very soon, and then you'll all be free to return home to your lives. I really wish these precautions weren't necessary, but I'm just not willing to put any of your lives in danger." He looked around at all of them, and he saw worry and a little fear but no resentment toward Chase, and that's what he'd been afraid of.

Liz stood up. "My goodness, look at me. I haven't even shown you your rooms yet." She was anxious and Devon knew she'd just hit the first nerve for Chase. He started to stand up when they were interrupted by the younger man.

"Mama, I don't want to start out on a bad feeling, but I need to be in the same room as Devon tonight." He looked his mother in the eye, his gaze never wavering, and it made Devon proud to see him stand up for himself.

"I have bad dreams, and they've been getting better"—he stood up a little straighter—"but my doctor says they'll probably get worse for a few days until I get used to everything, and the only thing that makes them stop is Devon talking to me."

Chase turned his head, seeking reassurance from Devon, and he smiled encouragingly.

"I don't want to argue with you, but that's the way it has to be. If that's not okay, we'll go somewhere else to sleep."

He stood and waited for his mother to speak, and Devon recognized the way he was standing, like he was waiting for the next blow to land but wouldn't back down.

Fortunately, Liz recognized it as well. She walked over and gently cradled Chase's cheek in her hand. "It's okay, baby. I wasn't planning on arguing with you." She reached around his neck then and pulled him in for a hug and whispered in his ear. "Whatever you need to get you through, Chase, I want you to have it."

Devon let out a sigh of relief as Chase nodded and hugged his mother again.

"I'm going to go out and grab the bags from the car." He turned and headed for the door as Tom called out to him.

"Here, let me come help you."

Devon smiled, and the two men went out to the driveway. Devon popped the trunk and waited for Tom to speak. He wasn't disappointed.

"I'm not trying to interfere, Devon, but are you sure you shouldn't be making Chase sleep alone now? What's he going to do when you're gone?" Devon could see the genuine concern in the other man's eyes, and so he answered as honestly as possible.

"I don't know what's for the best, Tom, but I'll be damned if I deny him any comfort I can offer him in the next couple of days." He reached into the trunk and grabbed Chase's suitcase. "When I'm not here, he can call me whenever he needs. I'll answer if I can. If not, you're going to have to be there for him. All of you."

He set down Chase's suitcase before grabbing a couple more bags and passing them to Tom. "He's come so far in the last while, but underneath, there's a part of him that's still the sixteen-year-old boy he was when he left." He looked up into Tom's eyes. "It'll be up to you to help your family understand where he's coming from. He's not able to express himself very well sometimes because he was never given the opportunity."

Tom nodded. "I understand."

"I hope so. His doctor says that he's basically suffering from a form of PTSD, and it can make his moods erratic. Mostly he's happy. I think that's his normal nature." He looked at Tom for confirmation.

"Yeah, he always was as a kid. He smiled all the time and was good to his friends and family without ever thinking about it." Tom frowned, obviously thinking. "I wish I'd pushed harder when he started to get quiet and withdrawn. Maybe I could have saved him from this."

Devon put his hand on Tom's shoulder. "You weren't much more than a kid yourself, Tom. Beating yourself up won't fix things."

Tom gave him a watery smile, and Devon continued. "Anyway, sometimes he gets sad… sometimes angry. He'd never do anything to hurt someone else, but I do worry about him hurting himself."

He shook his head at Tom's startled look. "No, not like that—at least not on purpose. But he stops eating, wants to stay in bed all the time." Devon blushed but kept talking. "Sometimes I have to get a little… um… bossy with him to bring him out of it."

He shrugged and reached for the two small bags left in the trunk before slamming the lid shut.

"Just keep an eye on him, and if you need help, then call me. I'll give you my new number. The phones Chase and I have are throwaways, and the asshole will have no way of tracking them."

Tom narrowed his eyes. "Can the bastard really do that?"

"I don't know." Devon sighed. "But I won't take the chance. There's nothing about this house that should lead him to you guys. Only the owner knows you're here, and he won't tell anyone, I can guarantee it." Devon ran his fingers through his hair and then picked up Chase's suitcase. "I just hope it's enough to keep you all safe."

The two men looked at each other for a few seconds, and then Devon took a deep breath. "Let's go in and get Chase settled. I wanna spend a couple of days having fun with him here before I have to go, okay?"

Tom nodded. "Okay."

They headed for the door, and Devon hoped it would all go as planned. Chase deserved this life.

Sixteen

DEVON CROUCHED beside the bed and looked at the handsome young man sleeping there. He'd managed to sneak out of bed and get ready without waking Chase, but soon he had to go, and he didn't want to leave without saying good-bye.

He wound a strand of Chase's hair around his finger before tucking it gently behind his ear. The other man was sleeping on his stomach, and the blanket had slipped down to pool around his waist, leaving his whole back exposed.

Devon could see all the scars that had been left behind by Kingston's abuse, and it made something in his chest clench in pain and anger. In his head, he knew everything that had happened to Chase wasn't his fault. Kingston was a delusional psychopath who didn't give a shit about the rules of society and who thought he should get everything he wanted and who would take whatever he wasn't given.

But in his heart, Devon felt like it was his job to protect Chase now, any way he could, and that meant making sure Kingston wouldn't ever be able to get his hands on Chase or anyone else ever again.

And so he would leave Chase here, in the arms of his family, and go back to New Orleans alone. And he would make Kingston pay for what he did to Chase and all the people he'd hurt.

Chase turned at Devon's touch, and those long lashes fluttered open. Being sleepy made Chase even more adorable than usual, and leaving was not going to be easy.

"Hey, sweetheart. How are you doing? Did you have a good sleep?" Despite the doctor's worries, there had been no nightmares the last two nights, and Devon was hoping that would continue when he left.

"Hmmm. Good… I'm good." He smiled sleepily, inching closer to Devon as the older man ran his fingers through Chase's silky soft hair.

"I'm glad." He leaned in and kissed Chase on the temple before pulling back. "My ride is going to be here any minute, baby. It's time for me to go."

Chase's full lips turned down in a pout, and Devon chuckled a little. He wasn't sure how Chase's mother ever said no to him when he was little. It was almost impossible for him to resist that face now.

"I don't want you to go." He slid one hand out from under him and grabbed one of Devon's. "I'm scared for you."

Devon smiled down at him gently. "I don't really want to go either, but I have to." He lifted Chase's fingers to kiss his knuckles. He didn't miss the shiver that went through Chase at the touch of his lips to Chase's skin. "I'll get this over with, and then we'll both be free. And he won't be able to hurt anyone ever again like he did you."

"He hurt you before…." Chase had rolled to his side and curled closer to Devon. "Don't let him do it again."

Devon shook his head. "I won't. And Andy and Joe and the rest won't either. Jax is one scary dude, you know… and Mike's certifiably crazy."

Chase smiled softly. "Mike's not so bad. He was always nice to me, and he's totally comfortable with who he is." He blushed and looked down. "And Jax sort of reminds me of an older version of you; handsome and smart and kinder underneath than he wants anyone to know."

Devon was proud of the way Chase had gotten to know his friends in the past months. And they had all taken Chase under their protection, his innate innocence and gentle soul charming them all into wanting to take care of him.

"You might be right." Devon leaned in to kiss Chase on the cheek, but the younger man moved quickly, sitting up and wrapping his hand around Devon's neck and pulling him in for a passionate kiss.

Devon was powerless to resist, letting Chase plunder his mouth for a few minutes before reluctantly pulling back.

Chase was the picture of decadence. His hair was a mess, his lips swollen and slick, and the sheet had fallen far enough that Devon could see exactly how much Chase was affected by the kisses.

He was fucking beautiful.

"I have to go, baby. You have your phone, and you can call or text me anytime. I'll answer as quickly as I can."

Chase's lip trembled, but he smiled a little. "Okay, just... be careful, okay?"

Devon nodded. "I will, the guys will make sure of it." He leaned in for one last kiss and then pulled away quickly, before he gave into the impulse to stay and climb right back into bed with Chase. He grabbed his bag and headed for the door. He opened it and then looked back. "I'll miss you."

Devon went down the stairs and out the front door, stopping once to nod at Chase's brother before heading out into the early morning and climbing into the car.

His phone dinged, and he looked down. *I'll miss you too. Make sure you come back soon so I can tell you I love you."*

Devon smiled and looked out the window. *As quick as I can, Chase.* Making promises to Chase was easy. He just hoped he could keep them.

WHEN THE taxi pulled up to the club, Devon got out and walked in the front door. No more hiding now. It was all about getting Kingston's attention and keeping it on him. If he could make him forget about Chase, it was all the better.

When he walked in, things were in full swing, getting everything ready for the party that was to take place that night. It would be the best way to get on Kingston's nerves.

The press was going to cover the event, billed as a fundraiser for a local women's shelter. And it would be. Devon was confident that almost two hundred thousand dollars would be donated to the worthwhile cause thanks to the auction that was going to be taking place that night.

But the main reason for the black tie masquerade party was so that Kingston would be able to attend and think he wouldn't be noticed. New Orleans loves a party, no matter the reason, and everyone would come to be shocked and awed by the activities they had planned.

The main room was decorated in black and white, accented with brilliant jewel colors. The St. Andrew's cross had been moved from the wall to the center of the room, and the whole place was glittering with lights and mirrors. It would be perfect.

Devon made his way to his office, knowing he only had a short time to get ready before they would be opening the doors. He wasn't surprised to find everyone already gathered there.

Jax, Mike, Scott, Andy, and Joe were all dressed in their tuxes and ready to go. Danielle was gorgeous in a red silk ball gown that Devon knew hid at least one small handgun, although he'd be damned if he knew where.

"Well, well, the gang's all here, huh?" Every head in the room lifted and turned toward him, and he couldn't help but smile at the fierce protectiveness he saw in all their faces.

Andy strode over to greet him and hugged him quickly before pulling back. "It's about time you got here. Thought you were gonna be late to your own party!"

"Not a chance. The sooner this is over the better. Is everything in place?" He walked to his desk and grabbed his tux off the hook behind it.

Jax nodded. "Yeah, everyone is where they're supposed to be. Kayley and Justin are watching Kingston's house and will let us know when he's on the move.

Devon wasn't happy about the young couple being involved, but they'd insisted on helping out, and surveillance was probably the safest thing they could be doing.

Devon nodded and stripped to his boxers. Every person in the room had seen him naked or close to it at one time or another, so getting dressed in front of them didn't bother him in the least.

Everyone was going over the details, and he asked questions here and there, making sure everything was ready. Once he was dressed, he passed out the masks everyone was to wear.

All the staff had the same black-and-gold mask except for Danielle, whose was red to match her dress, and Devon's, which was more elaborate, befitting his status as club owner. It also served to help him stand out from the crowd. It was black as well, but the front curved across his forehead and down one side of his face, leaving one green eye exposed completely. It was accented with gold jewels and gave Devon's face a feline look.

It was a mask meant to make people notice you, and it went well with the custom-made tux he was wearing. Black with a black vest and black silk shirt, the only color came from the dark-green tie that matched Devon's eyes.

The whole outfit made him look strong and powerful, and he knew it would piss Kingston off as soon as he saw it.

Jax looked at him, making sure everything was perfect, and then nodded approvingly. "That's gonna make him nuts... well, more nuts." He handed Devon his wallet and phone. "The tracking device I borrowed from my friend is sewn into the waistband of the pants. Try not to lose them, okay?"

Devon nodded thoughtfully. "So, Andy and Joe, you're gonna stay in the main room, keeping an eye on things there. Scott and Mike are going to be at the door, and the back entrance will be locked from the inside. Jax is going to be hanging around that area all night. We need people to be able to leave through that door because of the fire code, but I don't want Kingston sneaking in that way."

He looked around at all of them, making sure everyone understood their roles. "Danielle and I will patrol the back rooms, giving me a reason to be wandering down the halls. It has to look like I'm vulnerable." He could see that none of them were particularly happy with the plan, but it was all they had.

"I don't know how, but at some point he's going to go for it. I'm betting it will be after my little show in the main room. I'll have to fight back enough to make it look real, and then once he figures I'm subdued, I want him to only have one option of where to go. It has to be the empty playroom at the end, understand?"

He waited for their agreements before turning back to Mike. "You've got the cameras all set up?" The cameras were essential to the plan. Without them, they had no evidence, and they needed to prove what Kingston was doing to the one person who could do something about it.

Mike nodded. "You know it, boss. In the hall and in the room, all ready to pick up everything that happens and so we can keep an eye on you."

Devon clapped him on the shoulder. "Thanks, Mike." He turned to Jax. "And the security detail you hired is watching Chase and his family just in case?"

"Yep, just checked in with them, and it's all quiet." Devon could feel his friend's concerned gaze on him, but it didn't matter. Keeping Chase safe, that's what mattered.

"I guess we're good to go, then. The doors are going to be opening in about half an hour, so let's make sure everything's ready." He looked around the room at his friends. They were all taking a chance by helping him, and he didn't know of any possible way he could thank them. "You guys will never know how much I appreciate all of your help. Kingston's a dangerous man, and I know how much you're all putting on the line."

Danielle walked up and put her hand on his arm. "It's not all about you, you know. He's dangerous to a lot of people and a really bad representative of our community. He needs to be stopped."

He nodded and gave her a quick hug. "Okay, let's go. We all know where we need to be and what we need to do."

One by one they left the room after an acknowledging nod at Devon. He watched them go, marveling at how lucky he was to have such amazing friends.

He looked at his watch and pulled out his phone. He thought about sending a quick text to Chase but decided he'd better wait until it was all over. The less Chase knew about what was going on the better.

He grinned as he walked over to the mirror and fastened his mask. Only in New Orleans would you find high society attending a fundraiser at a BDSM club. Ordinary rules really didn't apply here. New Orleans always seemed to be a world apart, and this kind of event really solidified that.

He also couldn't deny that it was that exact element that had attracted him to this particular city in the first place. Creating a high-end BDSM club like Mystique had been a dream from the time he was a young man in Dallas, looking for a place he felt comfortable and never finding it. He wasn't going to let Kingston destroy everything he'd worked for, and he wasn't going to let him destroy Chase.

In almost two hours, he was going to be putting on a demonstration with a very willing young sub who shared a lot of physical characteristics with Chase. He hoped that seeing him dominate a tall, lean man with shaggy hair would be enough to drive Kingston into doing something stupid and finally give them something to work with.

Once the mask was in place, Devon left the office and made his way to the front of the club. After checking to make sure that everyone knew their places and that all the preparations were complete, it was time to start letting people in.

Devon stood at the bar, letting Andy and Joe handle the security team and the incoming guests. It wasn't long before people recognized him and started making their way over to chat with him.

He spoke to most people warmly, genuinely pleased at the turnout for a charity that was dear to his heart. It was important to him that women who were stuck in abusive relationships had a place to go for help. He'd seen a favorite aunt deteriorate before his eyes when he was a child, until one day she died. It wasn't until he was a teen that he found out she had been murdered by her husband for daring to leave him after he started beating on their children.

He looked around but didn't spot Kingston. There were so many elaborate masks in the crowd, however, that missing him was almost assured. He knew the man had left his mansion and arrived at the club because Kayley and Justin had reported when he left and then discreetly followed his limo until it had pulled up to the doors.

Andy had made sure that the invitations that went out didn't have the name of the invitee, so it would have been easy for Kingston's men to get a hold of one. So much planning had gone into this evening, and Devon was anxious for everything to work out.

Devon worked the room, smiling at some of the faces he recognized. He wondered how the mayor would feel to know that his sister was in attendance and bidding on a night with Mistress Danielle.

At eleven o'clock it was time for the show. Devon went to the back room, where the sub was waiting for him. The young man was naked except for black briefs, and it was a very good look for him.

Devon walked up, smiling appreciatively. "Hello, Mark, how are you?"

"I'm fine, Sir, thank you." His smile was genuine, and Devon could see that he was more than ready for the session to begin.

"Your safeword, Mark?" He always used the same one, but it was best for the Dom to check every time.

"Indigo, Sir." The sub kept his eyes on the floor, and Devon nodded in approval.

"Good." Devon picked up the collar that was sitting on the table behind Mark, slipped it on and buckled it. Mark was one of those amazing subs that fell into subspace almost as quickly as the collar was fastened.

"I'm not going to gag you tonight. I want you to make as much noise as you want… as long as it's respectful, understand? Remember, there are ladies in the audience." He walked around and grabbed the leather binders that would hold Mark's arms behind him from wrist to elbow. He laced them up, knowing exactly how tight was just enough.

"Yes, Sir. I'll remember." The sub stood docilely, making Devon smile with pleasure.

Devon picked up the long chain that was the leash and attached it to the collar. It had a leather handle at the end, but Devon just let it hang down Mark's back. It made a bigger statement when the sub followed along willingly.

"Keep your focus on me, and if you need to stop, don't hesitate to use your word. It's hard to do a scene in a room full of people, especially those from outside the community, and I don't want you becoming uncomfortable or afraid." Devon framed Mark's face with his hands and made the young man meet his gaze for a moment. "It doesn't make you weak to use your word to get out of something that's making you feel bad. It's harder to say you want out than it is to just go along with something. I'm trusting you to know your limits, understand?"

Mark nodded. "Yes, Sir. I understand."

Devon smiled and stroked the sub's cheek. "Good boy. I know you'll make me proud."

Mark preened at the compliment, and it made Devon laugh.

He turned and headed for the door, knowing Mark was right behind him, eyes down demurely as he followed the Master out into the crowd.

EVERY GAZE was on Devon and the sub as they made their way to the stage. Some were admiring, some hungry, and some were staring in titillated shock at what was about to happen.

Devon sensed one set of eyes on him almost like a touch. They radiated rage and frustration, and Devon could almost feel it drill into him as he stepped up onto the raised platform before reaching to help Mark up as well.

Once they were facing the crowd, the sub fell gracefully to his knees at Devon's feet, never lifting his eyes from the floor.

Devon reached down and used one finger to lift Mark's chin, letting everyone see the adoring gaze that blazed across the sub's face. He smiled, letting him know that everything was going to be fine, and then stood straight with his fingers sifting through Mark's hair.

The sub leaned into the touch, and Devon let him lean against his thigh for comfort as he addressed the crowd.

"This young man's name is Mark. He's a recent university graduate with a chemical engineering degree and has an IQ of 137 and was at the top of his class every year. In short... he's wicked smart." Devon looked down at the sub again, smiling at his blush. "He is also one of the most beautiful subs I have ever seen."

He walked over to a padded bench that had been set in the middle of the stage and motioned for Mark to come to him. The sub stood quickly and obeyed before dropping to his knees once more in front of the bench.

Devon continued to talk as he leaned Mark over the bench and secured him. It wasn't about keeping him still so much as it was about keeping him safe. If he jerked around too much during the demonstration, he could fall and hurt himself.

"Being a sub isn't about being stupid or weak." He tested the bonds then leaned over to whisper in Mark's ear, making him giggle, before looking at the crowd again.

"Being a sub isn't always about something that happened to you… something so bad that you need to be made to hurt so it can go away."

He straightened up and walked over to the table that Danielle had set up for him. He grabbed a light flogger, something that would sound good but not leave behind too many welts, before returning to the bound man.

"Being a sub is about giving and taking. You give yourself to someone… trust them to look after you… to know what you need." He let the flogger trail over the bare skin of Mark's back. "It's about taking what your Dom gives you and using it to let yourself go."

He let the strands of leather caress the soft skin of the sub's barely covered ass, and the man moaned quietly at the feel of it. "Don't ever think a sub is less just because he serves and obeys."

Devon let the first blow fall, watching as Mark shivered at the feel of it. "It takes strength and courage to trust so much… to give all the power to someone who could hurt you so easily."

He was speaking to the crowd, but the message was meant for only one man… and Devon hoped it was pushing Kingston closer to the edge all the time.

"Some Doms take advantage of that trust… they feel like they can force someone to submit to them." Mark's grunts and moans were coming louder and faster as the flogger struck him again and again, and Devon knew it wouldn't be long before the man was flying.

"True submission isn't taken, folks." He took his eyes off Mark for just a second to observe the crowd's reaction. "True submission is given freely. Otherwise, it's just slavery, and that's a whole other thing."

Some people looked very uncomfortable behind their masks, and he wondered if it was because they were disgusted or if it was because it was turning them on.

He turned his attention back to Mark, where it should be. He'd chosen this particular sub for the demonstration because Mark didn't get off sexually when he was with a Dom. He had a boyfriend for that… a young man who was in the back, waiting to take care of the man he loved when the scene was over.

Mark loved subbing because it gave him a sense of purpose and because being in subspace was completely freeing for him.

Devon stopped the flogging once in a while, leaning down to whisper to Mark, running his hand over the sub's shoulders and back, telling him how good he was being and how proud he was of him.

"This lifestyle isn't all about pain." A few more strikes with the flogger, and he could see all tension fall out of Mark's body as he let go. "It's not all about sex." He continued to let the flogger fall, smiling at the gorgeous red glow of Mark's ass. The man was clearly relaxed, his mind gone somewhere else while he trusted Devon to bring him back when it was time.

"It's about people finding what they need in a place without judgment, where the rules that are in place are for everyone's safety." He eased off on the blows before stopping completely and then tossed the flogger back on the table. He kept a hand on Mark's skin, knowing the young man needed the contact to help ground him.

"Safe, sane, and consensual. That's our community's motto. Anyone who doesn't like those rules isn't welcome here." He crouched beside Mark and started undoing the straps holding him down.

"Now, if you all will excuse me, I'm going to deliver this amazing young man into the arms of someone he loves and make sure that they have everything they need." He undid the bindings on Mark's arms, rubbing them gently to help get the circulation back into them.

"Please go take a look at the items up for bid in the silent auction, and make sure you spend some of your hard-earned money supporting a good cause." He smiled as the young man started to come around.

"Thank you all for coming, and I hope you enjoyed our little demonstration."

As he helped Mark sit up, there was no mistaking the bliss on the sub's face. Devon could see people staring curiously, no doubt wondering how something that looked so painful could feel so good.

Once Mark was turned toward him, the young man cuddled close to Devon's chest as he was helped to his feet. Devon kept him tucked into his side as he helped him off the stage and through the crowd. He was happy to see everyone moving back respectfully, although he was sure that the presence of his security team helped.

He could still feel those angry eyes on him, and he wanted to get Mark back to his boyfriend as quickly as possible so that the young sub wouldn't be caught in the crossfire. When they reached the hallway, he sent the security guards back to watch the party and helped Mark to the recovery room attached to his office.

He was glad to see the smiling face of Mark's boyfriend and was more than happy to pass over his aftercare to him. Mark thanked him sleepily, and they were so adorable together that Devon couldn't help hugging them both. He spent a few minutes making sure they had everything they needed and then slipped into the hallway.

He decided to continue down the hall, mostly to make sure no one was trying to make use of any of the rooms, but all the doors were locked. When he got to the last door, the one that had been set up for their trap, the door opened. When he looked in, he searched around, but he couldn't see any of the hidden cameras that Mike had set.

As he backed out of the room, he bumped into something solid. As he turned to see who it was, he was hit from behind and pushed back into the room. The last things he saw before the darkness took him were James Kingston's angry brown eyes.

Seventeen

DEVON CAME to slowly, his eyes blinking against the light that was shining on him.

He groaned as he realized that the thumping beat he was hearing actually came from inside his head as pain thudded in his skull. His stomach rolled as the pain increased when he tried to open his eyes fully.

Swallowing, he got the nausea under control and then tried lifting his eyelids again. As the haze receded, he realized his arms were bound above his head and he couldn't lift his feet from the ground.

His neck and shoulders ached from the weight of his unconscious body pulling on them after he'd been improperly hung from the ceiling.

"What the fuck?" The rasp of his own voice hurt his ears.

Looking around, he realized he was in one of the playrooms at his club, but he couldn't quite remember how he'd found himself in the very vulnerable position he was in.

"Andy?"

"I'm afraid that mangy mongrel isn't available to you right now."

The cruel voice brought everything back… the plan…. Chase… fucking Kingston.

"For fuck's sake, Kingston! What are you hoping to accomplish here… in my fucking club?" Devon let all the derision and loathing he felt for the other man show in his voice. He had to get him pissed off and talking for this clusterfuck of a plan to work.

Kingston chuckled. "Still so defiant, aren't you, my pretty little sub?"

Devon froze as the other man walked up behind him and snaked one arm around his waist. Then he relaxed and snorted. "You really are delusional, James. I'm not a sub... not by anyone's standards. If you haven't figured that out by now, you really are fucked in the head."

The slap to his face wasn't completely unexpected, and Devon never even flinched.

"You have something of mine, Devon... and I want him back." Kingston let go of Devon and walked around to stand in front of him. He lifted his hand and stroked Devon's face in a mockingly tender caress. "I wasn't quite finished with Chase yet. That deplorable toy needed to be disposed of properly."

"He was never yours, you sadistic bastard. If you have to take it by force, submission never really belongs to you. It's the biggest lesson you never learned." Devon smiled at the other man, enjoying the anger building in his expression. "Chase's gone, and you'll never find him. I've made sure of that."

The hand that had been caressing Devon's cheek suddenly grabbed Devon's jaw in a punishing grip. "I will find him... I promise you that. And when I do, I'm going to bring him in front of you and whip him till he bleeds. I'm going to fuck him while he calls out for you to come and save him, and then I'm going to let you look him in the eyes while I snap his fucking neck."

Devon was almost afraid of him at the moment. The way he spoke about torturing and killing Chase like it was nothing was absolutely terrifying.

"It's not gonna happen. He's safe forever... and that's a promise I'm making you!"

Kingston looked like he was about to stroke out. His face was red, and sweat fell freely down his cheek and neck, making the white dress shirt he was wearing cling to him damply.

Kingston tightened his grip on Devon's face almost enough to make him scream and then it abruptly fell away. The smile was back on Kingston's face. It was chilling.

"I'm not going to argue about it with you, Devon. When I'm through with you, you're going to be begging to tell me where Chase is." He walked over and picked up a large leather paddle. It was thick and heavy, with holes drilled in it, and it was made to cause extreme pain.

Devon closed his eyes for a second and prayed to God that someone had the good sense to keep Andy out of the office and not let him see what was going on... or that Joe had handcuffed him to the desk. They'd all agreed to wait for Devon's signal to come to his rescue, but it was going to be all but impossible for Andy to resist breaking down the door and beating Kingston to death.

When he opened his eyes again, his torturer was grinning down at him. He'd mistaken Devon's worry over Andy for fear, and it was adding to his maniacal behavior. "Finally afraid, Devon? Now that you're here at my mercy—or lack of it—and no one around to save you?"

"I'm not afraid of you, you fucking mental case. I'm just disgusted by you and your barbaric practices. It's people like you who have so many prejudiced against all of us in our community. You're a monster, and you'll never be my Master."

Devon knew that pushing him was just going to make this worse, but he wanted there to be no doubt about the depth of the man's madness. He knew the cops would have arrested Kingston with the footage Devon already had and kept him locked up for as long as they could... but Devon was after a more permanent solution.

Kingston was almost foaming at the mouth as he moved around behind him. He couldn't help flinching as the other man dragged his nails down Devon's naked back, no doubt leaving bloody welts in their wake.

When the first blow of the paddle came, he jerked just once but didn't scream. The blows that followed came fast and hard, and Devon just rode it out, sparing a brief thought to hope that the blows around his kidneys wouldn't have him pissing blood for a week.

When it stopped, Devon was amazed to find he was still alone in the room with Kingston. He figured that, cue word or no, there'd be no keeping his friends out now.

He could hear banging on the other side of the door, and when he examined it closely, he could see that the other man had jammed the lock with something, making it impossible to turn.

"Looking for your rescue, sub? It's not coming... not till I'm done with you." Kingston dropped the paddle and walked over to pick a cane up off the table.

Devon wondered how ironic it was that he was being tortured with tools he himself had provided. The thought made him chuckle, and the sound just infuriated Kingston even more.

He stood back, letting the first few hits catch Devon across the cheeks of his ass, and it hurt more than the paddle had, but it wasn't anything he couldn't handle.

"I'm not stupid, you know. I'm well aware that you wanted to trap me here, so...." He threw his arms up and twirled around. "Here I am! Call the cops... let them arrest me. I don't give a shit."

He swung the cane at Devon's back, catching him with the top edge, and it dug in, gouging a furrow out of his skin. The pain finally caused him to cry out, and the banging on the door got even louder.

"My dad's fucking lawyers will have me out of jail in a few hours, and you're still going to be a bleeding pile of dog shit on the floor, begging for my forgiveness." The cane came down, flaying off another bit of skin. Apparently Kingston was happy with the last blow and was trying for the same result.

Devon knew that if he didn't do something quick, he was going to be too injured to help himself. Looking up at the cuffs holding his hands, he saw that Kingston had used the ones from the club, obviously not knowing about the hidden escape latch he insisted be built into all of them.

Trying to ignore the pain as much as possible, he looked around for something to defend himself with before spotting the paddle on the floor. Knowing he would only have one chance at it, he closed his eyes and thought of Chase. This had to work or he would never be safe, and Devon couldn't allow that to happen.

Reaching his thumbs around, he disengaged pins holding the cuffs in place and squatted quickly, grabbing the paddle from the floor and pulling the pin from one of the ankle cuffs at the same time. He managed to push back to his feet just as Kingston swung the cane.

Devon grabbed it and pulled hard, bringing Kingston into hitting range. Devon swung out, catching the other man in the side of the head, and he dropped like a ton of bricks. Devon wasted no time pulling the other pin and getting himself completely free.

Even though he'd gone down hard, Kingston was almost back to his feet as Devon staggered for the door. He lunged at Devon, unintentionally pushing him the rest of the way there. Devon felt the piece of metal that had been jammed into the lock sink into his shoulder, and he couldn't help the angry howl that broke from him.

When he instinctively pulled back, he pulled the metal with him, and he had time for a fleeting prayer that the door would unlock now before the cane hit him in the side of the face.

He felt the skin break over his jaw, and blood started running down his neck, and he was enraged that this maniac had been able to leave more scars on his body.

He turned, and when the cane came at him again, he grabbed it and pulled it from Kingston's grip.

The man's eyes widened almost comically when he realized he was unarmed and Devon was coming at him.

"Never again, you fucking bastard." Devon growled the words as he brought the cane down on Kingston's head and shoulders.

The other man squealed as the cane hit him again and again. "No... don't... you can't."

"I can and I fucking will." Devon pulled his arm back, aiming another vicious blow at Kingston's shoulder. "And you're never going to hurt another person ever again."

He knew he should stop—be better than Kingston, but he kept seeing Chase's innocent face in his head, and it fueled his rage even further.

"My father's gonna fucking kill you!" The mad gleam in Kingston's eyes never faded at all. He was still convinced he was right and that anything he wanted could be gotten with money and his father's influence.

"Maybe, but I'm gonna make sure you feel every ounce of pain you've inflicted on Chase first." Devon was angrier than he'd been in his life, and underneath it all was more than a little fear. Fear of what could have happened and fear of what he could still do to Kingston.

He pulled back to rain more blows on the cowering man, but at that moment, the noise from the door reached deafening proportions and the door finally split from the frame.

Scott, Jax, and Mike all spilled into the room, and Devon could hear Andy screaming from the hallway. "Get off me, you stupid motherfuckers... I'm gonna beat the shit outta all of you."

Jax walked over quickly and grabbed the cane from Devon's hand, tossing it aside. They stood and stared at each other for a second, Devon panting and wild-eyed, Jax steady and waiting.

Devon looked at Kingston, now standing between Mike and Scott still screaming and ranting, and started toward him.

"Devon, don't." There was a strong hand on his arm, stopping him, and he looked at Jax. "Don't do this to yourself. There are people who need you here... not in jail... or dead."

Devon looked into the older Dom's eyes, saw the love and concern there, just like Chase said it was, and nodded. "Okay."

Kingston started to laugh. "You stupid fuckers. My father's going to destroy you all. You think you can get away with this bullshit?" He was kicking, so Jax swiftly grabbed a length of rope from the nearby table and nodded at Mike and Scott.

They pushed down on Kingston's shoulders, startling him enough that Jax could grab his legs and quickly and efficiently tie them together.

He stood, brushed off his hands and grinned at Devon. "You don't get to be one of the best Doms in the business without learning something about tying people up."

Devon grinned back at him, and Kingston started up with another round.

"My fucking father—" He was cut off by the arrival of another man walking through the splintered door.

"Your fucking father is gonna shut you the hell up."

Craig Kingston looked like the politician he was. His suit and tie were impeccable, and there wasn't a hair out of place on his head. The only thing that seemed off was the look of absolute fury on his face.

He walked up to his son as the man started sputtering again. "But, Dad, come on... these useless fuckers...."

The crack of the back of his father's hand against Kingston's cheek was startlingly loud. "I warned you, James. After the last time, no more, but you couldn't listen. Now you've taken it out of my hands."

His son paled. "Please... Dad... I'll do better...." He sounded like a pitiful animal as he begged his father, but no one in the room felt any sympathy for him at all.

His father glared at him grimly. "Yes, you will. But not here."

James wailed, but his father ignored him and turned to Devon. "Mr. West. I'm truly sorry for the pain and suffering James has caused you and your friend. I should have been paying better attention, but I'll admit he had me fooled. It won't happen again. You have my word on it."

Devon looked down as the other man extended his hand, and he grasped it in his own. "It better not. If he's ever seen in the southern states again, this video will go to every news outlet in America, and you have my word on that."

Craig's mouth pressed into a thin line, but he nodded and motioned to two men who'd been hovering outside the door. They came in and relieved Mike and Scott of their burden, one of them injecting something into the younger Kingston's arm. He quieted almost immediately, and they carried him out of the room.

Craig Kingston took one more look around and headed for the door as well. Devon called out to him.

"Good luck with the senate race, Mr. Kingston."

The other man faltered a little but didn't look back, disappearing as quickly as he'd come.

Once he was gone, Devon nodded to Jax, who smirked and headed to the doorway and into the hall. "Okay, guys, you can let him up now."

There was a roar and squeals of pain, and then Andy was running in the door, followed closely by Joe.

"That was not the deal, fuckhead. I was supposed to kick his ass, remember? You fucking promised!" Devon could hear the hurt under the anger, and he swayed as he reached out for his friend.

"I need you here." He swayed again, but Andy caught him before he could fall.

"Yeah… well… you shoulda let me kick him in the nuts at least." Andy was pouting, but Devon could deal with it.

"Andy? I hate to interrupt your bitching, but I think I need to lie down. And maybe see a doctor?" Things were starting to get a little hazy around the edges. "And find my fucking phone. I gotta call Chase."

They all looked around, and Joe found Devon's clothes in the corner. His phone was thankfully intact, and he dialed Chase's number as Jax brought a bathrobe he'd grabbed from Devon's bathroom and put it around his shoulders.

Chase answered on the first ring. "Hello? Devon? Are you okay?"

"I'm fine, Chase, just like I told you I'd be." He struggled to keep the pain out of his voice. No way did he want Chase knowing how badly he was hurt.

"As you sure? Your voice sounds funny." His soft voice and quiet concern was almost Devon's undoing. He had to get off the phone fast.

"I'm positive, sweetheart. It's all under control. He's never going to hurt you or anyone else ever again."

Chase drew a shuddering breath on the other end. "And you too, right? He can't hurt you any more either."

"No, baby, he can't." Devon was almost at the end of his rope. "I have to go, Chase. There's a few more things I need to take care of, so I'll call you tomorrow, okay? I want you to go to bed now and get some sleep."

"But, Devon…." Chase didn't whine, but the hurt in his voice was heartbreaking.

"If you can't sleep, then take one of your pills. You need to get some rest. Can you do that for me, Chase? Take care of yourself like I would?"

"I'll try… but no one takes care of me like you do."

Those simple, sweet words were like a balm to Devon's battered soul. "Good. I'll call you tomorrow. All right?"

Chase sighed. "Okay. Night, Dev."

Devon squeezed his eyes shut. "Night, baby. Sweet dreams."

He closed the phone and passed it back to Jax.

"Come on, hero. Doc Jones is waiting to fix your pretty face at the hospital. Let's get it done so I can get some sleep." Andy's snarky words were belied by his gentle tone.

"Yeah… that would be good." Devon was exhausted. He took two steps toward the door before everything went sideways. All the voices in the room faded to a dull roar in his ears, Jax's panicked "fuck" was the last thing he heard before the world went black for the second time that night.

Eighteen

THE TICKING of the grandfather clock in the hall and the whirring of his computer were the only sounds Devon could hear as he sat in his office, and it annoyed him. It was too quiet in his house these days.

Clicking Save on the document he was working on, Devon dropped his pen and lowered his aching head into his hands. It had been two months since his ordeal with Kingston, and the only lasting effect had been a tendency toward more headaches. He had a feeling stress had something to do with it.

Time had dragged for him, but it was something he'd have to get used to. So was missing Chase.

Devon hadn't seen him since he'd driven away from the safe house in Corpus Christi. It had been difficult to insist that Chase stay with his family and spend some time getting to know them, but he knew it was what was best for him.

He'd woken in the hospital, disoriented and pissed off and surrounded by worried faces. It didn't take long to get everything taken care of, and then he was home being watched over by a bossy Kayley and three protective dogs.

It took a few weeks to completely recover from the concussion he'd gotten when his head had hit the door. The damage had been mostly bruises and strained muscles, and those had healed quickly. However, there had been three long furrows across his back that were still red and would leave scars.

There was also the puncture wound from the metal in the lock that had pierced his shoulder. Fortunately, it hadn't hit anything important, and the doctors assured him that the pain in the muscle there was only temporary.

He had a thin red line on his jaw that Lisa Jones had worked on diligently, and he was confident that any mark left behind would be minimal at best.

He hadn't wanted Chase to see any of it. He didn't need any more guilt over confronting Kingston, so Devon had forbidden anyone from mentioning it to him. He knew Chase had been texting Andy and Jax, and he was glad Chase had been comfortable enough with the two men to keep in contact with them of his own accord.

Devon knew Chase had been unhappy with being made to stay with his family, but Devon was adamant. They needed a fair chance to get to know each other again without distance making it harder.

Devon was still convinced that once Chase had some time away, he'd get over his attachment to Devon and be able to move on to a life surrounded by his family.

It was only natural that Chase had clung to Devon after he'd rescued him—at least, that's what Devon kept telling himself.

They still talked. Devon kept getting random texts during the day that made him smile as Chase told him about something he'd seen that had excited him or how Zoe was making him laugh or a story that Tom had told about when he was a baby.

They talked on the phone once a week as well. It was all Devon would allow, and he knew he was being selfish with even that much contact, but he couldn't bring himself to cut Chase off completely.

He justified it by telling himself that he didn't want Chase thinking another person had just thrown him away, but the truth of the matter was that those conversations were the highlight of Devon's week.

Chase's laughter and soft voice were something Devon craved more than anything else in his life, and he wasn't sure how to reconcile himself with that.

Sighing, he looked at the clock, unsurprised to find that it was almost two in the morning. Sleep was elusive these days, and his friends had all been giving him worried looks for weeks.

Devon rubbed his hands over his face before getting up and walking over to the window to look out at the night.

For the first time since he was nineteen and had started training as a Dom, Devon was unsure about the direction of his life. All he knew was that not having Chase in his life and in his bed was something he wasn't sure he was ever going to get over.

Turning away from the window, he walked to his desk, shut the lid on his laptop, and turned off the lamp.

He wandered into the hall and toward his room, a vague idea of trying to get some sleep in his head.

The ringing of his cell phone brought him out of his thoughts, and he sprinted down the hall to his room to grab it.

His heart thudding, he looked at the phone to see Chase's number blinking up at him.

Pressing the answer button, he put the phone to his ear.

"Chase? What's wrong?" Phone calls in the middle of the night were never good news. "Are you okay?"

There was a hitched breath on the other end and then Chase's voice. "No… I mean… yeah, I'm fine, just…."

He trailed off, obviously unsure of what to say.

"Just what, baby? What's going on? Tell me." He let a note of command enter his voice, something telling him that Chase needed it.

"Do you not want me anymore? Is that what the problem is?" Pure frustration was pouring through the phone. "I mean, I know I'm not good enough… but I could learn, right? You told me I'm not stupid…." His voice faded again.

"Oh, Chase." Devon hated that he'd put this self-doubt into Chase's head. "Of course I want you. And you're more than good enough… you're perfect."

"Then why am I here instead of there, in bed with you?" Devon could here Chase struggling to get his breathing under control. "If you want me, I need you to come and get me. This isn't the place for me anymore."

Devon paced his bedroom, desperately trying to ignore his car keys sitting on the bedside table. "Chase, did something happen? Is someone giving you a hard time?"

"No. Everyone is being really nice, and I love them, I really do." Another pause and Devon knew he was gathering his thoughts. "And I know they love me, but… I can't be what they want me to be."

That had Devon stopping short. "What do you mean? Are they asking you to change?"

"I'm not their Chase anymore. They're looking for that sixteen-year-old boy they lost. I can't be him, Devon. I've…." Devon could hear him swallow. "I've been through too much to ever go back… and I don't want to."

Devon closed his eyes. He knew how much this was costing Chase… the risk he was taking and how it would be making him feel, but he still wasn't sure that what Chase needed was him. His connection to Kingston might make it hard for Chase to move on.

"Chase—"

Chase cut him off. "I need to know, Devon. I can't keep going the way I am. If you want me, come and get me, because, God, I wanna be yours."

Devon couldn't get his brain to work. He knew he needed to be saying something, but before he could, Chase continued. "But if you don't, please tell me so I can move on." His voice wasn't much more than a whisper.

That finally jolted Devon's mouth into gear. "What do you mean, move on? What are you saying, sweetheart?"

"I…." Chase's voice cracked. "I need someone, Devon… someone to give me what I need…."

The thought of someone else—of anyone else—putting Chase on his knees had the Dom in Devon standing up and howling in protest. In his mind's eye he could see another man's hands on Chase's beautiful skin, touching him and making him writhe in pleasure and pain below him, and it almost made Devon's heart stop.

Imagining someone else's marks on Chase, someone else soothing Chase's pain and cuddling him close, giving him everything that Devon wanted to be giving him.

He saw another man buckling his collar around Chase's long, graceful throat, and it was the last push he needed.

"*No!*" He was across the room and grabbing his keys and wallet in an instant before running out of the bedroom and down the stairs. "I'm grabbing the first flight I can get, and I'm bringing you home, Chase."

He slipped into the first shoes he could find and pushed into the garage.

"You're mine, you hear me? I want you." He started the car and waited until the garage door barely cleared the roof before reversing out into the night.

He let his voice drop a few notches. "You'd better be ready when I get there, because I'm not going to have the patience for packing."

"Devon...." Chase's voice was breathless. "I need you. Master, please...."

Christ, Chase was gonna kill him. "I know, baby. I'm sorry I took so long." Once he had the car pointed the right direction, he took off down the driveway and out onto the road.

"It's okay. You're coming now. That's all that matters." Chase's voice had a little gasp in it that Devon recognized.

"Chase, are you touching yourself?" He deliberately kept his voice low and rough. "You got your hand on that pretty cock of yours?"

Chase was panting. "No, Sir. Just my nipples." Chase moaned softly in his ear, and Devon almost drove into the ditch. "I... uh... borrowed those nipple clamps from your playroom. I've been putting them on when I need to feel close to you."

"Fuck." Devon shifted in his seat, trying to ease some of the sudden tightness in his jeans. Thank God he had hands-free in his car. "You have them on now?"

"N... no." He could hear the rustling of fabric, making him think Chase was in bed. "Was just gonna do it."

Devon smiled at the needy whine in Chase's voice. "Uh-uh, baby. Not yet." Chase's desperate whimper was beautiful. "You're gonna wait till I get there, and I'm gonna do it. I'm going to put you and all your stuff in the rental car, and after we leave your folks, I'm going to pull over to the side of the road."

"Oh God... Dev." Chase sounded like he'd been thoroughly fucked already, and Devon hadn't even touched him yet.

"I'm going to unbutton your shirt and get my mouth on them. Gonna suck 'em till they're aching 'cause you always taste so good."

The twenty-minute drive to the airport was going to take forever. The sound of Chase panting in his ear was the sweetest thing he'd heard in a long time.

"You want that, baby? My mouth on you... my teeth pulling at your skin?" Just the thought of it had Devon salivating, and if he didn't end this call soon, he was never going to get his body under control long enough to get on the plane.

"Please... Devon... love your mouth on me. Want it so bad...." There was no guile in Chase's voice, only desperation, devotion, and love.

"I'll put them on so you can feel them pulling as we drive. Gonna leave your shirt open all the way to the airport so I can play with them, tugging so I can hear those sweet sounds you make." He knew Chase was still playing with his nipples by the breathy sounds he was making.

"I need to come... please, Dev... I gotta."

Devon grinned. "No you don't, sweetheart. You want to wait for me to get there, don't you? It'll be so much better with my hands on you, stroking your cock, licking you clean. You're gonna keep that for me, aren't you, Chase?"

Chase was keening into the phone, but Devon knew he had him. He waited as Chase got a hold of his emotions and calmed down enough to talk again.

"Hurry, Dev. I miss you so much." His voice was soft and sweet again, much to Devon's delight. His boy was being so good.

"I'll be there as quickly as I can. I'll text you when I get a flight time, okay?" Devon could see the first sign for the airport up ahead. "It shouldn't be more than three or four hours. Can you be ready by then? Do you want to wait for me to talk to your parents?"

"I'll be ready, don't worry." Chase sighed. "I'm going to go and wake them up and talk to them as soon as I'm packed. I think my brother will back me up. He's the one who convinced me to call you."

Devon would have preferred to be there, but it wasn't his call to make. "Okay. Just remember, though, I love you and I'm coming for you."

"I know. I love you too. Be careful and get here soon. I wanna kiss you." Devon could hear the happiness in Chase's voice and knew he was doing the right thing.

"Bye, Chase." He hung up just as the lights of the airport came into view. Punching another button had his phone dialing out.

"Hello?" Andy sounded sleepy and grumpy, but Devon didn't care.

"Andy, get your ass on the computer and get me booked on the next fucking flight to San Antonio."

"Fuck you very much, West!" Andy mumbled to someone and then came back. "Finally come to your senses, huh?"

Devon chuckled. "Yep. He called me and asked me to come get him. He's coming home."

Andy grunted in his ear. "Good, I'm tired of your sorry-assed, mopey face around the club all the time. It's bad for business." Devon could hear the clicking of computer keys.

"Shut up, asshole. I pay you good money to put up with my bitchy face." Devon was sure he was going to be teased for months over this, but it was worth it.

Andy was quiet for a moment as he searched for a flight. "Here you go, sweets. Next flight going to San Antonio leaves in forty-five minutes. How close are you to the airport?"

"Five minutes out. Book it!" Devon couldn't even find it in himself to complain about the hated nickname.

"You sure you're the Dom, Dev? You're running after him awfully hard." Dev knew he was only teasing so he didn't let it get to him.

Devon took the overpass to the airport, glad he'd managed to get there without running into any cops. He'd definitely been speeding.

"He's worth it, Andy, trust me."

Andy hesitated slightly at Devon's serious attitude before answering him. "I know he is, Dev. And I know he loves you a lot. That's all that matters to me."

"Thanks, Andy." He pulled into the parking garage and quickly found a spot to park.

Andy cleared his throat. "It's all booked. I'll send the details to your phone. Bring him to see us as soon as you're ready to leave the playroom."

Devon huffed out a laugh. "I will. Bye."

He hung up the phone and grabbed a jacket he'd spotted lying in the backseat before locking the car and heading into the airport.

He heard his phone ding and looked down to see the message from Andy had come through. He forwarded it to Chase so he'd know that Devon really was on his way to pick him up.

The flight would take about an hour and the drive to Chase's folks another thirty minutes. He looked at his watch. It was going to be a long two hours.

DEVON PULLED up in front of the Mackenzies' house and was surprised to see Chase and his brother standing on the sidewalk. Chase was smiling shyly as Devon stopped the car and got out.

He walked toward them, his eyes never leaving Chase, but he addressed Tom first. "Everything okay, Tom?" Chase didn't seem upset, so he wasn't too worried, but he had to make sure.

"Yeah, it's all good. My little brother is just a little excited to see you, and Mom and Dad...." He paused for a moment, glancing at Chase before continuing. "Well, they aren't really happy about Chase leaving."

Devon opened his mouth, but Chase cut him off. "They're not mad, just disappointed. They understand better than I thought they did." He shook his head a little. "They said to just give them some time to get over it. They love me and like you a lot... they'll get over it, I know it."

Devon stood in front of Chase and wrapped his arms around him before finally looking at Tom. The other man shrugged and gestured toward the house. "They'll be fine. We're just gonna miss him, that's all." He patted Chase's shoulder and headed for the house.

He looked back as he opened the screen door. "Take care of him, Devon. We only just got him back."

Devon nodded. "I will. You have my word."

Tom gazed at them a moment longer and then went in, letting the door close behind him.

Devon pulled back from Chase a bit and used one hand to lift his head so he could look into those beautiful hazel eyes and smiled. "Hi...."

Chase blushed. "Hi... I missed you." He was adorable, and Devon couldn't resist kissing him. Chase opened for him immediately, taking the kiss deeper than Devon had intended while he was standing in Chase's parents' yard.

His mouth was soft and pliant, letting Devon have complete control, and the hard-on that Devon had managed to quell on the flight came raging back. He broke the kiss, letting his forehead rest against Chase's until they both got their breathing under control again.

"I missed you too." He kissed him again and then stood up straight. "Let's get this stuff in the car, yeah?"

Chase nodded and grabbed one of the bags. Devon loved that he didn't even try to use it to cover up his arousal, just carried it by his side to the trunk of the car.

Once it was all loaded, Devon pulled him close and kissed him again, gripped his hair and pulled, extending Chase's neck. He licked over his pulse point before sucking hard, pulling the blood to the surface enough to leave a mark.

Chase whimpered but only tried to move closer. "That's my mark on you, baby... the first of many. Everyone's gonna see it and know you're mine." He sucked again on the same spot, smiling against the soft skin as Chase bucked his hips against Devon's.

He kissed the bruise he'd created and reluctantly backed away, pulling Chase by the hand to the passenger door. He opened it and let Chase get in before going around to the driver's side and sliding behind the wheel. He took Chase's hand and pressed it to his lips, then smiled at him. "Let's go home."

Chase's answering grin was blinding, and it made Devon's heart feel too big for his chest. They put on their seat belts, and he started the car and headed for the airport.

After a few blocks, however, he pulled off into a deserted-looking alleyway and killed the engine. Devon looked at Chase to see him holding up something he'd been clutching in his hand.

"You promised...."

Devon's cock twitched when he realized Chase was holding the nipple clamps he'd taken from Devon's house.

Devon grabbed Chase by the back of the neck, reeling him in for a desperate kiss before letting him go and lifting the clamps from his palm.

"You're right, baby, I did." He rubbed his thumb over the hard peak of a nipple under the soft cotton covering Chase's chest. "You better get this undone for me."

Chase's fingers were pulling at the buttons before Devon had even finished speaking. He didn't stop until they were all undone, and he shrugged the fabric off his shoulders so it bunched around his biceps, effectively pinning them to his sides.

"Please.... Dev... I need...." Chase licked his lips, an unconscious movement that Devon copied, watching as it made Chase's eyes even darker with lust.

Devon pinched one nipple between his knuckles and rubbed. Chase bowed his back as he gasped and shuddered.

"Don't worry. Gonna give it to you." He leaned in and sucked the pebbled flesh into his mouth, pulling hard.

Chase cried out and his head fell back against the seat, and it was everything Devon had imagined it would be.

"Dev...." Chase only seemed capable of panting his name, and it made Devon's cock throb in his jeans.

He nipped at the tender flesh, being careful not to bruise him, as it would make the clamps too painful.

Opening the clamp with practiced fingers, he pulled back to watch Chase's face as he let it close on Chase's skin.

Chase's eyes shot open wide, and he grunted in surprised pain. Then they slid shut again as he relaxed and breathed through it.

Devon moved to the other nipple, teasing it mercilessly until he noticed that Chase's hands were clenched into fists, his nails digging relentlessly into his palms.

Devon reached for one hand and carefully straightened the fingers before taking the other and doing the same thing. He kissed them both and set them on Chase's thighs before resuming his torture.

The noises spilling from Chase's mouth were addictive, and it took all Devon's self-control to stop himself from reaching down and palming Chase's cock until he came in his jeans. That wasn't how he wanted this to go.

When the second clamp closed on him, Chase keened and his hips lurched, but he slowly relaxed as Devon kissed his neck and stroked his hands up and down Chase's arms.

"How's that, baby. Not too tight?" He loved how the chain that hooked the two clamps together looked brushing against the tanned skin of Chase's chest. Maybe they'd see about getting Chase's nipples pierced.

Chase shook his head frantically, moaning when the movement caused the chain to swing. "Feels so good…."

Devon smiled and kissed him again, softly brushing a finger over one of the clamps just to hear the whine Chase would make. Pulling back reluctantly, he reached for Chase's shirt and tugged it over his shoulders, freeing his arms.

"I wanna get you home." He straightened up behind the steering wheel and started the car before looking back at Chase. He was slumped in the seat next to Devon, quiet and relaxed even though his cock was hard and leaking so badly he had a wet spot on the front of his jeans. "Ready?"

Chase nodded. "Let's go." His voice was back to being soft and sweet, and it was so fucking hot that Devon felt like his own cock was being strangled.

Pulling back onto the road, he headed for the airport. He wanted to talk to Chase about how things went with his family, but he wanted to do it at home where he could give him the attention he needed.

For now he was content to let Chase take his hand and play with his fingers and stare at him. Most people would find such an intense scrutiny uncomfortable, but Devon understood.

He was happy to let Chase look his fill and hoped he'd come to realize that Devon wasn't going anywhere without him again. Now that Devon had let himself accept that Chase really did love him and it wasn't all about gratitude and hero worship, he was ready to step into all the roles Chase needed him to fill.

Friend. Lover. Dom.

"Did you eat anything this morning?" Devon had just realized he had run out and hadn't stopped for anything, not even a coffee, and his body was starting to protest.

Chase shook his head. "No. I was too keyed up."

Nodding, Devon started looking for someplace to get some breakfast. "I need some coffee at the very least. Any suggestions?"

"Yeah, there's a little twenty-four-hour diner a few blocks ahead. It's got a really good breakfast." He was stroking the inside of Devon's wrist as he spoke, smiling as he did.

"I'll take your word for it." He chuckled when Chase's stomach growled. "And it sounds like it had better be soon."

Chase shrugged. "I haven't been really hungry lately." He finally looked away from Devon's face, letting his gaze fall to their entwined hands in his lap. "I'm sorry. I know I told you I'd eat and stuff... I just didn't feel like it much."

Devon gave the chain a little tug, making Chase gasp. "It's okay. We're gonna talk about all this when we get home."

Chase looked at him, and Devon smiled encouragingly. Chase smiled shyly back and squeezed Devon's hand. He looked out the window.

"The diner is just over there." He pointed to the right, and Devon pulled into the parking lot as they reached it.

Devon gently tugged the chain again before letting go and reaching for the buttons of Chase's shirt. He did it up most of the way so that the chain and clamps were hidden, but the white cotton didn't do much to disguise them.

Looking around, he spotted a hoodie Chase had tossed into the backseat, and he passed it to him. "Better put this on." He wanted everyone to see that Chase was his and he'd bet money that Chase would like it too, but they were in Texas, and it was better to be safe than sorry.

Chase slipped the hoodie over his head, his eyes widening when he realized that the heavy material would rub over the sensitive nubs on his chest. Devon could see him moving, testing to see if it was too painful.

"You want me to take them off?" He would if Chase needed it. Real injury wasn't the goal here, but Chase just looked at him like he was crazy and lifted his hands to cover his chest.

"No... it's okay... I like it." He blushed as he said it, and it delighted Devon as much as it had the first time he'd seen it.

Devon kissed him quickly and then got out of the car, motioning for Chase to do the same. They walked into the diner, Chase on his heels, and when they stood waiting to be seated, he probably stood a little closer than was necessary, but Devon didn't say anything. He knew Chase would be feeling as vulnerable as he did aroused and needed the physical connection to Devon to ground him.

The older woman who came to seat them noticed Chase's closeness, but she just smiled and winked at Devon as she ushered them to a corner booth. He let Chase slide in first then slid in beside him, glad that the vinyl tablecloth would make it so no one could see the hand Chase had clenched onto Devon's thigh.

Devon ordered coffee for himself, and Chase quietly asked for sweet tea before seconding Devon's order for the breakfast special. Once the coffee had been poured and the tea brought to the table, she left them alone with another smile.

Chase pressed up along Devon's side as he looked down at the table and chatted quietly. He asked about the club and how Kayley was doing, but Devon could see he was distracted and starting to get uncomfortable.

When the meals came, they both ate quickly, and Devon was happy to see Chase eat almost his whole breakfast, even with his growing discomfort.

Devon decided it was time to go when Chase accidentally leaned his chest against the table as he reached for his tea and it caused him to whimper in pain.

Standing quickly, he pulled enough money out of his jeans to cover the bill and the tip and hustled Chase out of the diner and into the car.

He pulled the car around the back for a little privacy and then turned to Chase. "Take the hoodie off… carefully."

Chase did as he was told, slipping it off and throwing it into the backseat. Devon reached up and undid the buttons of Chase's shirt and pushed it back.

His nipples were red and a little swollen but not too bad, and Devon knew most of the discomfort came from the fact that Chase wasn't used to the clamps being on for longer periods of time.

"Gonna take them off now." He reached for one of them, but Chase shook his head.

"No, I can do this… I want to be good." He sounded so earnest, and Devon hurried to assure him that this wasn't a failure.

"Sweetheart, you're so good… you're making me proud already." He framed Chase's face with his hands, kissing him thoroughly until they were both breathless.

Devon slid his hands down, grabbed Chase's hands and put them on his shoulders, and then quickly released both clamps, his eyes never leaving Chase's as the blood rushed back in.

Chase gave one sharp cry, and then Devon could see him let the pain catch and take him as he breathed through it and found that place in his head that turned the right kind of pain to pleasure.

His head fell back against the seat as he gripped Devon's shoulders, and small whimpers fell from lips that were red and shiny from being bitten.

Devon put his hands around Chase's rib cage, his thumbs resting against the muscle just under his nipples, and he massaged around them gently, helping soothe the tingling ache that he knew Chase was feeling.

After a few minutes, he could feel all the tension bleeding from Chase's body until Devon brushed a careful thumb over a still-hard peak. Chase jolted but immediately relaxed again, so Devon leaned in closer and licked over the other nipple, soft swipes that made Chase whine quietly.

"So beautiful, Chase. Look at you, your poor little nipples red and swollen." He sucked on one gently, pleased when Chase slid his hands into Devon's hair to hold him in place.

He blew over the abused skin, watching as a shudder crawled through Chase. "Feels good now, doesn't it, baby? Bet you could almost come from this, couldn't you?"

"God... yes.... Devon, please." Chase's needy voice made Devon want to push him back and pull his cock out of his jeans and suck him until he came down Devon's throat.

"No... not yet, sweet boy." He licked over the other nipple, every touch of his tongue making Chase twitch. Sitting up, he pulled Chase against him, cuddling him for a few minutes before pushing him back against his seat.

Devon reached down to adjust his jeans, trying to get more comfortable, when he heard Chase sigh.

Looking over, he saw Chase's eyes fixed firmly on the bulge in Devon's jeans as he licked his lips. Devon smiled wickedly as he palmed his cock teasingly.

"See something you want, Chase?" He popped the button on his jeans and slowly pulled down the zipper. Chase nodded absently as he tracked every movement.

"Fuck... I'm so hard it hurts, and it's all because of you." Devon pulled himself out through the slit in his underwear. He slid his hand up and down his cock, moaning at the feeling. "You wanna help me out?"

"Devon... please... let me suck you. I wanna so bad...." Chase loved sucking cock like no one Devon had ever met, and Devon had no qualms about indulging his fetish.

He pulled Chase's head down, grinning as he practically fell on Devon. "No hands now, mind you. Let's see if that tongue is as talented as I remember."

Chase didn't say a word, just hummed in pleasure as he licked up Devon's shaft and then sucked the head in before sinking all the way down.

Devon knew he wasn't going to last long. He'd been too keyed up to start with, and he fisted his hand in Chase's hair, not really directing, just holding him in place as he fucked up into his mouth.

Chase moaned like it was the best thing he'd ever felt, and Devon could feel the vibrations traveling up his spine.

"Jesus, Chase… perfect fucking mouth on you." Chase seemed to relax his throat and let him slide in until his nose was bumping against Devon's stomach every time he bobbed down. He was drooling and his eyes were tearing up, but when he looked up at Devon, those hazel eyes radiated pure happiness.

Devon could feel his orgasm starting to build in his balls. "Gonna come, Chase… right down your throat. You ready for it?"

Chase didn't even slow down, just hummed a little louder. Devon reached under him and flicked over one sore nipple, and Chase choked for a second. The fluttering of his throat was all Devon could take, and he gripped Chase's hair hard, pulling him back enough to catch it all as Devon gave in and flooded his mouth.

He shoved into Chase's mouth a couple of more times and then watched as Chase shuddered and stiffened as he came in his jeans just from Devon fucking his mouth.

It was the hottest thing Devon had ever seen.

Chase pulled off and rested his forehead against Devon's stomach as he licked him clean until Devon's oversensitive cock couldn't take it anymore.

Devon petted Chase's hair, letting him rest for a few minutes. Indulging Chase's needs was so easy, and he wondered at how everything he was used to was so different with someone you loved.

Before Chase, Devon had always tried to be careful with his subs, making sure all their needs were met, but he'd always been able to maintain a professional distance. There had never been anyone he'd wanted to take things further with… no one he wanted in his home and his heart.

Chase had gotten under his skin from the very beginning, and it had never occurred to Devon to mind. Everything had always felt right when they were together, even when Devon was fighting his own emotions, and now that he'd stopped going against his nature, everything was even better.

Looking down, he realized Chase was on the verge of falling asleep. "Uh-uh, baby. It's not naptime yet. We need to get to the airport and get you cleaned up before we get on the plane."

Chase sighed but sat up, obviously reluctant to lose contact. He carefully tucked Devon back into his jeans and zipped him up before retreating to his own seat. "Yeah. I'm just a little sleepy."

Devon smiled and stroked Chase's cheek before starting the car and getting it moving. "Just a few more hours, then we can sleep for two days if you want."

Chase smiled sleepily. "Hey, Dev?"

Devon glanced over at him. "Yeah?"

"I love you. Thanks for coming for me." Chase's voice was rough and sweet, and the blush was back. He was gorgeous.

"Love you too, sweetheart. You're mine, and I'll always come for you." Chase's happy smile was all the answer he needed.

Nineteen

ON THE way back to the house, Devon called Kayley and told her to take the next couple of days off. He knew that an audience would only make Chase feel awkward and uncomfortable, and that was the last thing he wanted.

When they walked in the door, the dogs went nuts, clambering all over the both of them. Cammy was in heaven with Chase scratching at her ears, and it was hard to get the three animals corralled and into the back yard.

Once that was done, Devon sent Chase upstairs to have a shower while he locked up.

Going up the stairs, he stopped and stuck his head into the guest room, but there was no sound of running water coming from the bathroom there.

He continued to his room and the en suite bathroom, stripping off his clothes along the way. He was naked when he walked in, and he could see Chase in the shower, the clear glass door not hiding anything.

Chase was so beautiful, and it never failed to take Devon's breath away. He crossed the room, pulled the door open, and joined Chase under the water, closing the door quickly to keep the heat in.

"Devon...." Chase's voice was soft, barely heard over the running of the water. "I'm so glad to be home."

Devon wrapped his arms around Chase's waist, relishing the feeling of his water-warmed skin against his. "I'm glad you're home too."

Chase rested his head on Devon's shoulder. "Are we going to the playroom now?" He didn't sound scared, but Devon could see he was nervous.

Devon shook his head. "The only place we're going is to bed for a nap. Neither of us has had enough sleep in the last little while. Then we'll see." He stroked Chase's back, loving how he melted against him and trusted Devon to take care of him. "Nothing happens that you don't want, baby."

"I know you'd never hurt me, Dev… not in any way I didn't want you to." Chase mumbled the words into Devon's neck, almost asleep on his feet.

Devon smiled and kissed Chase's hair. "Let me get cleaned up, and then let's get you to bed. You're definitely too big to carry."

Chase nodded and leaned back against the wall while Devon quickly soaped himself and rinsed off. He was more than half-hard by the time he was finished but too tired to do anything about it.

Turning off the water, he pushed Chase out onto the rug in the middle of the floor. The younger man just stood there, pliant and sweet, as Devon dried him off before toweling off himself and then urged him toward the bedroom.

When they reached the bed, Devon pulled back the covers, and Chase crawled in, snuggling into the pillow as Devon spooned up behind him.

Once they were covered up, Devon worked his arm under Chase's head until he was resting on it, and with his other hand he gathered both of Chase's wrists together in a firm grip, holding them close to his chest. He smiled as Chase stiffened for barely a second and then relaxed completely, humming his satisfaction at the restraint as he drifted off to sleep.

"Love you, sweet boy." Chase shivered softly as Devon whispered in his ear. "I'm so lucky to have you."

Devon drifted off with the scent of Chase tickling his nose and the quiet thump of his heartbeat under his fingers.

WHEN DEVON blinked his eyes open six hours later, Chase had flipped over and was curled into Devon's side, his head pillowed on his chest. He looked smaller than any man as tall as Chase had a right to, and it made Devon want to protect him as much as he wanted to dominate him.

He would have lain there watching him for longer, but it was like Chase had sensed that he'd woken up, and soon he was blinking sleepily up at him. "Dev? Everything okay?"

Devon ran his fingers through Chase's hair before gripping the back of it and using it to pull him up for a kiss.

Chase opened up for it immediately, letting Devon push his tongue inside, letting him explore as much as he wanted before pulling away. Chase tried to follow that clever mouth with his, and Devon chuckled at him as he began to pout at being denied.

Devon got off the bed and walked over to the tall dresser just inside the door, and he could feel Chase's eyes tracking him the whole way. Devon opened the bottom drawer, reached inside, and pulled out a slim, square box, and Chase's eyes widened when he saw it.

Turning back to the bed, he watched as Chase scrambled off the mattress and slipped to his knees, head down, legs spread and arms clasped behind his back. It was the first time he didn't look sad and scared as he fell into presentation, and Devon could see there was pride in his stance now.

Devon stopped in front of Chase and put his hand on his head, petting him lovingly. "Look at you, kneeling so pretty for me." Chase pushed into the touch, practically purring with happiness. "I'm so proud of you, baby."

Reaching down, he lifted Chase's chin so he could look into his eyes. "I have something for you, if you want it." The intense want and need in Chase's gaze gave him his answer, but he needed to be sure. Devon crouched down so he wasn't towering over Chase as he spoke to him.

"You don't have to accept this right now. I'm willing to wait until you're ready, whenever that might be. I will always want this with you, so no for now doesn't mean no forever." He leaned in and kissed Chase's forehead before pulling back to look at him again.

Chase's eyes shined at him as he smiled. "I've wanted this from you since you saved me. And not just because of that. You're everything any sub could want in a Master, and it's something I never thought I deserved or would ever get."

He swallowed and licked his lips before continuing. "You showed me I was wrong... about myself... about so many things, and this is where I want to be... for as long as you'll let me."

Devon smiled and kissed him gently and then stood up. He opened the box and pulled out a slim leather collar with silver accents. He unbuckled it and showed Chase the writing that had been inscribed into the inside of the collar. It said "sweet boy."

"Dev...." Chase smiled brightly before sobering. "Master, please... I'd like the honor of wearing your collar." He bent his head once more and waited for Devon.

"It's you who's honoring me, Chase." Devon slipped the collar around Chase's neck and did it up carefully, making it tight enough for Chase to feel when he swallowed without choking him.

Once it was properly fastened, Devon hooked one finger over it and used it to angle Chase's head as he leaned down and plundered his mouth with a savage kiss. He bit at Chase's mouth, the possessiveness he felt roaring to life at the eager whimpers falling from his sub's throat.

Pulling back, he couldn't hide the satisfaction he felt when he saw how shiny and kiss-swollen Chase's lips were, and the happy, dazed expression on his face just added fuel to the fire.

"As much as I want to continue this, we're going to go down to the kitchen and eat before anything else happens. You're going to need to keep your strength up...." He let the promise hang in the air as he turned from Chase and grabbed a pair of jeans that were hanging over the back of a chair and slipped them on.

He walked over to the dresser, grabbed a pair of underwear from the drawer, and returned to give them to Chase.

Devon took one hand and pulled Chase to his feet, then knelt to help him put the underwear on. Chase looked down on him with awe as Devon directed him to lift one foot and then the other before sliding them up Chase's long legs and over the cheeks of his ass.

The black jockstrap left Chase completely exposed from behind, while the front cradled his hard cock, the tip peeking out over the top of the waistband.

Chase never moved, letting Devon do as he pleased, with only soft, contented sighs to show how happy he was.

Devon stood and walked behind Chase, admiring the view. He couldn't resist giving the pale, silky flesh a hard swat and grinned at Chase's yelp. "Such a gorgeous ass."

He turned and walked to the door, unsurprised when Chase fell in behind him like he was already leashed and followed him down the stairs.

When they reached the kitchen, Devon sent Chase to let the dogs in and smiled indulgently as he watched Chase love all over them for a few minutes.

After turning on the coffeemaker, he walked to the fridge and opened it, delighted to find a fruit-and-cheese platter Kayley had prepared for them before leaving. He chuckled when he saw the sticky note on top with nothing but a smiley face and the words "about time" written on it.

Devon made toast while waiting for the coffee and put everything together on a tray. He handed Chase the coffee cups and carried the tray into the living room. He set it on the side table and then took the cups from Chase, setting them there as well.

Sitting in the corner of the couch, he waited for Chase to sit beside him and found himself happily surprised when he sunk to the floor at Devon's feet and rested his head on his knee.

Devon settled one hand into Chase's hair, petting him gently. "So good for me, Chase." He slid his hand down to curl around Chase's cheek, and he leaned into the touch before turning his head and kissing the palm of Devon's hand.

The black collar stuck out in stark relief against Chase's skin, and just looking at it had Devon growling possessively and leaning down to nip at the tender skin above the leather.

Chase arched his neck and gave Devon all the access he demanded. "Master, please... God... love you."

Devon pulled back to look into Chase's eyes. "I love you too, sweetheart."

Chase smiled shyly and cuddled closer to Devon's legs. "Thank you."

Devon patted his cheek and then reached for the plate of fruit. Kayley made it all bite-sized, which suited Devon perfectly.

He picked up a piece of pineapple and held it in front of Chase's mouth. He took it carefully, his pink tongue reaching out to lick a stray drop of juice from Devon's skin, causing Devon's cock to twitch in his jeans.

Chase's eyes never left Devon's face as they shared the fruit. Devon knew Chase loved the stuff and had once told him that he'd not really been given more than a few apples when he lived at Kingston's. It was the reason he didn't like them now.

Devon held his patience, feeding Chase bites of mango and peaches, strawberries and more pineapple, because he knew it was Chase's favorite.

He ate some himself but was too wrapped up in taking care of Chase to have much of an appetite.

Grabbing the toast off the table, he fed that to Chase as well, relishing the sweet torture of him licking the butter from Devon's fingertips.

They drank their coffee, but Devon let Chase handle that himself. He didn't want to take the chance of spilling the hot liquid on Chase's bare skin. He was still a little wary of anything that might burn him, and Devon didn't want him worrying about it.

Talking quietly, Chase told him more about his time with his parents, how it was awkward at first, especially with his father. Chase had been sure his father was upset with him sometimes, but after some late-night talks mediated by his mom, he found out his father was just frustrated with the situation and feeling guilty about not finding Chase himself.

After they'd got it out in the open, and Chase had reassured his dad it wasn't his fault in the least, things went better for all of them.

Once the food was finished, Devon put a finger under Chase's chin and gently urged him into a full kneel. Chase went quickly, that pride shining from him once again as he presented for his Master.

Devon got up from the couch and took the dishes to the kitchen, tidying up before going back to the living room. He touched Chase's shoulder, and when he looked up, Devon motioned him to stand.

Chase got gracefully to his feet and followed when Devon turned and walked to the playroom door.

Devon stopped and turned to face Chase before opening the door. "You're sure you're ready for this?"

Chase nodded and then shyly kissed Devon. "I need it... from you."

Devon wrapped both arms around Chase's waist and pulled him in hard. He slid one hand up Chase's back and tangled it in his hair, using it as leverage to drag him down for a blistering kiss. When he stopped, they were both panting for breath, and Chase had the most beautiful blush creeping up his chest and neck.

Taking Chase's hand, he opened the door and led him down the stairs.

WHEN THEY reached the basement, Devon directed Chase to stand in the middle of the room while he walked around him and took stock. Deciding what was appropriate for Chase would be difficult because of his history, and he didn't want to ruin the experience for either of them.

Chase stood quietly, arms once again behind his back, hands clasped over his elbows and his eyes lowered to the floor.

"Eyes up, sweet boy." Devon kept his voice low and deep, and he didn't miss the shiver that rolled through Chase as his eyes found Devon's.

"For now, I want to see your face. No looking at the floor unless I tell you to." Chase nodded as Devon walked behind him and stood close enough that they almost touched but not quite. He used his foot to push Chase's feet a little farther apart and then trailed his hand down to caress the silky smooth skin of Chase's ass.

Chase moaned, barely audible, and Devon pulled his hand back before slapping one cheek hard, hoping for a louder reaction. He wasn't disappointed. Chase cried out and pushed his ass back, looking for more, but Devon wasn't quite ready for that yet.

"We'll get to that." He slid his finger between Chase's cheeks and ghosted them over his hole. It twitched against the touch, and Chase moaned louder.

"Master, please…." Chase swayed back, and Devon could see that keeping still was something that was difficult for him.

He could work with that.

Walking to the cabinet, he opened one of the drawers and pulled out a set of cuffs that were attached by a length of chain. The cuffs were wide and made of leather. They were padded on the inside so that Chase couldn't rub his wrists raw as he struggled, and that suited Devon fine.

Chase didn't say anything when he saw them, just looked wide-eyed at Devon for a moment.

"Before we go any further, we need to talk about your words. I know Kingston ignored them, but I won't. It's important that you know that." Devon took a deep breath before reaching for Chase's hand.

"What do you mean, *words*? Isn't there just one? The safeword?" Chase offered his hand to Devon and watched as he attached one of the cuffs, his eyes crinkling in confusion.

Devon shook his head. "No, I want you to have three. Sometimes you're just going to want to stop immediately. Let's use red for now, until you can think of something else if you want."

Chase offered his other hand, and Devon buckled the other cuff on as he continued. "Then there's going to be times when you like what we're doing but maybe it's too much or too fast and you want to slow down without stopping completely. So you need a word for that. Again, we'll go with yellow until you come up with something else."

Devon grabbed a wooden stool from beside the wall and brought it behind Chase. He climbed up and attached the chain to another chain that hung from the ceiling, high enough that Chase was stretched out with his feet barely flat on the floor.

Devon got down and moved the stool back to the wall before returning to smooth his hands down Chase's arms and torso. He pushed up behind him and wrapped an arm around his waist, pulling him close.

Chase let his head fall back onto Devon's shoulder, and Devon couldn't resist the long, tempting expanse of Chase's neck. He leaned in and pressed a line of kisses there as he ground his denim-covered cock against the cleft of Chase's ass.

"One more word, sweet boy." He pulled away and moved around in front of Chase, smirking at the disappointed whine that followed. "After you've called yellow, you need a word to let me know you're ready to continue. Again, something simple, we'll use green for now."

Devon couldn't stop touching Chase's smooth skin, running his hands over his chest and pinching his nipples. Chase whimpered and moved restlessly every time, and the sound went right to Devon's cock.

"What if I'm gagged?" Chase let his eyes fall to the floor, and Devon knew that being gagged wasn't something Chase was looking forward to.

"Baby, right now I'm loving those sweet sounds you make. I wanna hear them and have no intention of denying myself that pleasure." He put his hands on Chase's hips and leaned up to kiss him, biting down on his lower lip before thrusting his tongue in.

"If the time ever comes that we both want that then we'll work out a sign for stop."

Chase's chest was heaving like Devon had stolen the breath from his lungs, but he still remembered his manners. "Thank you, Master."

"I told you before, sweetheart, this is about both of us, not just me. And I won't force you to do anything you really don't want to." Devon stepped back, wanting Chase to clear his head a little.

"I know things are going to scare you, Chase, and that's okay. I just hope you'll trust me enough to try some of them knowing I won't let anything bad happen to you."

Chase's expressive eyes showed Devon everything: the fear, the longing, the neediness, and it was a powerful feeling to know that Chase wanted to be there with him even after everything he'd been through.

"There's no punishment for using your words, so don't be afraid to use them if you have to." Devon walked to the cabinet and pulled a blindfold out of one of the drawers before returning to Chase. "You have to be honest with me at all times. If I ask you how you feel or if you like something, then tell me the truth. I'm asking questions so I can make things work for us, and if you're saying what you think I want to hear, I could do something you don't like without meaning to."

Chase trembled as Devon slipped the blindfold over his head and fastened it securely. "Are you okay with not being able to see?"

Chase started to shake his head but then he stopped. "I don't know, but I think I'd like to try."

Devon rubbed a soothing hand over Chase's back. "Good boy. I'm proud of you for giving it a chance."

Chase beamed at the praise, and Devon rewarded him with another kiss. His boy loved kissing and he was happy to indulge him with it as often as possible.

"Having your eyes covered makes you use your other senses more. It makes everything you feel or hear sharper... more intense." Devon picked a small flogger out of the cabinet and brought it to Chase. It looked like a long leather fringe that had been rolled together and stuck on a handle. This one wasn't really designed for causing pain, but it could nicely warm someone's skin after a while.

Chase whimpered when Devon trailed it over his back, letting the leather fall softly on his skin as he moved it over his shoulders and down his chest.

"How does that feel, Chase? You want me to stop?" Devon pulled his arm back and let the ends of the flogger slap gently across Chase's nipple, causing him to cry out.

When he realized what he'd done, he started babbling. "Don't stop... sorry, Master... it feels good... please don't stop."

Devon let the leather fall a few more times without any real force, watching as Chase shook with each touch.

Looking down, he could see Chase's cock straining against the cotton of the underwear and let the leather strands brush against it carefully.

Chase twisted against the bonds, trying to get more friction, but Devon pulled away. "You're so beautiful like this, Chase. Your sweetness and submission shine from you, and I'm so proud you're giving it to me."

"I love you, Master... I have to give it to you." Chase's voice was quiet but sure, and it made Devon's heart feel like bursting from his chest.

Devon moved behind him and leaned up to kiss the back of Chase's shoulders. "Thank you, sweet boy."

Pulling the strips of leather into his free hand, he stepped back and struck out with the flogger a little harder, letting it land across the swell of Chase's ass.

He moaned and pushed his ass out a little more, so Devon gave him what he wanted. He knew from experience that there would be no real sting from the leather, just a gentle heat that would build and build until the skin was so sensitive just the slightest touch would be overwhelming.

The leather strips fell in a random pattern, crisscrossing Chase's ass and upper thighs until he was almost sobbing with overstimulation and begging Devon to give him more.

Devon would stop every few minutes and run his hand over the reddening skin as though he could rub the warmth in deeper. The wet spot on the front of the cotton jock was getting larger all the time, and suddenly Devon needed to have them gone.

He laid the flogger on a small table and knelt in front of Chase before carefully pulling the waistband over his weeping cock and down his legs. Chase shook as he obediently lifted first one foot and then the other so Devon could remove the underwear completely.

Devon ran one finger over the head of Chase's cock and across the slit, causing Chase to keen. "This all for me, sweet boy?"

He leaned in and licked over the smooth head, just one swipe, but it had Chase begging. "Please... God, Master... I'm gonna... gotta stop."

Devon smiled. It was the perfect time for a lesson. He kept licking over Chase's cock, tiny kitten licks that had Chase shuddering with the effort to hold back his orgasm. "You want me to stop, Chase?"

He watched as Chase shook his head even as he begged, like his body and his mouth just couldn't come to an agreement.

"Use your words, baby. What do you want me to do?" He hadn't touched Chase other than the licks, and he decided to up the stakes. Reaching up with one hand, he rolled Chase's balls in his palm and tugged gently. The result was instantaneous.

"Yellow! Oh please, Master…."

Devon pulled his hand away immediately and stopped licking. He pushed himself to his feet and reached up to cradle Chase's face in his hands. "That's so good, sweet boy." He kissed his lips, drinking in the whimpers pushing up from Chase's throat.

Chase melted against him, and Devon held him close. "Now, why didn't you want to come?"

Chase nuzzled his face into Devon's neck. "You hadn't said I could. I didn't want to disappoint you."

Devon smiled, pleased with Chase's confession. "That makes me so proud, baby." He reached down and stroked Chase's cock, making him whine. "But I want you to come… whenever you need to."

Chase nodded. "Yes, Master. Green."

Devon kissed him until Chase was breathless and then sunk to his knees. He sucked the head of Chase's cock back into his mouth and reached around to grab both cheeks of his ass.

Chase gasped at the rough touch and he bucked forward, but Devon was ready for him. He relaxed his throat and let him plunge in to the root. He sucked hard as Chase tried desperately to pull back but was unable to because of Devon's grip on him.

"Devon… oh God, it hurts… please… don't stop." Chase's body was shaking hard as the sensations overwhelmed him.

Devon pulled off to breathe and leaned down to lick the velvet-soft skin of Chase's sac, using his tongue to tease and manipulate it.

He knew Chase was right on the edge, and he knew just how to push him over.

Devon turned him around and grabbed his ass cheeks, pulling them apart. He brushed his stubbled cheek across the still-red skin before pushing his tongue in to lick at Chase's twitching hole.

"Dev… fuck…."

Devon pulled at the rim with both thumbs to create a little burn and then shoved as much of his tongue into Chase's ass as he could.

It was too much for Chase, and his whole body stiffened as he shot pulse after pulse of come all over the floor. Smaller spurts leaked down the side of his cock, and Devon let go of his ass with one hand to reach around and jack him slowly, drawing out the pleasure as long as possible.

All the muscles in Chase's body seemed to let go at once, and if Devon hadn't caught him, he would have been hanging from the chains, his legs no longer able to hold him.

Devon stood up and pulled Chase against him with one arm as he worked at the buckles of the cuffs with his other hand. Once his arms were free, Devon carefully removed the blindfold and led a barely conscious Chase to the big bed in the corner.

Pulling back the covers, he pushed him into the bed and urged him to scoot over and lie on his stomach.

Devon hurriedly got out of his jeans and climbed in after him, running his hands over the still-sensitive skin and making sure Chase wasn't really hurt.

Chase turned his head to look blearily at Devon.

"Hey, sweet boy. You okay?" He pushed the hair out of Chase's eyes, and Chase lifted one hand and grabbed Devon's arm, trying to pull him down on his back.

"I'm good. Want you to fuck me, though. Need to feel you on my skin."

Devon's cock was definitely interested, squeezing out precome until it was running down the sides. He levered himself up over Chase before he nestled his dick in the crease of Chase's ass.

Lowering himself, he blanketed Chase's back, reaching up to tangle their fingers together as he whispered in his ear.

"How about I just do this? Gonna rub my cock all over the pretty red ass, mark you all up." He sucked at the skin behind Chase's ear as he ground himself against Chase.

Chase responded by groaning and lifting his hips as much as he could, giving Devon more friction. "Yes... do it...."

It wasn't going to take long. Devon was too wound up from watching Chase. A few hard thrusts and Chase's pleading for it had Devon coming all over Chase's ass and lower back. The come smeared between them until they were both sticky with it, and Devon loved how it felt.

When he couldn't hold himself up on his elbows anymore, he let himself fall to the side before rolling onto his back. Chase immediately wiggled closer to drape himself over Devon's chest, tucking his head under his chin and nuzzling into his neck.

Devon grabbed some tissues and used them to wipe Chase's back down before cleaning himself and tossing them to the floor.

"Sleepy, sweet boy?" Chase nodded and hummed, but that was it. "You can rest for a bit. I'll wake you up in an hour."

"'Kay. Love you, Dev." Chase was like a big snuggly puppy after sex, and before him, Devon would have been annoyed by it. Apparently everything was different with Chase.

"Love you too, Chase." He waited until he was sure Chase was asleep before slipping out of bed and into the shower in the adjoining bathroom.

He had some big plans for his boy tonight. He'd better be ready when Chase was done with his nap.

Twenty

CHASE WOKE to the delicious feeling of a warm, slick hand on his cock. His hips bucked up instinctively, pushing into the amazing pressure, and he moaned at how good it felt.

"Devon...." Chase planted his feet on the mattress, using the leverage to get a good rhythm going as he fucked Devon's hand.

"Look so gorgeous like this, baby." Devon's gravelly voice seemed to crawl up Chase's spine, and he snapped his eyes open to meet Devon's gaze.

"Don't you come, sweet boy. I have plans for you, and I'll be upset if you mess them up." Devon's tone was light, but the meaning bled through Chase's pleasurable haze, and he tried to pull out of Devon's grip but couldn't.

Devon kept stroking, sweeping his thumb over the head, and Chase whined as the effort of trying not to come became almost painful.

"Dev, please." Chase needed him to stop or he was going to come whether he wanted to or not.

"You need some help, sweetheart?" Devon leaned down and licked at the drops welling up from Chase's slit.

Chase cried out. "Yes. Master, please... I can't... don't make me...."

Devon grinned and took one more lick before pulling away. "Such a good boy for me, Chase. You beg so pretty."

Devon ran the fingers of his clean hand through Chase's hair for a few minutes, and Chase realized his Dom was letting him get control of himself before continuing with the scene.

As he took stock of what was going on around him, he realized that Devon had cleaned him up while he was sleeping, and he'd also buckled the leather cuffs back around Chase's wrists. He flexed his arms, relishing the feeling of the restraints and wondering what they were for.

Chase smiled at Devon and was rewarded with a kiss before being pulled up off the bed.

Devon wiped his hand on a damp towel and walked to the opposite corner of the room with Chase following him. Chase was curious and excited about what was going to happen next.

Chase knew that most people who were aware of what happened to him thought he'd be afraid of Devon and the life he led, but it wasn't true.

He was still a little nervous about what could happen, but Devon had never been anything but exactly what Chase needed, and he'd risked his life and his freedom to help Chase.

His family liked Devon and appreciated him bringing Chase back to them, but they were worried he was taking advantage of Chase somehow. It wasn't true, though.

Chase was safe here and loved. He could see it every single time Devon looked at him. There was nothing hiding in Devon's eyes, and Chase knew he loved Devon more than he ever thought he could love anyone.

Talking to his therapist had helped a lot, and the man had seemed to understand that Chase was capable of making his own decisions. He'd questioned him endlessly about his feelings and if he felt obligated to Devon and whether that was why he wanted to submit to him.

It wasn't that, though. Now that he could see things for himself, he'd realized how screwed up Kingston's version of the Dom/sub lifestyle was. For Kingston it had all been about ownership, pain, and humiliation. And Chase knew some people wanted that from their Masters, but it was up to the Dom to know the difference between those who just wanted to submit and those who needed some of the darker aspects of the relationship.

Kingston hadn't known. He was broken in ways that Chase couldn't even begin to understand, and he'd wanted to break Chase and Devon as well.

Chase used to think there was something twisted in him for wanting this, to be controlled and sometimes used. Devon had helped him understand that there was nothing wrong with him and that he understood why Chase needed what he did.

It made Chase smile when he thought about all the times Devon had talked to him about what this kind of lifestyle should be, how passionate he was about the duties a Dom had to his sub.

Chase looked up, and his eyes widened when he saw the leather swing in front of him. It looked stiff and new, and it hung from chains that were attached to a black metal frame and a pulley system that had been mounted to the ceiling.

On a table set away from the swing, leather straps and metal clips had been piled up, waiting for Devon to use them how he saw fit.

Devon turned and slipped his arms around Chase, pulling him in for a kiss as he maneuvered Chase around so that his back was to the swing. Chase remained relaxed and pliant, letting Devon move him as he pleased.

His eyes never left Devon's face as the cuffs on his wrists were attached to the chain and then as Devon knelt and wrapped padded leather cuffs around his legs, just above the knee.

Devon pressed a kiss to Chase's hip and stood up. When he lowered Chase into the swing, Chase didn't resist. He trusted Devon to not let him fall.

When it was done, Chase was suspended in the air, his arms held above his head, with his hands hanging freely. The straps attached to the cuffs on his legs had been adjusted so that his knees were lifted and spread, unable to close, exposing his cock and ass and leaving them open to whatever Devon had in mind.

Chase was as vulnerable as he'd ever been in his life, but he knew he was safe, and that was all that mattered. Everything else, he could let go of, and he could just let Devon take care of him. He knew it would take some time for Devon to trust that Chase knew his own limits, but he was looking forward to the exploration.

"Chase, look at me." Chase was startled when Devon's voice broke the quiet surrounding them. He hadn't realized he'd closed his eyes as Devon had adjusted everything, and he opened them to find Devon standing by his head, looking down at him with love and concern. "You okay?"

Chase smiled at him, feeling almost like he was floating. "Yes, Sir." When Devon smiled at him and stroked his hair, Chase tilted his head, shamelessly begging for another kiss. Devon bent and rewarded him with one, biting at his lips like he wanted to swallow him whole.

"So proud of you, Chase." Another lingering kiss and Devon stood back up. "You make it so easy to spoil you." He slid one hand under Chase's head, supporting it as he did something Chase couldn't see. His head was lowered and tipped back a little until he was eye level with the bulge in the front of Devon's jeans.

Devon reached down and rubbed his cock, and Chase could see how hard he was. His mouth started to water as the smell of Devon's arousal reached him, and he was desperate to have all that smooth, silky skin free of its restraints and lying on his tongue.

When Devon's hand reached for his zipper, Chase whimpered and looked up at his Master pleadingly. "Please… let me…."

Devon pulled his cock out of his jeans and stroked it. "You want this, sweet boy? Wanna suck my cock? Let me fuck your mouth till I come?"

Chase whined and licked his lips. "Please… Master. Wanna taste you."

Devon's cock twitched in his hand. "Look at you, begging to be choking on my dick." He moved closer, and Chase closed his eyes as Devon rubbed the head over his lips. He flicked his tongue out to lick the precome Devon had left behind.

He was gratified by Devon's grunt of pleasure when Chase's tongue finally found the tip of his cock. Chase didn't try to lift his head.

He would take what he was given, and he knew if he was a good boy, his Master would reward him.

Humming his pleasure, he licked over the velvety skin, his tongue barely able to reach until he felt the head pressed between his willing lips. Devon fucked into his mouth, reaching down to cradle Chase's head as he did.

He felt surrounded by Devon. His nose was buried between Devon's legs, and the smell of him was overwhelming there. When he pulled out until just the tip of his cock was in Chase's mouth and then pushed back in, Chase felt stuffed full again, breathless in the best way.

"So goddamned beautiful, sweet boy. Your mouth is fucking amazing." The satisfaction in his voice urged Chase on, and he sucked his Master a little harder.

He knew he was gasping and moaning around Devon's cock, but Devon had told him over and over how much he loved the sounds he made, so he didn't even try to stifle them.

His own cock was aching, but he barely noticed, so caught up in Devon's pleasure and taking some of it for his own.

"Gonna come, Chase. You want that? Gonna drink down everything I give you?" Devon's thrusts were getting erratic, but he never lost control, even as he finally used him in the way Chase had been dreaming of since they'd met.

Chase moaned his agreement, swallowing on Devon's next thrust so that the muscles in his throat milked his cock. Devon groaned and pulled out so that just the head was still in Chase's mouth as he started to come.

The hand in Chase's hair tightened almost painfully, but he was too busy swallowing to really pay attention. Devon grunted as pulse after pulse landed on Chase's tongue and a few stray drops made their way out of his mouth and trickled down his chin.

When he'd finished shuddering through his orgasm, Devon dropped to his knees and kissed Chase desperately before licking his face clean. He let his forehead rest against Chase's for a moment as they both got their breath back, the hand on the back of his head never faltering in its support even once.

It was silent in the room as Devon stood, bending for another kiss before he once again adjusted the chains so that the hammock was supporting Chase's head, leaving him free to walk around to Chase's feet.

Chase's eyes tracked him, his attention focused so completely on his Dom's face that he was unaware that Devon was reaching for him until one teasing finger slid up from his balls to the tip of his cock.

He cried out, trying to arch into the touch, but he had no leverage at all and was unable to move. He was completely at his Dom's mercy.

"Love your big cock all hard for me." He reached down and fondled Chase's balls, tugging them until it was just shy of painful. "I'm gonna play with your ass, maybe tie up your cock… see how far I can push you before you come."

A suddenly slick finger was rubbing over his hole and then pushing in slowly. "And after you come, I'm gonna get you hard again and fuck you… just like this." He gave the swing a little push, letting his finger come almost all the way out before the momentum impaled Chase on it once more.

"You want that, baby?" Devon's finger crooked just the right way and found Chase's prostate. He cried out, sure he was going to come and not wanting to disappoint his Dom, but suddenly Devon's other hand was there, squeezing the base of his cock tightly. "Don't you dare, sweet boy. I haven't even begun to have my fun yet."

Devon pulled his finger free and walked over to the table. He picked up a dildo and a bottle of lube and brought them back to Chase. The dildo was flesh colored and long but not as big around as Devon's cock. "Let's start with this. I think you might like it." He trailed the tip of it down Chase's chest, and when it was right over his nipple, it started to vibrate, causing Chase to moan and try to arch his body. "I know I'm going to."

The vibrating stopped, and the vibrator continued its journey down Chase's body. Chase's eyes never left Devon's face as he watched the emotions play out there. Devon's eyes were hungry as he teased the vibrator over the tip of Chase's cock. The way Devon looked at him made him feel like he was the most important thing in Devon's world, and he liked it.

Chase's body tensed up as he waited for the vibrating to start, but Devon just looked up at him and grinned as he let it slip over the slit and down the underside of the shaft. "Bet you can't wait to come, can you, baby?" He popped the lube open and tipped it so that it slowly dripped over Chase's balls and Chase could feel the cool liquid slide down over his ass. "I love how you look when the pleasure hits you." He ran the vibrator through the slick mess until it gleamed when he lifted it into Chase's view, and Chase could feel his hole clenching in anticipation of having it inside him.

"This is gonna feel so good, Chase." Devon pushed the silicone into Chase slowly, and without prep the burn was almost overwhelming, but it didn't take long for it to fade into the fullness he'd been craving.

"Dev… oh… please." Chase was trying to be good, but the frustration of not being able to move was starting to get to him. "Fuck me with it. I gotta come."

He realized how he sounded just as Devon's hand smacked hard against the meat of his ass. The stinging heat just added to his need but also reminded him of his place.

"Who's in charge here, Chase?" The use of his name was deliberate, showing Devon's displeasure with Chase's behavior.

"You are—" The words caught in his throat as Devon's hand came down again. "Devon… I'm sorry." He got it out just as the third blow landed, and Chase knew if he could move, he'd be trying to move into the punishment instead of away.

Devon nodded and smoothed his hand over Chase, soothing the sting away. "I know you are." He pulled the vibrator out a little and changed the angle as he pushed it back in. It scraped over Chase's prostate, and he cried out as sparks went off behind his eyes. "Do you trust me to take care of you, sweet boy? Will you let me get you where you need to go?"

Devon's bright green eyes seemed to stare right into him as his Dom waited for him to answer.

"Yes… I trust you, Dev."

Chase could feel Devon searching for something in his eyes, and when he found it, he nodded in satisfaction. "Good." He looked around and spotted something on the table and walked over to get it. When he came back, he had what looked like a couple of leather straps in his hand, and he was smiling wickedly.

"For being such a good boy, I'm gonna help you out, baby." He grabbed Chase's cock and wrapped the leather around it quickly and efficiently. When he was done, there was a ring around his cock and one that pulled his balls away from his body, making it almost impossible for him to come without Devon freeing him.

It felt strange, but Chase was grateful. Without it, he would have come within a couple of minutes at best. Devon checked the fit and then leaned down to suck Chase's cock into his mouth until his nose was almost buried in Chase's pubic hair before pulling off with an obscene pop.

Chase keened as his cock throbbed with trapped blood. "Had to make sure it was going to work." Devon's voice was rough, and the sound had Chase shivering. He felt like he was drifting with only Devon anchoring him, and he loved it. He let go of everything—all his worries, all his fears—and just gave himself to his Master.

Devon's hands were on Chase's thighs, his gentle touch soothing the quivering muscles until he was completely still. "Such a good boy for me." The soft touches continued as Devon walked out from between his legs and around his body. "So proud of you. You're letting it all go, aren't you?" He didn't wait for an answer, just kept talking. "Look at me, Chase."

Chase turned, almost surprised to find Devon standing beside his head. His Master's long fingers slid into his hair, and it seemed like Chase's whole world had shrunk until there was nothing left but Devon and the way he touched Chase.

"You ready to soar, sweet boy?" Devon's hand tightened in his hair, and the brief sting helped Chase focus enough to answer.

"Yes. Please... anything." Looking up into Devon's eyes, he saw everything he'd been looking for his whole life.

Devon nodded and then stepped back before pulling something out of the pocket of his jeans. Just as Chase recognized what it was, Devon pushed the button on the remote, and Chase only had a second to breathe before it hit him.

The vibrator started pulsing, drilling relentlessly against his prostate. His whole body tightened, but without anything to hang on to, there was nowhere for the tension to go, and it flowed through him.

He was distantly aware of it crawling up his spine as his body tried to find release, but the strap around his cock kept him on the edge without letting him go over.

The vibrations sped up and slowed down, Devon playing him perfectly, judging his reactions and slowing everything down just when it got to be too much.

Pleasure and pain were twisted up and pulling at him from all directions, and it was the most amazing thing he'd ever felt in his life. At one point, Devon turned the vibrations down low and spanked Chase's ass until it was glowing red, every blow feeling like he was being fucked as it landed on the base of the dildo.

"Devon. Oh fuck!" He was screaming, but he couldn't stop it. He wasn't aware of anything but the bliss rolling through his body.

"You had enough?" The words being whispered into his ear startled him, and he forced himself to listen. "You wanna come, baby? All you have to do is ask."

Chase didn't ask... he begged. "Please... letmeletmeletme... oh God...." Chase's hands flopped uselessly, desperate for something to hang on to, and the smell of Devon was overwhelming.

Devon's hand was in his hair, arching his neck back to kiss him brutally as the vibrations inside him ramped up even higher. Chase wailed as Devon pulled away and released the pressure from around his cock and balls before whispering in his ear once more.

"Come."

Chase's world exploded as his orgasm overtook him.

"CHASE."

The first thing Chase became aware of was his Dom's voice calling to him. He made himself open his eyes and looked up to see Devon smiling down at him, his eyes full of pride and love.

"There you are." He was petting Chase's hair, and Chase leaned in to nuzzle against his hand. "Feeling okay?"

Chase swallowed and licked his lips as he tried to clear his head. "Fuck...."

Devon frowned. "What's wrong? Are you hurt—?"

Chase cut him off. "No." Chase realized his wrist cuffs had been unhooked from the chains, and he reached for Devon, grabbed his hand, and pulled him closer. "You were supposed to fuck me."

Devon grinned but shook his head. "Chase. You need time—"

Chase shook his head frantically and pouted. "No, you promised. Fuck me." Chase knew he sounded like a petulant child, but his self-control had been mangled by his orgasm. Devon pulled back his hand and smacked Chase's ass, causing him to yelp.

"Mind your manners, sweet boy." Devon's tone was playful but had an edge.

"Please fuck me... I've waited so long." Chase was desperate to have Devon inside him, and it was making him reckless.

Devon wheeled around abruptly and walked away, and for a moment Chase was worried he'd pushed too far, but he was back in a second, the bottle of lube and a condom in his hand. His jeans were unbuttoned, like he'd needed to relieve the pressure while he'd been tormenting Chase, and he pushed them down and kicked them off.

He ripped the condom open, rolled it on, and then slicked himself up quickly. Moving between Chase's legs, he pulled the dildo out slowly, and Chase whined at the emptiness it left behind.

"Shhh. I'll fill you back up." Devon watched as he slowly pressed his cock into Chase, and Chase was fascinated by the look on his face, like he was giving him some kind of gift.

"Dev, please." Chase hadn't meant to speak, but his words had Devon's gaze rising to meet his. He was still lying helpless in the swing, and all he could do was wait for Devon to give him what he needed.

Reaching down, Devon guided Chase's hands to the chains closest to his head and then leaned down to whisper in his ear. "Don't let go unless I tell you."

Chase swallowed, his mouth suddenly dry, and he nodded. "Okay." For just a second it was so still and silent as Devon looked down at him hungrily that Chase could feel the throb of his Dom's heartbeat where they were connected.

Then he grabbed Chase's hips in a bruising grip and slowly pulled out until only the head of his cock was holding Chase open for him. He pushed back in just as slowly until he was balls deep and grinding hard against Chase's ass.

Keeping the pace torturously slow, Devon used the motion of the swing to his advantage, making sure the angle was perfect so that he was hitting Chase's overly sensitive prostate with every thrust.

"So fucking tight... God, Chase." Devon ground out the words through gritted teeth.

Chase was dimly aware of the amount of control Devon was exercising as he fucked him, but the only thing that registered was the pleasure humming through his body. It almost seemed impossible when his cock started to harden, and Chase started to reach for it, but his hand was slapped away by Devon. "Told you to not let go."

Chase put his hand back on the chain automatically, earning a satisfied nod from Devon. Chase closed his eyes and let himself ride the wave of feeling that was rolling over him, only to have them flying open when Devon's slick hand wrapped around his dick and started to stroke.

It was almost painful, and he instinctively tried to pull away, but he only succeeded in jostling the swing enough to have him crashing back against Devon's hips even harder. They both grunted with pleasure, and it was the only sound in the room besides the slapping of skin on skin.

It didn't take long. The orgasm that overtook Chase was almost more intense than the first one, and he screamed his release. Devon rode him through it, his hips never ceasing as he wrung Chase dry.

Then his hand was back on Chase's hip, and he used his grip to hold him still as he finally let go and pounded into him until his own orgasm roared through his body.

Devon came hard, and Chase could feel pulse after pulse of liquid heat filling the condom inside him, and he wished fiercely that he could feel it splashing against his insides.

Trembling with exhaustion, Devon pulled out carefully and removed the condom, tying it off and tossing it toward the trashcan. Reaching up, he carefully released Chase's legs from the cuffs and lowered them, rubbing them gently to calm the shaking muscles. He murmured in Chase's ear, but Chase was too out of it to understand the words. He pulled Chase's hands from the chains and half carried and half dragged him to the bed, laying him down on his stomach carefully.

Chase turned his head, looking up at Devon from hooded eyes as he examined Chase and unbuckled the cuffs from his arms. Chase could see that Devon was as tired as he was and was amazed when the Dom got off the bed and walked over to the bathroom. He came back with a warm cloth and a bottle.

After he cleaned the come and lube from Chase's skin, he opened the bottle and poured some of the contents into his hand. He smoothed it over the muscles in Chase's arms and legs before getting up on his knees beside him on the bed and rubbing the lotion into his back.

"You were amazing, Chase." Devon leaned down, and Chase felt soft kisses being pressed into the back of his neck. "Perfect sub for me... so proud you're wearing my collar." His strong hands felt like heaven as they rubbed the soreness out of muscles that had been well used. "So lucky to have you in my life."

Chase could feel tears pressing against the back of his eyes at Devon's words, and he let them fall shamelessly.

"You're such a good man... can't wait to see you grow... see who you become." Devon licked at the tears running down Chase's cheek, his whole body blanketing Chase in comfort. "No more tears now, baby. No more looking back at the past. From now on, we go on to our future, okay?"

Chase sniffed and took a deep breath, trying to get himself under control. When Devon moved to get off him, Chase reached back and held him in place. "Stay... it feels good. I like the weight of you holding me down."

Devon chuckled in his ear. "I don't want to hold you down, Chase. Just want to give you a place to be anchored."

Chase smiled and snuggled closer to Devon. "My safe place… you're my home." He took a deep breath, liking how it was an effort with Devon on top of him. "Love you, Dev."

"Love you too. Now go to sleep."

Chase could hear the amused fondness in Devon's voice, and it made him smile.

"Okay." Turning his head, he kissed Devon's jaw and then let his head fall against the pillow. "Dev?"

"Yes, Chase?" Devon's voice seemed to be coming from far away.

"I wanna go back to school."

He could feel Devon smiling against the back of his neck as he drifted off. "Anything you want, sweet boy… anything you want."

Twenty-One

WHEN CHASE pulled up to the old farmhouse, the first thing he saw was the huge porch, and he knew it was the perfect place for his family. The dogs would love the big yard, and there was a paddock and a large meadow that meant they might be able to get the horses he and Devon had been talking about.

He'd been surprised when Devon texted him at school and asked him to meet him at the old farm outside of town. They'd only been discussing moving for a few weeks, and Chase hadn't even been aware that Devon had been looking at properties.

In the months since their first session in the playroom, time seemed to have flown by. Chase was well on his way to getting his high school diploma, and he was talking with Devon and his therapist about what he wanted to do after that. He also spent time getting to know his family better and was feeling good about his life.

Getting out of the car, he saw the side door to the huge barn was open a little, and he could hear music spilling out from inside. He walked over and pulled on the door, swinging it wide, and stepped in before calling out.

"Devon?" He ventured in a little farther and looked around before spotting another door. The music was playing in the other room, and he smiled, wondering what Devon was up to.

Striding to the door, he noticed it slid open on rails rather than having hinges, and he pulled it open, wincing at the way it squealed.

This room was dimly lit and had no windows, the only light coming from a lantern that had been set on the floor in the far corner. Stepping inside, he called out again.

"Dev? Uhm, I'm starting to get freaked out here." There was nothing in the room except a few bales of hay and a tarp that had been hung from the ceiling. His instincts told him to run, and he had half turned when he heard a groan from behind the tarp.

"Devon?" He ran over and pulled the tarp back and was horrified to find his boyfriend, bound and gagged and hanging from the ceiling by ropes that had been tied around his wrists. "Fuck.... *Devon!*"

He started to move toward him but was brought up short by the loud clang of the door slamming shut behind him. Almost paralyzed with terror, he turned slowly and found himself looking into the smiling face of James Kingston.

THE SOUND of someone calling his name brought Devon back to consciousness. It took a second for him to realize it was Chase. He tried to call out and warn him that it was a trap but couldn't find enough air in his lungs to do more than groan. He knew it was a mistake as soon as the sound left his throat. It only drew Chase to him instead of warning him away.

When he got to the club that morning, he'd been hit from behind, the blow to his head knocking him out cold. When he woke up, he'd found himself naked and hanging from his wrists for the second time in eight months, and he was pissed as hell. His ankles were cuffed to a spreader bar that had been chained to the floor, and he'd never been in a more vulnerable position in his life.

But the first whisper from behind him had left no doubt as to the identity of his kidnapper.

"Hello, Devon... it's been a while." Kingston stepped in front of him, his smile only branding him as more of a madman. "I bet it was your idea to have my father lock me away, wasn't it?"

He didn't wait for an answer, just backhanded Devon across the face, making his ears ring. "Too bad for you that he underestimated me as usual... and too bad for him. I made sure he'll never have another chance to do it again." The look in his eyes left no doubt that Kingston's father was dead. Devon would have felt bad for him if he hadn't been aware that the man's overindulgence of his son had been the catalyst for his own death.

"Man, I hate that I'm going to have to tell Andy he was right." Devon's lip was swollen and bleeding from Kingston's blow.

Kingston grinned. "He was right about what?"

Devon spit the blood pooling in his mouth onto the floor before answering. "I should have let him kill you...."

Kingston chuckled before pulling his belt open and sliding it out of the loops. He wrapped the ends around his hand and brought it down hard across Devon's shoulders. Devon managed to stop himself from crying out, but just barely.

There wasn't much talking after that... only pain and anger, and Devon started to scream after he lost count of the blows raining down on him like streaks of fire falling from the sky. The skin on his back and shoulders was welted and broken in some spots, and it felt like he'd been burned.

When Kingston brought out the heavy leather paddle with the holes drilled into it, Devon began to babble. He begged Kingston to stop... but he never once caved in to the grunted demands that Devon call him Master. He'd passed out during the beating, but not before realizing that his ass and thighs were covered in cuts and scrapes from the rough edges of the holes that Kingston had apparently drilled himself.

The only comfort he had was that the man seemed determined to not injure Devon's cock or balls, and Kingston fondled them possessively as he hit Devon over and over.

When he came to, every muscle in his body seemed to scream in agony, but it was Chase's voice that brought him completely around. The effects of the beating were nothing compared to the realization that Chase was here and there was nothing he could do to protect him from the misery that was waiting for him.

The shock and horror on Chase's face when he'd spotted him made Devon want to hide away from him, except just seeing the person he loved most in the world suddenly made him feel better.

That was all ripped away when Kingston appeared behind him with a gun in his hand.

"Hello, Chase... it's about time you got here."

Chase shuddered at the sound of Kingston's voice, and he seemed to shrink down into himself.

"Come to see your pitiful excuse of a Master, you useless piece of shit? Go ahead... take a look at him. It's about time you both learned that he isn't fit to be anyone's Master." Kingston pushed the barrel of the gun into Chase's chest and used it to urge him toward Devon. "He's a sub who needs to be shown his place, nothing more."

Devon looked into Chase's eyes and was devastated by the despair he saw there. He could see the Chase he'd come to know and love slipping away little by little and the scared, broken boy he'd once been coming back.

"Chase...." Devon's voice was wrecked from screaming, and he saw Chase flinch at the sound of it. He turned his head to look at Kingston. "Leave him alone you demented fuck. You've got me, you don't need him."

Kingston smiled and nodded. "You're right, I don't. He's nothing to me. But to you he's everything, and that makes him valuable... at least for a few hours." Reaching down, he grabbed Chase's cock though his jeans, squeezing cruelly until Chase cried out and fell to his knees.

"See, he's remembering how to behave already." He twisted his fingers into Chase's hair and sharply pulled his head back, exposing the black-and-silver chain he wore around his neck. Most people wouldn't have recognized it as a collar, but the sight of it made Kingston chuckle.

"Really, Dev? You collared him? It's meaningless, of course, but you could have done so much better." He grasped the chain with his free hand and pulled, breaking the clasp before tossing it into the dirt. He reached into his jacket pocket and pulled out a thick black-leather collar and dropped it in front of Chase. "Get up and put it on him."

Chase just looked at the dirt floor and didn't move. Kingston got tired of waiting and kicked Chase in the side, then pushed his head down until it touched the dirt.

Devon started screaming. "Don't you fucking touch him! I'll kill you with my bare hands." He pulled on the ropes binding his wrists, oblivious to the blood coursing down his arms as they dug into his skin. "Chase... oh God, baby, I'm so sorry."

Kingston let go of Chase's head and walked over to stand behind Devon. He wrapped his arm around Devon's neck and pulled back hard, cutting off his airway. "Shut the fuck up, Dev. It's about time you learned that you're not in charge of anything."

Once Devon was quiet, he moved to Devon's side, keeping the gun in one hand. He picked up the leather paddle with the other hand and brought it down hard across the tops of Devon's thighs, causing him to scream. Chase's head jerked up, and his gaze locked with Devon's as Kingston swung it again and again.

Devon tried to concentrate on Chase, tried to ignore the pain Kingston was inflicting, but it was starting to become impossible. Every slap of leather against his skin felt like knives carving into him.

Chase flinched with every blow, and Devon's biggest wish wasn't to stop the pain but to make it so Chase didn't have to see it. He could deal with everything Kingston was doing to him if only he knew Chase would be safe.

Chase's chest heaved as he watched, and to Devon it looked like he was descending into one of the panic attacks that sometimes plagued him. As the beating continued, Devon could no longer hold back his cries of pain, and it was killing him to see Chase flinch with every scream.

"See, Chase? Devon's no more a Master than you are." Kingston was sweating heavily as his arm flew. "He's nothing but my property, to use and abuse as I see fit." The madness in his voice was bordering on hysteria, and Devon knew that this time, Kingston would kill him, and then he'd kill Chase.

Devon couldn't take the look in Chase's eyes and let his own eyes slide shut. "I'm so sorry, Chase." Devon's voice was so raw he didn't even recognize it anymore. "I love you."

Kingston let out a roar of rage at Devon's barely whispered words. "Stop fucking saying that!"

Dropping the leather paddle, he picked up a cane that had been lying half-hidden in the dirt and swung it toward Devon's back. Devon watched as Chase's eyes widened, and for the first time, something other than fear filled them.

As the cane landed on his back, Devon's scream of pain was overshadowed by Chase crying out as he launched himself at Kingston. "*No!* Leave him the fuck alone!"

Chase caught him in midswing, and Kingston fell backward as the gun and the cane both clattered to the ground. Devon twisted to try and see them, but he was trapped facing the other way and could only hang there helplessly as Chase struggled for their lives.

Devon could hear grunts of pain, and at one point someone shrieked, but he couldn't be sure who it was.

"Chase! Oh God, please. *Chase!*" His throat was so wrecked that he could barely be heard, but it didn't stop him from trying.

"Get the fuck off me, you piece of shit!" That was definitely Kingston, and he sounded scared.

In the distance, Devon could make out sirens, and he desperately hoped they were the cavalry coming to their rescue.

He heard a couple of loud thuds and then Chase's voice. "You're not hurting us anymore!" There was a loud sizzling sound, and Kingston's voice was making a weird, vibrating staccato. Then there was nothing but silence except for the sound of heavy breathing behind him and sirens getting closer.

"Chase."

"Hang on, Devon." Another few seconds of barely being able to breathe and suddenly Chase was there in front of him cradling his face and crying.

"Shhhhh, baby, we're okay." The words sounded ridiculous coming from his raw throat, but Chase smiled at him anyway.

"I have a knife. I'm gonna cut the ropes, okay?" Chase waited until Devon nodded and then cut his wrists free, catching him in his arms before lowering him gently to the ground. "Oh, Dev." Chase looked devastated as he gingerly unwrapped the ropes and threw them to the side. He quickly unbuckled the cuffs from around Devon's ankles and looked around frantically, like he was hoping help was coming from somewhere.

"What can I do for you?" Tears were running unchecked down Chase's face, and it was breaking Devon's heart. Ignoring the burning pain in his back and legs, he reached up to wipe them away and smiled.

"You did it already. You're my hero, baby." Devon frowned as he turned his head to find Kingston twitching on the floor. "What did you do to him?"

Chase chuckled weakly. "Taser."

Devon arched an eyebrow as he looked at his beautiful boy. "And where did you get a Taser?"

Chase shrugged. "From Jax. He said it would help me feel better about walking around the campus, especially when it was dark."

"Guess it came in handy, huh?" Devon took another deep breath and let it out. "Do you have your cell phone? I think I'm gonna need an ambulance."

Chase cocked his head, as if listening. "I think it's almost here."

Sure enough, the sirens pulled up outside the building, and then there was the sound of car doors slamming and voices calling their names.

Chase shouted back. "We're in here!"

Devon figured he must have blinked or something, because the next thing he knew, light filled the room as a huge sliding door on one wall opened and people came flooding in. The cops came in first as they surveyed the scene and then the EMTs right after them. He found himself being lifted away from Chase, and he couldn't help the whimpers that broke free.

At that moment Chase's voice lifted over all the other noise. "It's okay, Dev. I'm right here. Not going anywhere."

Devon smiled and reached out, his hand making contact with Chase's and holding tight.

The cops had tried to cuff Kingston's hands in front of him before letting the paramedics look him over but the medical personnel were insisting they be allowed to look him over first. Once they declared him fit to travel, a young police officer leaned over to help him up.

The next few minutes seemed to happen in slow motion. Devon watched in horror as Kingston lurched to his feet and seemed to stumble into the officer trying to help him up. The momentum had them both falling into the cop next to him, knocking the gun he was still holding out of his hand. Kingston had landed on his knees next to the weapon and he grabbed it before bouncing to his feet.

"Look out!"

Every gun in the room was pointed at Kingston, but he'd grabbed the ponytail of the female paramedic who had been tending him. She'd frozen in place, making it easy for him to hold her and shove the gun into the base of her neck.

"I'm leaving, and if anyone tries to stop me, she's dead." He backed out the door on shaking legs.

Devon couldn't see anything for a moment because Chase had moved in front him, effectively blocking him from Kingston's view. Devon tugged on Chase's hand and he moved automatically, finally letting Devon get a look at what was going on.

Kingston was backing down the road, apparently too disoriented to realize he could have gotten into one of the vehicles and gotten away faster. The paramedic looked more mad than scared, and Devon could see she was just waiting for her moment.

It came when a familiar truck roared into the farmyard. The noise distracted Kingston, making him look back over his shoulder. The girl elbowed him hard enough in the ribs to make him let go, and she started to run toward the cops, still too much in the way for the officers to fire.

Kingston raised his gun and had it pointed at the girl as the truck headed straight for him. He must have realized at the last moment that the truck wasn't slowing down and turned again to look.

The expression on his face would haunt Devon for a long time. He didn't look scared, just completely enraged. As it dawned on Devon's sluggish brain that the truck belonged to Andy, Kingston swung the gun around and fired, shattering the windshield. Devon and Chase both screamed, but the truck kept coming.

Devon could clearly see the look of complete disbelief on Kingston's face as the truck hit him, throwing him up into the air. He bounced off the hood and then onto the ground and landed in a heap on the driver's side of the vehicle, his head at an unnatural angle.

People exploded out of the room, but all Devon could see was the front of the truck, and he prayed for one more miracle.

Chase was sobbing beside him, and Devon used the grip he still had on his hand to pull him down so his head was resting on Devon's chest. Devon closed his eyes and ran his fingers through Chase's hair, and he could feel his heart shattering at the thought of losing his friend.

There was the squeak of the truck door and the babbling of what seemed to be a hundred voices, but then a familiar Texas twang rose over all of it.

"I told you if you hurt him again I'd fucking kill you, didn't I, you bastard?"

Chase shot upright, and Devon's eyes flew open to see Andy pushing his way through the throng of people.

Chase pulled away from Devon, threw himself at Andy, wrapped his arms around his neck, and held him tight. Devon smiled as the much shorter Andy tucked Chase close to his body and maneuvered him back to where Devon lay on the gurney.

Devon grabbed Andy's hand, unwilling to pull him away from the comfort he was giving Chase. "I've never been so glad to see you in my whole fucking life."

Andy winced at the sound of Devon's voice, and Devon knew those blue eyes were cataloguing every ounce of Devon's pain. "He's dead, sweets. He isn't ever going to hurt either of you again."

Devon nodded, unable to speak around the lump in his throat.

Most men would have looked ridiculous trying to hold someone who was six inches taller than they were, but Andy pulled it off as he held Chase, letting him cry into his shoulder. "It's okay, darlin'. I'm fine, and Dev's gonna get all fixed up." He looked over his shoulder at the truck. "And Joe is gonna rip me a new one when he finds out what I did."

Chase chuckled and finally pulled away, moving beside Devon as the paramedics made their way back and began loading him into the ambulance. They tried to keep Chase out, but a few growled words from Andy had them quickly changing their minds.

"I'll meet you guys at the hospital." Andy sighed as he was tapped on the shoulder by a cop. "After I finish talking to these guys."

Devon nodded and squeezed his hand one more time before letting go. Andy leaned over him, kissing him on the forehead. "Don't you ever fucking scare me like that again!"

"Ditto."

Devon looked into the face of his oldest friend. His blue eyes glittered with unshed tears, and it was then that Devon realized how terrified his friend had been. "Thank you."

Andy patted his arm and then smiled at Chase before walking away with a police officer.

Once both men were settled in the ambulance, the doors were quickly closed, and they were on their way. The sirens blared through his head, making it throb with pain.

"Am I dying?" The paramedic looked surprised by the question but quickly answered him.

"Nope. I won't lie. You're going to be mighty uncomfortable for a while, but you'll live."

"Then can we cut the siren? My head feels like it's going to explode any fucking second." He wanted to be polite, he really did. But he figured that today he'd earned the right to be a grumpy asshole for a while.

The pain in his back was starting to become unbearable, and he was grateful when the paramedic started an IV and then injected a syringe full of medication into it. "There, the doctor told us you could have something for the pain." She smiled at him before looking over at Chase. "He'd going to be pretty loopy in a minute or two."

Chase smiled back at her. "I'll take him any way I can get him."

Devon smiled as the pain meds started to kick in. He let himself relax and drift off, secure in the knowledge that Kingston was dead and Chase was safe. It was all that mattered.

DEVON WOKE up on his stomach in a hospital bed, the smell of antiseptic and blood sharp in his nose. Turning his head, he spotted Chase asleep in a chair that he'd obviously dragged over beside the bed. He was wearing hospital scrubs, and his hair and face looked freshly washed, and Devon was glad someone was making sure Chase took care of himself.

Still dead tired, he was about to let himself fall under again when he heard the sound of someone snoring, and he couldn't help but smile. He'd know the sound of Andy sawing logs anywhere after a lifetime of sleepovers, camping out, and drunken parties where they ended up crashing on the couch together.

A small sound by the door had him looking up into Jax Logan's face as the older man smiled down at him. He opened his mouth to speak, but Devon slowly lifted his finger to his lips, shushing him, before pointing at Chase. Jax nodded and pointed down the hall, then mimed drinking coffee.

Devon grinned and let his eyes fall shut once more, feeling safe, knowing Jax was there keeping watch as the three exhausted men slept.

The next time he woke, Liz Mackenzie was sitting beside him, reading a novel. He tried to move his head to look around for Chase, but pain flared along his shoulders, and he groaned.

"Now, you just lie still, Devon. If you're moaning in pain when Chase gets back, he's going to have my hide."

Opening his mouth, he tried to ask where Chase was, but all that came out was a broken croak.

"Would you like a drink?" Devon nodded shallowly, and she stood up and reached for a bottle of water. After twisting it open, she popped a straw into it and then held it so he could take a sip.

He hadn't realized how dry he felt until he started drinking, and he whined when Liz pulled it away far too soon.

"That's enough for now. You don't want to be getting a stomachache." She looked nervous but genuinely concerned.

He licked his lips and tried to ask her about Chase again.

"Chase?"

Liz reached over and patted his arm. "I made him and Andy go home to have a proper shower and change their clothes. I don't imagine Chase's daddy will be able to keep them away much longer than that."

"Okay." His eyes slipped closed for a moment, but he forced them open. "Why am I so sleepy?"

Liz chuckled. "I imagine it's the drugs they keep giving you for pain. Every time you so much as breathe loudly, Chase's pushing them to give you more."

Devon smiled. "Make him ease up a little, huh? I wanna be able to stay awake for more than five minutes."

"I'll see what I can do." She looked at him closely and then seemed to make up her mind about something. "Devon, I'm sorry about the way we acted when Chase left with you. We just couldn't understand how he could want... that kind of relationship, even with someone as kind as you. He'd been gone so long, and we just wanted to keep him safe."

Devon smiled softly at her. "I know. I feel the same every day." He frowned as his mind rolled over the memories of his kidnapping. "When he walked into that barn, I would have done anything to be able to make him safe. But I was helpless. He had to save me."

Liz reached over and ran her fingers through Devon's hair. "I know you would have, honey. And so does Chase, so stop beating yourself up over it. I think that monster did enough of that."

She opened her mouth to speak again but was cut off by Chase rushing into the room.

"Dev." Chase sounded close to tears but managed to smile at Devon.

"Hey, sweet boy. I missed you."

Chase dropped to his knees beside the bed so he could lay his head on Devon's pillow. Devon inched his hand over to take Chase's and pulled it to his lips, kissing his fingers tenderly.

Chase frowned, and shadows filled his eyes. "I'm sorry."

"Chase, what on earth could you possibly have to be sorry for?" Devon was wondering if maybe his brain had been more scrambled than he realized.

"I let him...." He stopped and swallowed before continuing. "I let him hit you, over and over. And he took off the collar you gave me. He didn't have the right, Dev." Chase trembled next to him, and it was breaking Devon's heart.

"You saved me, baby. You saved us both. I was so scared for you, but you overcame your fear and stopped him. It was amazing." Devon could hear a sob, and it took him a second to realize it was coming from Chase's mother.

He looked up at her, begging her to understand. She nodded and gathered up her things. "I'm just going to get a coffee. I'll be back to check on you both later."

She left the room, giving them the privacy they needed.

"It was the cane." Chase voice wasn't much more than a whisper. "When I saw it, all I could think about was all the times he used it on me. It hurt so bad, Dev, and I couldn't let him do that to you."

"Shhh, it's okay. You stopped him, and now he's dead. He can't ever hurt us again." Devon wanted so much to be able to pull Chase into his arms and never let him go again. Maybe he could do the next best thing.

"Stand up, sweet boy."

Chase rose to his feet gracefully and waited as Devon painfully inched his way to one side of the bed. "Dev... don't. You shouldn't—"

"Get up here. This bed is totally uncomfortable. I need a better pillow." Chase looked at him in shock, and Devon just raised his eyebrow. "And lose the shirt while you're at it."

Chase blushed but didn't argue. He pulled his T-shirt off and carefully climbed onto the bed, settling on his back beside Devon and then stilling. Devon managed to lift himself enough to sprawl over Chase's chest. It took a few minutes to find a position that didn't make his back protest too much, but soon the feeling of Chase's warm skin under his cheek and the smell of his cologne had Devon relaxed and humming happily.

"I'll get you a new collar, Chase, something special, okay?" Chase rubbed his hand soothingly up and down Devon's arm before he tangled their fingers together on Chase's chest. "I'm so glad you're here with me. I love you so much."

"Love you too, Dev. Now go to sleep. The sooner you're better the sooner you can take me home."

Devon grinned and kissed Chase's chest before snuggling closer. "Okay." He closed his eyes and was almost asleep when a random thought hit him. "How did the cops and Andy find us?"

"Oh, well. That was Jax too. He gave me this safety-button thing. It was in my pocket. When I pushed the button, it turned on the GPS in it and called 911. It also alerted the central office to call Andy and Jax and tell them where I was." He sounded embarrassed, but Devon was touched by the care that his friends had shown Chase.

"That's awesome. Just… make sure you don't activate it by accident, okay? That could really be awkward." There were more things he wanted to ask, but for the moment all he could care about was Chase being beside him, and he finally let himself sleep.

Epilogue

DEVON WALKED into the house and tossed his keys onto the small table by the door. He'd spent the afternoon running errands, and after three hours at the DMV, he was glad to be home.

It had been four months since his and Chase's final ordeal with Kingston, and things were just now getting back to what passed as normal for them.

There had been a lot to explain to the cops, but they hadn't been pushed too hard, especially when the details of Kingston's father's death started to emerge.

Kingston's father had been visiting the Italian headquarters of his corporation, and he'd been to see his son earlier in the day. They'd argued, and when it had turned physical, the older man had left, and his son had been furious. Hours later, Kingston had broken free of the men guarding him and had gone to his father's office, where he'd been working alone, after hours. The fight and the brutal murder that had followed had been caught on the building's security cameras. Kingston had taken hundreds of thousands of dollars in cash from his father's safe and had found his passport there as well.

From there he went to the airport and hopped on the first available flight back to the States. How he'd made his way from New York to New Orleans was still a mystery, but from the little the police could find out, it had been clear that getting to Devon and Chase had been his only priority.

Andy had been cleared of any wrongdoing in Kingston's death, and the look of satisfaction hadn't left his face for weeks. Joe still looked pissed off at Andy half the time, but Devon hadn't decided if it was because of the chance that Andy took or because Joe hadn't gotten to be a part of it.

Devon looked around, suddenly aware that he wasn't being molested by three hyperactive dogs, and it made him curious. He walked down the hall toward the kitchen, intending to look in the backyard, where he expected to find Chase playing with the dogs.

As he rounded the corner, however, he was brought up short by the sight of Chase on his knees, naked, with his head bowed and his legs splayed wide. His arms were straight out in front of him, and in his hands he held his collar, the first one Devon had given him. It was still Chase's favorite, and now he held it out to his Master. He was the most perfect picture of a sub that Devon had ever seen.

Walking forward, he took the offering and crouched down in front of Chase. He lifted Chase's chin so he could look into those gorgeous hazel eyes.

"Look at you, sweet boy, waiting so pretty for me." Devon leaned in and softly pressed his lips to Chase's, pulling back before Chase could deepen the kiss. He smiled when Chase whimpered in frustration but didn't move otherwise. "I'm a lucky Master, coming home to a gift like this. I didn't forget an anniversary or anything, did I?"

Chase smiled and shook his head. "No, Sir." Now that Devon had taken the collar, Chase put his hands behind his back and gripped his elbows. As usual, his presentation was flawless.

They had talked about it, and they'd decided that getting Chase's nipples pierced would be worth giving up the nipple clamps for. They'd had them done about a month after their ordeal, and although it had almost killed Devon to not touch the tender nubs for the required healing time, the way they made Chase react had been worth the long wait.

Chase usually wore silver barbells in the piercings and had taken to wearing tighter-than-usual shirts so they could always be seen. He loved it when Devon played with them in public, and whenever they kissed, one of Devon's hands would inevitably find their way to

Chase's chest. He just couldn't get enough of the breathy moans that fell from Chase's lips with every tug.

Right now his nipples were already peaked around the cool metal, and Devon couldn't wait to get his mouth on them.

"Then what have I done to warrant this lovely invitation?" He ran his fingers up Chase's cheek and into his hair, pulling a little. Chase grunted in pleasure and leaned into the touch.

"Nothing, really." Chase shrugged. "And everything." Every time he moved, the muscles rippled under his skin.

In the last four months, Chase had really begun to fill out. He worked out in the gym almost every day, and his lean body had built up muscle all over, but especially in his arms and chest.

Devon knew Chase had been a little worried that if he got too big, Devon wouldn't want him for his sub anymore, but it was a groundless fear.

Devon knew that body size meant very little in the BDSM world. It was all about the attitude and need of the people involved. It was how a small woman like Danielle was able to have huge men quivering in fear and anticipation at her feet.

"I don't know, Chase. You've done just as much for me." Devon stood and buckled the collar around Chase's neck. Once it was fastened, Chase lowered his head to the floor and lifted his ass a little higher. Devon walked around him, trailing his fingers over tanned, bare skin until he was behind Chase. Letting one finger slide down between the cheeks of Chase's ass, he discovered that Chase was ready for him in more ways than one.

"I see someone's been touching my things without asking again." It was a kind of joke with them. Devon had never forbidden Chase from touching himself, knowing he'd spent too many years without any control over his sexual feelings. But Chase liked it when Devon acted possessive about him, and Devon loved possessing Chase.

"I've been a bad boy, Dev. Maybe you should punish me." The hopeful note in his voice made Devon chuckle.

"I don't know, sweet boy. I'm not sure the punishments are really effective. Sometimes I think you might even like them a little." He swatted Chase on the ass just hard enough to leave a red handprint.

Chase moaned and pushed his ass back even more, begging with his body even as he began to beg with his mouth.

"Please, Dev. Need it."

And Devon knew it was true. Of all the things they'd explored together, spankings were Chase's favorite. He told Devon that, for whatever reason he couldn't put into words, the feeling of Devon bending him over his knee and spanking him until his skin was hot and red made him feel safe and loved. Devon would never deny him that feeling for long.

Devon slid his finger over Chase's hole, noting how relaxed and loose it was. "What did you use, baby?"

He couldn't see Chase's face, but there was no missing the flush that stole over his neck and upper back. "The dildo you bought me. The black one."

Devon eased two fingers in and encountered barely any resistance at all. "I think that one's become your favorite. Mine too." Leaning over Chase, he hooked his finger under the collar and gave a gentle tug. Chase sat up immediately, and Devon took advantage of the position to turn his head for a kiss. By the time he pulled away, they were both panting.

"Let's take this upstairs."

Chase looked faintly surprised but got to his feet and followed Devon up the stairs. When they reached the bedroom, Devon stripped down to just his jeans and crawled onto the bed, arranging himself so that he was sitting against the headboard.

He looked at Chase and patted his lap. "Come on, get comfortable."

Chase scrambled to comply. Getting on the bed, he knee-walked over to Devon before arranging himself face down over Devon's legs. His cock was nestled between Devon's thighs, and the feel of the soft denim rubbing against it had Chase rock hard in seconds.

Devon smoothed his hands down Chase's back and over his ass. With the weight Chase had put on and the time he'd been spending in the sun, most of the scars Kingston left behind were barely visible—at least the ones on the outside.

The scars left behind on Chase's heart and mind were going to take longer to heal. He still fell into occasional bouts of severe depression and self-doubt, but not as often as he used to.

His nightmares didn't come as often either, but when he had one, Chase never thrashed or screamed in his sleep. He was more likely to wake and lie beside Devon terrified and trembling. After the first few times, Devon had extracted Chase's promise that if he was awakened by a bad dream, he would wake Devon up right away. Devon assured him that he wanted to know when Chase was scared or sad and that taking care of him was way more important than a few lost hours of sleep.

Devon suffered through a few nightmares of his own, but they didn't take long to fade in the face of Chase's love and his undemanding need for Devon to take care of him.

He loved watching as Chase's confidence bloomed as he took accounting courses at the local college. He was determined to help Devon with the running of the club, and Devon had to admit that the prospect of handing the paperwork he despised over to Chase was very appealing.

Chase had also started working at the club behind the bar. When they had talked about it, Chase had told Devon it would be a good way for him to get used to being around other people who were involved in the lifestyle while giving him something to do besides just hang on to Devon.

Of course Devon made absolutely sure it was obvious to everyone that Chase was his boy and his alone. All the staff kept a fond eye on him, although they tried to not make it obvious. He'd been adopted into the family that Devon had made for himself, and as far as they were concerned, Chase was their favorite little brother.

Things with Chase's family had been improving as well. While his parents were still a little concerned about some of the aspects of their relationship, they couldn't deny Devon's overwhelming love and respect for their son.

His brother, Tom, had come down to the club a couple of times, and while he wasn't interested in joining in, he had admitted he could see the appeal of certain aspects of Dom/sub relationship dynamics.

Chase's sister, Zoe, had been the first to adapt. She was just happy to have her brother back, and the fact that Devon tended to spoil her when she visited had helped. She had also become quite attached to Kayley and Justin and tended to spend as much time with them as she did with Chase and Devon.

An impatient whine from Chase brought Devon out of his musing, and he smiled at the pout Chase threw him over his shoulder.

"A little impatient are we, baby?" Chase squirming in his lap wasn't doing much for his own patience. He smacked him on the back of his thigh. "Settle now."

Chase froze and then relaxed completely. "Yes, Sir."

Devon soothed him with a few more touches until the only sign that he wasn't sleeping was the frantic beating of his heart that Devon could feel throbbing under his hands.

"Good boy." Running his hand down one more time, he caressed the curve of Chase's ass cheek. "How many, sweet boy?"

"As many as you think I need, Devon." Chase was lying with his head resting on his arms, his face turned to look at Devon.

"Hmmm, I think you need to figure it out for yourself. How about I start, and you tell me when to stop?" They'd been working on figuring out Chase's limits. He was so used to having to just endure the beatings he'd been put through, he sometimes forgot that with Devon, he really did have a say in what was enough.

"Okay." Chase sounded nervous, and Devon pulled him up to kiss him softly. When Chase was boneless against him, he urged him back to his position across Devon's legs.

He waited until Chase's head had fallen onto his arms again. "Ready?"

Chase nodded, and Devon pulled his hand back and delivered a light swat to his ass, causing Chase to yelp. "Words, Chase. Use your words for me."

"Yes, Dev, I'm ready."

Devon put one hand on the back of Chase's neck, not really holding him down, just offering reassurance. The sound of the first hard slap of skin against skin was almost deafening in the quiet room. The muscles under Devon's hand tightened a little, but that was all.

"That's one, Chase. Have you decided how many you want yet?" Just because it was Chase's decision didn't mean Devon wasn't going to remind him to make one.

Chase shook his head. "No, not yet."

Devon pulled his hand back, letting it fall a couple more times. Chase grunted, and Devon could see he was biting his lip to hold back more.

"Uh-uh, Chase. I wanna hear those sweet sounds you make. No holding back on me." A couple more blows, these a little harder, had Chase moaning and rubbing his cock against Devon's thigh.

"More. Please... Devon. Need more." He moved his hands behind his back, silently asking Devon for what he needed. Devon slid the hand on Chase's neck down to wrap it around both of Chase's wrists. He could get free if he really wanted to, but Devon knew that wasn't the point.

Devon let four more hard ones fall, and Chase cried out louder with each one. His ass was turning a pleasant shade of dark pink, and Devon liked how Chase shuddered when Devon rubbed over the handprints littering his skin. "So fucking pretty, sweet boy."

He let his hand fall harder, twice this time, and Chase jolted and tensed after the second one, and Devon wondered if he was about to come. After a second the tension slowly left Chase's body, and he relaxed against Devon again.

"How many, Chase? You'd better not come until I'm deep inside you." Chase's fingers were flexing in Devon's grip, but he made no move to get them free.

"I won't, Dev." He took a deep breath and looked Devon in the eye. "Five more... can you do five more?"

"Yeah, baby. I can do that."

Chase exhaled and smiled shyly. He had sweat rolling down his face, and his hair was sticking to his head. His ass was so red it almost glowed, and he looked absolutely content.

"That's my good boy." Giving Chase's wrists a squeeze, he let the last five blows fall, getting a little softer every time they landed.

Devon whimpered with each one, but his eyes had fallen shut, and his face showed nothing but pure bliss. He must have been counting, though, because after the last one fell, he opened his eyes and looked at Devon with eyes that shone with love.

"I'm so proud of you. You did so good for me, baby." Devon let go of Chase's wrists. "Scoot off me so I can take care of you."

Chase groaned but lifted himself to his hands and knees, crawling carefully off Devon before collapsing on the bed.

Devon got off the bed and went to the washroom, came back with a cool cloth and wiped Chase down with it, being especially gentle over the heated skin of his ass.

Once he was done, he tossed the cloth in the general direction of the bathroom and stripped out of his jeans and underwear. Urging Chase to lift his hips, Devon slid a pillow under them and then pressed him down.

Devon waited for him to relax before he pushed his legs apart and crawled up between them. Using the lube on the nightstand, he slicked his cock and wiped his hand on the sheets.

When he used his hands to pull apart the cheeks of Chase's ass, the heat pouring off the reddened skin hadn't abated much at all. Chase moaned but didn't move as Devon positioned himself against his hole and slowly started pushing in.

They'd done away with condoms months ago, after being tested, and Devon relished the feeling of sliding into Chase without any barriers between them.

"You feel so good, sweet boy. So hot and tight, even after working yourself open." He blanketed Chase with his body, knowing the pressure would cause the heat of Chase's ass to burn even hotter.

He buried his face in the side of Chase's neck, sucking the marks he knew Chase craved into his skin, while sliding his hands up Chase's arms to tangle their fingers together. Chase always held on so tight, but Devon never complained. It was what Chase needed, and Devon would always give it to him.

He had intended to fuck Chase hard and fast, but once he was settled against his back, he found himself barely moving, pulling out just a little and then grinding down. He knew his cock was in almost constant contact with Chase's prostate, causing pleasure to ripple through his boy in waves.

Chase's breathy moans and bitten off cries made Devon feel protective and possessive at the same time, gentling his kisses against the delicate skin of Chase's throat, licking over the marks he'd already left behind.

"Gonna take you to the club soon. Put your leash on you and let it hang down your back." He lifted away a little, letting go of one of Chase's hands to trail a finger down his spine. "You're so beautiful, they're all gonna want you, but they can't have you." He slipped his hand back up to curl around the back of Chase's collar, tugging gently. "This tells them that you're mine, doesn't it, baby?"

Chase groaned and pulled against the grip Devon had on his collar a little. Devon knew it was because he wanted to feel it more, not because he wanted to get away.

"All yours, Devon. Always." Chase's voice was roughened by the pressure against his throat.

Devon let go of the collar and slid his hand to wrap around the front of Chase's neck. He used his grip to pull Chase's head back, knowing that the restriction it put on his breathing would bring Chase close to the breaking point fast.

"So fucking gorgeous." Sliding his hand up, Devon turned Chase's face to take his mouth in a wet kiss. "Gonna come for me, baby? Just from me fucking you?"

Chase nodded frantically, unable to speak as he panted for air.

"Good boy." Devon got both of Chase's hands in his, stretching them back over his head. He gave up trying to talk and sank his teeth into Chase's shoulder as he ground down even harder.

Chase cried out as his orgasm tore through him, and Devon could feel every spasm of it. He kept grinding until the tension went out of Chase's body, then freed his hands and pulled Chase's hips up.

He spread Chase's cheeks apart and plunged back in, thrusting three more times before he came hard as sparks flew behind his eyes.

Falling forward, he barely managed to move to the side and flip on his back to avoid crushing Chase. Ignoring the ruined sheets, he urged Chase up until he was resting with his head on Devon's chest.

Devon smiled as he carded his fingers through Chase's long, shaggy hair. Every time the younger man mentioned getting it cut,

Devon distracted him until he forgot about it again. He loved having it in his hands, letting the silky strands run through his fingers. He loved how Chase moaned so sweetly when Devon pulled on it gently as he sucked Devon's cock.

"You're petting me again." Chase's voice wasn't more than a whisper against his skin.

"That's because you're like a big cat, pushing into my touch and purring contentedly when I run my fingers through your hair."

Chase growled low in his throat and nipped at the skin under his cheek before licking over the small hurt.

Devon chuckled. "Okay, more like my very own tiger than a cat." He gave the hair wrapped around his fingers a little tug, and Chase's growl turned into a happy sigh.

Devon knew they had to get up and shower soon. They were both sticky, and if they didn't, they'd be very uncomfortable when they woke up. When Chase curled in closer, however, he decided it could wait a little longer.

"Are you really going to take me to the club like that? Parade me around and show everyone who I belong to?" Devon couldn't quite read Chase's mood, so he tried to answer carefully.

"I'd like that very much, but only if you want it too."

Chase tensed a little beside him, and Devon stroked his free hand up and down Chase's arm as he waited for what he would say.

"I bet some people are mad about your new rules."

Devon had decided there would be no more intimate contact between him and the subs that came to the club. The ones there for anything sexual would be sent to other Doms. He would keep a few of his regular clients—like Miles Smallwood—but for the most part, he would stick to running the club and training other Doms.

Some people had resented Chase for it, but he'd never asked Devon to do it. He hadn't known about the changes at all until Devon pulled him into his office one night to tell him.

Chase had thanked him by sucking him dry in his desk chair before pulling him into one of the playrooms and begging Devon to flog him.

"It was my choice to make. I don't need anyone else but you." Devon could feel Chase smile against his chest. He hadn't asked Devon to quit, but Devon knew his boyfriend was happy about his decision.

"Then it would be my honor to be presented to the club in any fashion you choose, Master." Chase's voice was full of love and respect, and to Devon's delight, a little bit of sass.

Devon grinned and kissed the top of Chase's head. "All right, you brat, go get the shower warmed up."

Chase snuggled in closer, apparently determined to stay in bed. Devon lifted his hand and gave him a playful swat on one of his still-red ass cheeks, grinning as Chase yelped and jumped up out of bed. Rubbing the spot Devon had just hit, he looked over his shoulder and pouted before sticking his tongue out.

When Devon started to get up, Chase turned and sauntered to the bathroom, deliberately teasing him. Watching his sub walk away wearing nothing but Devon's collar and the handprints he'd left on Chase's ass was a sight he was never going to get tired of.

As he got off the bed to follow Chase to the shower, he realized that, as much as Chase belonged to him, he belonged to Chase right back.

It was a good feeling.

CINDY SUTHERLAND is a first-time author in her early forties who never thought that getting involved in a fandom would lead to being published. She is an avid reader who would take in anything she could get her hands on, having inherited a love of books from both her parents. She wrote in secret as a young adult, with only her family for an audience, and now is over the moon at the thought of sharing her love of writing with a few more people. Her favorite stress-busting activity besides writing is singing karaoke at her hometown bar, and she is passing on her love of reading to her daughter. Cindy thanks God every day for an errant YouTube recommendation that led to her having the best group of friends she's ever had in her life, and she is looking forward to seeing where the rest of this journey will take her; and, hopefully, more stories to tell.

You can e-mail Cindy at cindyls_3@hotmail.com, contact her on Facebook at https://www.facebook.com/pages/Cindy-Sutherland-Dreamspinner-Author/313915495374744?ref=stream, and follow her blog at http://cindylsblog.wordpress.com/.

Romance by CINDY SUTHERLAND

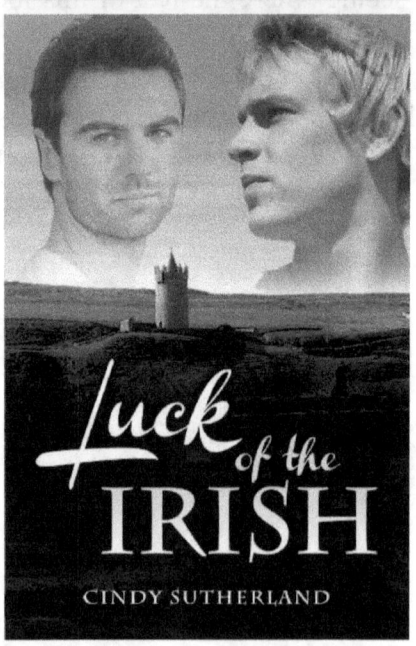

http://www.dreamspinnerpress.com

Romance by CINDY SUTHERLAND

http://www.dreamspinnerpress.com

www.ingramcontent.com/pod-product-compliance
Lightning Source LLC
Chambersburg PA
CBHW051638260626
47170CB00004B/1233